DEATH IN AN ENGLISH GARDEN

DEATH IN AN ENGLISH GARDEN

BOOK SIX IN THE MURDER ON LOCATION SERIES

SARA ROSETT

DEATH IN AN ENGLISH GARDEN
Book Six in the *Murder on Location* series
An English Village Murder Mystery
Published by McGuffin Ink

❀ Created with Vellum

ABOUT DEATH IN AN ENGLISH GARDEN

A COMMON, GARDEN-VARIETY MURDER...

Location scout Kate Sharp is enjoying the gorgeous springtime in her favorite idyllic English village while coordinating locations for a Jane Austen documentary, but when she's assigned to manage a difficult star who has received threats, Kate discovers that danger and death aren't always on screen. After a tragic accident in the star's beautiful English garden, Kate suspects murder. With a sly and secretive murderer intent on putting suspicion on Kate, she must find the culprit before she's led down the garden path.

Death in an English Garden is the sixth entry in the popular Murder on Location series, which is perfect for cozy mystery readers who want to indulge their inner Anglophile. Will appeal to fans of M. C. Beaton, Stephanie Barron, and Marty Wingate.

PROLOGUE

INTHEKNOW.COM/CELEBRITYNEWS

EXCLUSIVE:
SCARY RIDE FOR ARABELLA EMSLEY

It was a close call for Arabella Emsley, star of the recently released The Right People, when the brakes went out on her Range Rover Tuesday night. "It was terrifying," the doe-eyed star said.

She left Zini's after dinner with a friend, but almost didn't make it home. Unable to stop, Emsley steered the car off the road and into a ditch. A mechanical failure was to blame for the scare, and Emsley says she feels lucky to have escaped unharmed.

Emsley is off to the English countryside to film an interview on site at the elegant stately home, Parkview Hall, where she will discuss her role in the feature film reboot of Jane Austen's clueless rich girl busybody, Emma.

CHAPTER 1

"*B*ODYGUARD?" ELISE'S HEAD SNAPPED UP so quickly that her bun of grayish brown hair, which was pinned haphazardly at the nape of her neck, slipped down to the collar of her black shirt. Her tone caused everyone in the room to pause.

Sharp outbursts from the producer of the Jane Austen documentary weren't unusual. You'd think that after working with Elise for almost a year, I would have gotten used to her rather forceful personality, but I still tensed when she used that caustic tone. I was glad that—for once—she wasn't unhappy with me.

Paul, the Assistant Director and focus of her attention, looked unperturbed. He removed the pencil that he kept tucked behind his ear and tapped his clipboard. "Actually, bodyguards. Plural."

"That's absurd." Elise shook her head. The bun traveled down another inch. "Impossible."

"That's not all." Paul shifted the clipboard and consulted his computer tablet. He spent his days juggling the clipboard, tablet, and Elise's bad moods. "The reserved accommodations for Ms. Emsley are no longer suitable," he read. "She needs space for the two security personnel as well as her assistant. She needs the new

3

location to be secluded and secure." Paul hesitated for a second then added, "And arranged as soon as possible. She wants to arrive early."

I turned back to study the image on my phone. Troubleshooting issues related to the location were part of my job; issues related to the talent weren't my responsibility. "A little to the left," I said.

Freya, the production's general gofer, moved a lacquer screen a few inches closer to the canopied bed. She was a sturdy girl with a round face and unflagging energy, an invaluable quality on the set.

Freya and I were returning a bedroom in the stately home of Parkview Hall to the exact arrangement we'd found it in before we began filming. Earlier in the day, we'd filmed a scene from *Emma* in the Oriental room, named for the imported Chinese wallpaper that inspired the decorating theme.

I checked my phone, comparing the room to the pictures I'd taken before we began filming. "That's good. Okay, now let's do the chest of drawers." I moved on to my next set of photos. "We need the Chinese vase and the matching lamps with gold bases."

I tucked my phone into the back pocket of my jeans and moved across the room to the carefully packed boxes where we had placed the items that had to be removed before filming began. We often had to move furniture and decor, sometimes even strip a room completely and change everything, so I always took hundreds of pictures—wide shots, close-ups, and everything in between before we began—so I knew exactly where to replace each item.

Elise's voice carried over the loud crackle of unfolding paper as Freya and I removed the items from their protective nests. "Absolutely not. Everything was arranged months ago. Her people signed off. We can't change anything at this point. What could she possibly need one bodyguard for, let alone two?"

"Probably for that vicious ex of hers," Freya said so quietly that only I could hear her.

I raised my eyebrows. Arabella Emsley was the new "it" girl for historical drama. *The Red Poppy*, a drama set during World War I had been her breakout role a few years ago. She'd landed several other historical roles after that, including the role of Emma in a new feature film adaption of Austen's novel. Arabella's appearance in our little documentary was connected to publicity for the *Emma* movie. She would be interviewed for one of the *Jane in the Modern World* segments and tell viewers how it felt to bring an Austen character to life in the movie.

In addition to the interview, we had two days scheduled for her to dress in period costume and be filmed in several locations both indoors and out around Parkview Hall. If everything went according to plan, the documentary was set to air a week before the release of the new *Emma* movie. It was a nice symbiotic promotional scheme, but it meant that we would have a genuine star on our hands. We typically used local actors for the depictions of Jane Austen's life and incidents from her books. Those scenes were used with voice-overs from our interviews with experts discussing specific topics. The reenactments illustrated points from interviews and kept the documentary visually interesting.

Freya wrinkled her upturned nose. "Bit of a sod, that one. Her ex, I mean. I read all about it in the paper last week. He'd been spotted with another woman for weeks, but Arabella defended him and said everything was fine. Then the day before her new movie released, he announced he was engaged to some waitress. She sounded a bit of a twit—the waitress. She couldn't even put a sentence together when they interviewed her. She just giggled and flashed a pink diamond the size of a Cadbury egg."

I carefully positioned the Chinese vase in the middle of the dresser. "The new version of *Emma*? That's out? I thought it came out later."

"No, you're right. The new *Emma* comes out in the fall. This was last week when *The Right People* released. You must have heard about it—a family saga set in the 1920s."

"I do remember seeing something about it." I'd seen a tabloid with the bold headline *The Wronged Woman* over a picture of Arabella, her expression somber and her dark eyes appearing even more enormous than usual against her fair skin. "That is horrible, for her husband to behave that way." Elise and Paul were still in the room, discussing what to do about Arabella's request. I lowered my voice as I added, "I can't believe I'm agreeing with Elise, but I don't see how something like that means Arabella needs a bodyguard."

"Not her husband," Freya said. "Ex-boyfriend. They were together ages and ages. You know, like you and Alex. At least for a year or two."

"I see." I plugged in one of the lamps, suddenly feeling quite a bit older than Freya, even though there couldn't be more than five, maybe six, years between us. Alex and I had been dating for almost a year, but I always shied away from counting our time together. I didn't want to jinx anything.

Freya paused, a lampshade in her hand. "Where is Alex? I haven't seen him all day."

"He's on his way to Chawton." We had finished filming on location in several areas around Bath a few days ago. He'd stayed behind to wrap up there. Now he was traveling with a small crew to the village where Jane Austen had lived when she revised her earlier novels and wrote her last three novels. The cottage was now a museum, and we had permission to film in and around the cottage and had interviews scheduled with several of the museum trustees.

"Do you miss him?" Freya asked with a grin.

"Like crazy." Without intending to let things get serious, Alex had somehow filtered into my day-to-day routine, and now I was amazed at how many gaps there were in my life when we were apart. I'd wanted to go with him to see Austen's house, but we were in the final press to finish filming and our little production couldn't afford to pack up and take the whole crew to Chawton.

My visit there would have to wait until we had some time off, which wouldn't be that long from now. In a few short weeks, the bulk of the location work would be done, and my calendar would be wide open after that. It was an unsettling thought. I had immersed myself in my work on the Austen documentary series. But I would have to surface from it soon and figure out what I was doing next.

I removed the next bundle of wrapping paper and pushed the thought of the future away. Something always came up, and I had plenty to do right now. As helpful and nice as she was, I didn't want to discuss my love life with Freya so I said, "Still, it doesn't sound like Arabella would need extra security."

Freya crumpled a wad of packing paper noisily then stuffed it back into the box. "But he's Stevie Lund." Seeing that the name didn't register with me, she added, "His uncle is Porter Lund," as if that fact alone clenched her argument.

I compared the replaced items on the chest of drawers to the pictures I'd taken and gave a nod of my head, indicating it looked perfect, before her words registered. "You mean the guy involved in those drug raids? *That* Porter Lund? The one who got off because the police didn't get the right authorization in the beginning?"

His name had been all over the news when I moved to Nether Woodsmoor last spring and again recently when the case against him and several other people had fallen apart. I didn't remember all the details, and since I was a temporarily transplanted American, I didn't have a great knowledge of the UK legal system, but I did remember the case had been thrown out because the attorney general hadn't approved it at the right time. It had caught my attention because of the words "attorney general." Since there were so many tiny differences between British English and American English, I'd been surprised that the same term was used in both countries.

Freya picked up the empty box. "That's the one. Stevie is his nephew, and he's dodgy. You can tell just by looking at him. Slimy, if you know what I mean. I wouldn't want to be in Arabella's shoes, especially after she threatened to sue him."

"What for?" I asked, realizing that I was getting swept up in the tabloid tale, but it was hard not to. That's why the tabloids sold so well, I guessed.

"The property. They bought a flat in London together."

"That could be worth suing someone for." If the flat were located in one of the swanky parts of London, it would be worth millions.

"Oh, it is," Freya said. "Arabella said they had been secretly engaged for something like *six months*. Since they bought the flat together, she said they should sell it and split the money."

"Hmm. Six months. That is an eternity in the movie industry. Sounds very Jane Austen," I said with a smile. "The secret engagement part," I added, but her blank look didn't clear. "Lots of secret engagements in Austen's books—Frank Churchill and Jane Fairfax, Lucy Steele and Edward Ferrars. And everyone assumed Marianne and Willoughby were engaged. Interesting how Austen used actual secret engagements and false assumptions about engagements in her plots."

"Ah—yeah. Do you want me to get the next box?"

"No, I can get that. Why don't you find Melissa and tell her we're ready for the dressmaker dummy and the undergarments." Tours came through these rooms regularly and one of the most popular features was a dressmaker's dummy outfitted in the undergarments the ladies wore in the early 1800s. My friend Melissa worked in Costume and had taken charge of the corset, chemise, and whatever else was on the dummy when we had to move it out of the room.

"That sounds rather tarty," Freya said.

"You didn't see it earlier?"

"No, I was down in the drawing room, helping with the lights."

"There's nothing risqué about it," I said. "In fact, once all the underwear is on it that dummy will be more covered up than I am when I wear a sleeveless summer dress."

"Okay, one *not* scantily clad dressmaker's dummy coming right up."

I went to work putting a delicate writing desk back in place. I positioned an antique inkwell desk set and a hand-painted papier-mâché box inlaid with mother-of-pearl on the surface. Behind me, Paul and Elise's voices continued, but I tuned them out. I added the modern lamp, the last touch to the desk, then stepped back and bumped into someone.

"Sorry, Freya—oh, Mr. Takagi, I didn't realize you were behind me." This wasn't the first time I'd turned around and been surprised to find our new director had silently entered the vicinity.

"Kate," he said in a mock-scolding tone, "you simply *must* call me Ren. In the first place, the word *mister* makes me feel quite elderly. And, second, if you keep calling me Mr. Takagi, I could get an inflated sense of my own importance." His features were Asian, but his accent was as crisply upper class as Elise's accent. His publicity bio stated he was forty-two, but he looked a decade younger. Rento Takagi was his full name, but he asked everyone to call him Ren.

"I don't think there is any danger of that, but I will try...Ren," I said, finding it hard to use his first name because he was so courteous and had such a dignified manner. It made me want to speak to him more formally, even though he was standing there holding the dressmaker's dummy by the torso. He'd probably met Freya on the way up the stairs and offered to carry it for her. He was always pitching in, getting things done no matter how small the task. "Here let me take that from you."

"It's fine," he said. "Where do you want it?"

"Over there, by the window."

We crossed Elise's line of sight, and she bore down on us.

"Ren," she snapped, clearly not feeling the reserve I did toward the director. "We have an issue. Arabella Emsley." A shade of satisfaction edged her words. Elise had never been fond of the features that were included in the documentary that discussed the modern pop culture enthusiasm for Austen and her work. If Elise had her way, the documentary would be a pure academic dissection of Austen's works. "She's demanding new accommodations."

Paul cleared his throat. "That's not all. If we don't change Ms. Emsley's reservations, she's canceling."

Elise looked at the ornate molding around the ceiling. "*This* is why I do documentaries, so I don't have to deal with spoilt movie stars." She looked at Ren. "What do you say to this? It was your idea to bring on the starlet."

As always, Ren waited a beat before he spoke. "The idea came from above me, if you'll remember." He sent Elise a quick smile, and her triumphant look faded.

It always amazed me that Ren's calm manner seemed to overcome Elise's rages. Elise and our last director had not had a good working relationship—to put it mildly—and we were all a little worried about how Ren and Elise would "get on" as my friend Louise said.

But Ren had arrived, and in his reserved way, set about getting the work done, something that Elise appreciated. When points of contention came up, he let her vent. He listened, his face impassive, and then in the end, he did exactly what he wanted. And somehow, it worked.

"Many people will be unhappy if Mrs. Emsley refuses to come," Ren said.

"Then it's on her," Elise said quickly. "It's not our fault if she throws a tantrum."

"But then we'd have several gaps to fill," Ren said, and Elise's mouth pinched. I could tell that she didn't like it, but he made a good point.

"Is there anywhere else in the area that would meet the criteria?" Ren's expectant gaze shifted to me.

I was the location scout, after all. I had to find locations for filming as well as accommodations for the talent and crew. I opened my mouth to reply that there was nothing, but paused. "There is Tate House," I said slowly. "It would be rather unusual. I don't know if it's even available."

Tate House stood on the wooded hill above the village with only its gables visible above the treetops.

"It certainly is secluded enough," Elise said. "But wasn't it sold?"

"Yes. The buyer did some renovations and put it right back on the market. Louise said it was also available for a holiday rental. I haven't seen anyone at the house, so maybe it's available to rent for a few days."

I lived on a lane of cottages on the lower portion of the hill. For a few weeks, the shrill whine of electric saws and the dull thud of hammering had filtered down through the trees. But once the workmen had packed up and departed, it had been quiet.

Of course I wouldn't have known if someone had moved in because the road to reach the house was actually around the other side of the hill. Anyone living there would usually arrive and depart that way. But a footpath ran behind the cottages and curved up the hill where it divided. One branch of the path climbed through the trees to Tate House while the other branch continued around the hill. It dropped down to meet the road that took ramblers to one of the old stone bridges that crossed over the river.

The previous owner of Tate House had often used the footpath to get to the village instead of driving down, so I thought if someone had moved in, I would have at least caught a glimpse of a newcomer. But so far this spring I'd only seen visiting ramblers and cyclists on the footpath. "It's been sitting there, empty, for months," I said. "No one's even come for a weekend. Or, at least that's what Louise says."

"She would know if anything had changed," Ren said. "She knew who I was before I even checked into the inn." As the owner of the White Duck pub, Louise picked up all sorts of local news and heard quite a bit of gossip, too, but she only passed on the news and kept the gossip to herself. I was sure that was why people confided in her.

"I suggest we attempt to fulfill some of the requests." Ren said, his casual tone further deflating Elise's indignation. "Then we can negotiate from there. Let's not escalate the situation. Give them a bit, and not go into the arena of ultimatums. Nothing beneficial ever happens when ultimatums are thrown out."

Elise let out a long breath through her nose. She looked as though she were about to force herself to eat a food she particularly disliked. "I'd rather not give privileges, but I suppose in this case, we must at least appear to try, the schedule being what it is. Kate, get on this right away."

"I better finish here. I can call the estate agent—"

"Go on," Elise said, cutting me off. "I'm sure...er...that thickset girl can wrap up things in here. After all, it's only putting it back the way it was before. Nothing spectacularly difficult."

Freya came in the room, and I hoped she hadn't heard Elise's comment on her build. Deciding that arguing with Elise about Freya's body type wouldn't help things, I tightened my jaw muscles as I said, "I'll take care of it," trying to channel some of Ren's soft-spoken manner.

Paul tapped on his tablet. "I'll forward you the contact information for Ms. Emsley's assistant, Torrie Mayes, since she wants you to handle everything."

"You should probably call her back, if you've been working with her," I said.

"But Ms. Emsley's last requirement is that her assistant work exclusively with you."

CHAPTER 2

"*M*E? ARE YOU SURE?" I asked.

Paul nodded. "Requested you by name. Her assistant said Ms. Emsley is set on you."

"But...that makes no sense. Why me? That's not even my job." I looked around the half-finished room from the dressmaker's dummy to the bare wall on the far side of the room where several pieces of furniture and decor still needed to be replaced.

Paul finished tapping on his tablet then shrugged. "I don't know why, but she asked for you specifically." He twisted his tablet around and pointed to my name in the email.

"You're famous." Freya put down the base of the dressmaker's dummy beside the torso. "I bet it's because of what happened in Bath. You were in the news."

I thought I heard Elise murmur something that sounded a lot like *infamous*, but when I looked at her, she smiled in her mechanical way and said, "Excellent. That will work out well, won't it? Give—um—your assistant instructions about finishing here." She shifted her attention back to Ren. "Now, about the gardens, let's go down and take a look. I want it set up exactly as

I…" Her voice faded as she strode away with Ren at her side and Paul trailing behind them.

~

"You live in the cottages in the lane down below, don't you?" Claire Montrose asked as she unlocked the front door of Tate House an hour later.

"Yes, Cottage Lane." I pulled my camera clear of the lapels of my raincoat and looked through the viewfinder at the front of the house. The day was mild and sunny with a predicted high of about seventeen degrees Celsius, which meant temperatures in the sixties—no matter how hard I tried to adjust to European measurements, I still thought in Fahrenheit—but I couldn't quite shake my Southern California roots. To my mind, sixty degrees qualified as cool. The weather was variable here, to say the least. I knew the flat, silvery-edged clouds in the distance could multiply, sweep in, and cast a gray tinge over the village. I wanted to get some photos while the light was clear. With the surrounding trees casting deep shadows, the area around Tate House was already dark enough.

Unlike the cottages in the lane with their carefully tended gardens and bursts of flowers, the front of Tate House had no flowers, no garden, and no lawn, just a sweep of a tarmac drive that rose from a pair of impressive gates that had swung back when Claire clicked a remote control. The drive curved through a dense grove of gnarled oaks whose canopy cast a deep shadow over the undergrowth. Drifts of fallen leaves carpeted the ground between the trees. "That brick wall on either side of the gate, how far does it go?" I asked.

"Around the whole property. It transitions to a dry-stone wall after several meters."

"Good to know." While I was sure that a determined person

could scale it, the five-foot wall would keep casual ramblers from trespassing.

"The wall encloses the top of the hill, but most of the area is wooded and not easily accessible. Of course, the house and back garden are so stunning that I doubt your client will want to leave it...except for filming, I assume?"

"Perhaps." When we spoke on the phone, Claire had tried to pry as many details out of me as she could about why I was looking at the property, but I wasn't giving away anything that I didn't have to. She knew it was related to the documentary, and had been so eager to show me the inside of the house that she'd nearly rear-ended me when she zoomed up the hill and rounded the drive's blind turn to find me sitting in my borrowed car, waiting in front of the closed gate. While Alex was out of town, I was using his vintage MG Midget to get around, and I was so glad she'd braked in time. I did not want to have to call Alex and tell him his car was in for repairs.

I didn't drive much, but I had conquered my knee-weakening nerves about driving on the opposite side of the road, and now I could actually navigate without breaking out in a cold sweat. I'd even considered getting a car of my own, but I couldn't justify the expense, especially with Alex living only a few cottages down the lane and offering me a lift to work every day. He also let me use his car whenever I needed to run to Upper Benning or points farther away, which wasn't often. I just had to ignore the sticky notes that dotted the dash. Instead of an app on his phone or a paper calendar, Alex used sticky notes to keep track of appointments and contacts. I didn't understand it, but I'd come to realize that it was a system and—somehow—it worked for him.

I focused the camera lens on the exterior of the house and took several photos. Thick pelts of ivy crisscrossed the façade, nearly obscuring the mellow golden stone, typical of so many of the buildings in the area.

Claire pushed open the front door, its leaded glass inset flashing as it reflected a ray of sun that penetrated through the trees. "It's more modern than the cottages. Completely updated inside." The front door opened into a wide room with a fireplace directly opposite the doorway. "This is the sitting room." Claire's heels clicked across the pale blond floorboards. "Several walls were knocked out to create one large room."

"It's not quite what I expected." While the exterior of the house felt like a scene from *The Secret Garden*, the inside reminded me of a doctor's waiting room.

Streamlined furniture in shades of tan, gray, and pale purple were grouped around the room. An abstract painting hung over the intricately carved fireplace mantle and sleek side tables of chrome and glass made the decor of pottery bowls and woven baskets look as if they were hovering in mid-air. A staircase of frosted glass steps suspended on silver wires floated to the left of the fireplace.

"Isn't it wonderful? As I said, total renovation."

"Yes, you did." I lifted my camera and snapped some photos. I'd discovered that my ideas about what qualified as "new" versus "old," were quite different from most of the inhabitants of Nether Woodsmoor. To me, anything from before the Civil War was "old." Louise had agreed with me until she realized I was talking about the American Civil War, not England's Civil War.

"I was expecting something from the turn of the century—the nineteenth century, that is." I let my camera drop back and swing from the cord around my neck. I took out my Moleskine journal to make a few notes.

She smiled at my little joke. "No. Tate House is very up to the minute. It has a very nice security system. The new owner added home automation control. The lights and security system are now controlled through online apps."

"What type of security system?" I asked.

"High-end. Exterior cameras at the gate and front entrance, all connected to monitors. You can view through an app on your phone, or there's a dedicated monitor in the study."

That should please Arabella Emsley, I thought.

"The security system was the only thing that was in good shape," Claire said. "Basically, everything else in the house has been replaced—plumbing, electrical, appliances. The flooring is new throughout the house." She waved a hand at the glossy pale boards. "And it's been freshly painted." She tilted her head to the fireplace. "Of course, the owner left the unique historic touches. The mantle is Edwardian. Gives the place the feel of history, doesn't it? But it's not your normal boring historic home. It's an *edgy* historic home."

I made a murmur that might have sounded like agreement. The mixture of modern with antique felt jarring to me, but maybe that was the idea. I'd take my cottage, which was unabashedly Old World and cozy, over edgy historic any day. I followed her up the glass staircase that swayed slightly. "That's on purpose," Claire assured me. "The architect says it reflects the insecurity and angst of our modern society."

"I see." I gripped the wire that functioned as a bannister tightly.

The upstairs was more traditional. The hallway had a country home feel with oil paintings covering the walls from the chair rail to the ceiling. Narrow tables and chairs with delicate curved legs filled the space between the bedroom doors along with glass display cabinets showing off delicate china. What looked to be a genuine elephant foot umbrella stand sat in one corner by a grandfather clock.

There were more than enough spacious bedrooms to house Arabella's entourage. The bathrooms were completely updated with huge tubs and separate showers, and the kitchen, with miles of stainless steel and a huge gas stovetop in a marble-topped island, looked like something transplanted from a restaurant. The only indication of the age of the house in the kitchen was a closed door that Claire pointed out, which hid the back staircase. It had once been the servant's staircase and went to the upper floors.

Claire walked down a short hallway that connected the kitchen with the dining room and the sitting room where we'd entered. She stopped in the dining room and pushed open the sliding glass doors that made up one wall. "The kitchen has a door that opens onto the terrace as well." She stepped outside. "And...the back garden." She flourished her hand.

A wide flagstone terrace stretched across the back of the house. I walked around a pair of lounge chairs to the edge, expecting more trees. Instead, I saw masses of blooms and bursts of color. A breeze swept through the trees with a sound like running water.

Shallow stairs in the same flagstone dropped down from the level of the house to a path that wound through an amazing garden that spilled down the slope behind the house. I walked down a few steps, dropping into a kaleidoscope of vivid blooms. A swath of low-growing purple blooms buzzing with bees gave way to a profusion of fuchsia flowers then to a carpet of tiny white blooms. "I really should learn more about gardening and flowers," I said.

Claire, still on the flagstone terrace above me, caught her hair away from her face as the wind picked up. "I don't suppose you get these types of plants in California?"

My head was level with her feet, and I had to tilt my head back to see her. Only the edge of the terrace and the gabled roof of Tate House were visible from where I stood. "No. Nothing like this."

I did recognize a few of the flowers in the garden. Lupines shivered on their stalks, a mix of pale pink, lilac, blood red, coral, deep purple, and cream. Roses filled one area while in another space farther down the hill lily pads floated on a pond with goldfish flickering below the shimmering surface. A yew walk filled one side of the garden, the only area with a regimented and formal landscape. A wall of beech trees encircled the entire garden. Against the tree line, ferns and ivy dominated the shadows.

"So, what do you think? Beautiful, isn't it?" Claire asked.

"Gorgeous," I said between clicks of the camera shutter. Whether or not it worked out so that Arabella could stay here, I wanted to record the cascade of color and the contrast of light and shadow. The garden was mostly in the sun. It seemed as if a giant hand had scooped out a swath of trees to make room for the garden. "I had no idea this garden was part of the house." I walked down to the next landing and focused the camera on a pale pink rosebud that bobbed gently as a bee made its way across the petals.

"It was a bit run down when the current owner bought it. He's had quite a bit of work done to bring it up to this standard." She leaned toward me and lowered her voice, despite the fact that we were clearly alone, the only sounds the faint buzz of the bee and the wind. "Between you and me, we have a major landscape magazine interested in doing a story on it. With the exposure from an article like that...well, I doubt it will be on the market much longer."

I reluctantly let my camera drop back onto the cord and took out my Moleskine journal from one of the large pockets on my raincoat. I climbed up the steps to the terrace. "Let's talk about a few details."

"Certainly. Why don't we go over here?" She stepped off the terrace and led me around to a square of lawn, which was tucked up against one of the walls of the house with a turret-like curve. A splash of sunshine warmed the iron table and the surrounding grass, while a few feet away the thick trunks of ash and beech trees rose higher than the house, sheltering us from the wind.

We settled down at the table, and I went over dates and requirements. She whipped out contracts and made calls. I countered with my own phone calls to Paul and Elise. The end result was that Arabella and her entourage could occupy the house beginning in two days and stay on through the end of filming. Elise was adamant that Arabella had to pick up the difference in cost between Tate House and the lodging we'd originally arranged for her. As Elise would have said in her understated British way, the difference in cost was not insignificant.

Claire got another call and went back to the terrace to discuss something in private so I took a deep breath and dialed the number for Arabella's assistant, mentally reminding myself to negotiate as Ren had said. No ultimatums.

I wasn't good at identifying accents, not like my friend Melissa. She could pinpoint a person's origin after hearing only a sentence or two. I couldn't do that, but as soon as the voice came on the line, I recognized that this woman didn't have the careful pronunciation style that I heard from Elise as well as from news broadcasters. I said, "Torrie Mayes, please."

"Yes? What?"

Her tone was impatient, and I spoke quickly before she could hang up. "I'm Kate Sharp with the Jane Austen documentary production. I may have found an alternative location for Ms. Emsley, but we need to work out a few issues." I gave her the details about Tate House, quoting the size of the house and describing the location, including the extensive grounds, the gated entrance, and the wall that surrounded it. "If you give me your email, I'll send you photos of the house."

"That's not necessary. How much?"

"The cost to make the change, you mean?"

"Yes," she said, and I was sure from her tone that she was

rolling her eyes. I named a figure and without a pause she said, "Fine. Do it. Send us the contracts, whatever you need." She rattled off an email and fax number that I barely had time to write down before she said, "We'll arrive the day after tomorrow," and hung up.

CHAPTER 3

*C*ONSIDERING THE LAST-MINUTE NATURE of the switch in Arabella's lodging situation, it was all done with a minimum of fuss, except for Elise's constant reminders that the whole thing was "highly irregular." Faxes and emails whipped back and forth between Arabella Emsley's people and our team. For the better part of a day, my email dinged constantly because I was copied on every piece of correspondence.

I'd hoped that once the new lodging was arranged I might be able to slip out of the role of go-between, but Torrie emphasized that Arabella wanted me involved in everything that went on between her and the Jane Austen production. So, two days later, I stood on the drive at Tate House in the shade of the trees as a black SUV rolled into view. A very specific email had arrived in my inbox yesterday with their arrival time as well as the information that Ms. Emsley wanted me to be on site at Tate House—and no one else. I'd puzzled over the last line of the email, not sure it was serious. I opened my email on my phone and reread it. "When Hibbert arrives the code word is *ocean.*"

While people had entrusted me with their homes and workplaces for filming, no one had ever gone so far as to give me a code word—or even a secret handshake—so I couldn't help but wonder if it was some sort of joke. Was there a camera hidden somewhere in the vicinity to record my gullibility? But then again, it could be completely serious. I didn't deal with movie stars often, but I'd heard from other people in the business that they could be quite paranoid.

A man in a dark suit and white shirt with an open collar emerged from the driver's seat, and I went to meet him. From a distance, he looked the very picture of corporate casual, but as I got closer, I saw a small silver hoop in one earlobe. He tugged on his shirt collar and shifted his neck, which made me think that the suit wasn't his favorite choice of attire. I held out my hand. "Hello, I'm Kate Sharp."

"Chester Hibbert. Ms. Emsley's security detail." Dark eyes under dark brows scanned my face as he crushed my hand in a quick shake then shifted his attention to the treed area around the front of the house. He was probably in his late thirties. He had a slightly crooked nose and a shaved head, which was balanced with a layer of stubble on his face. He was a few inches shorter than me, but what he lacked in height, he made up for in width. His shoulders and chest indicated he spent long hours at the gym.

He seemed to be waiting for me to say something else. It had to be the code word thing, but I suddenly realized that I had no idea how the code word worked. Was I supposed to say the word or ask him to tell me the word? "The code word...?" I said, tentatively.

His face cleared, and he raised his eyebrows expectantly, clearly waiting for me to finish the sentence.

"Ocean," I said, and he nodded approvingly as if I'd answered a difficult question correctly in class.

"You're it?" he asked. "No one else around?"

"Just me. You're American?" I asked, surprised by his lack of accent. I'd expected a Brit.

"Canadian." He tilted his shaved head down toward the drive. "How long has that gate been open?"

"Only since I came up here. Ten minutes or so."

"And no one else entered after you?"

"No." I glanced toward the SUV, looking for Arabella and Torrie, but the doors remained closed. I couldn't see anything through the dark tinted windows.

"Good."

Seeing my glance at the SUV, he said, "That's the decoy. Ms. Emsley will be here as soon as I give the all-clear. If you'll wait here, I'll check the perimeter and house."

"Oh, I see," I said, but I didn't understand at all. Did an actress need security this tight? Even if she had annoyed her thuggish ex-boyfriend?

"Have you been inside?"

"Yes. I checked everything." Habits die hard, and I'd made a quick tour of the house before the arrival time. I made sure everything was in place and took additional pictures of the rooms. It was an impulse that came from being a location scout. Even though I knew we wouldn't be filming in the house, I wanted a record of the rooms before Arabella arrived. I was pretty sure that once they left, it would be my job to make sure everything was in order before Claire did a walk-through of the house.

"I'll do the same. Key?" He held out a beefy hand.

"It's unlocked."

He frowned, but didn't say anything except, "Can you close the gate from here? Do you have a remote?"

"Yes, right here." I pulled it out from the bundle of keys. Claire had reluctantly handed everything over to me that morning in front of the gate along with the codes that unlocked the gates and the doors. I'd jotted everything down in my notebook and said, "Okay, we're good to go," but she didn't take the hint. She'd wanted to be on the property and show Arabella through the house herself. I practically had to shove Claire into her car—apologizing all the while—but reminding her that I was only following instructions.

I hit the button on the remote to close the gate as Chester strode off across the bit of green lawn that ringed the house. He disappeared around the side of Tate House, and I inched close enough to the SUV that I could see through the tinted windows. No other passengers waited inside, but luggage filled the back. I could just make out the distinctive Louis Vuitton pattern on the luggage.

I stepped back and waited until he appeared on the opposite side of the house. He went to the front door and disappeared inside. I crossed the tarmac and followed him inside. "Everything should be fine," I said.

"Right." He continued through the rooms. I trailed behind him as he checked each room, opening closet doors and checking locks on exterior windows and doors. I made a few more attempts at conversation, but each time I got a one-word reply like "fine," or "good." I stopped talking and simply followed.

When we'd made a complete circuit, he nodded to me again and made a call on his cell phone. "It's clear," he said and hung up. Definitely a man of few words.

I followed him outside. He opened the back of the SUV and heaved out the luggage. I blinked as he stacked overnight bags, suitcases of every size, a huge travel trunk, and even a circular hatbox. "That's an impressive amount of luggage for a few days."

"Yes." Chester slung the strap of one of the smaller bags over his shoulder, picked up a suitcase in either hand, and carried them into the house.

The sound of a car engine filled the air and then a sharp blast on a horn sounded. Arabella had arrived. I clicked the button, the gate swung back, and a second black SUV roared up the incline. The front passenger door opened, and a small dark-haired woman hopped to the ground. For a second, I thought it was Arabella, but then I saw her face and realized it wasn't her. This must be Torrie Mayes, Arabella's assistant.

This woman's chin was too pointed and, while her hair was cut in the same chin-length bob that Arabella favored, her hair was streaked with thick gold highlights and cut in a more severe style of a stacked bob. There was something else about her that was different. At least on screen, Arabella had an air of fragility, as if she were as delicate as a porcelain figurine. This woman had a sharpness, a hard aggressive edge that was evident from the way she lifted her chin and marched toward me. "You're the assistant?"

"Kate Sharp." I extended my hand. "Location scout, temporarily on loan to help you out."

"Brill." She bent her head over her bag and muttered, "Where did I—? Ah, here they are." She took out a pack of cigarettes, shook one out, and put it between her lips. I mentally cringed. Smoking had not been covered in the contract, but I was sure that Claire, not to mention the owner of Tate House, would have a fit if they knew one of the temporary residents was a smoker. I began mentally trying out different ways to tell Torrie that there was no smoking in the house.

She spoke around the cigarette as she lit it. "As long as you're Kate Sharp, that's all Arabella cares about." She took a long drag then blew out smoke. She closed her eyes for a second. "That's better. Such a long drive." She tilted the pack of cigarettes toward me. "You smoke?"

I shook my head, and she quirked her lips to the side. "I shouldn't either. My life would be so much easier if I didn't. Arabella hates the smell of the smoke. She won't let me smoke in the car, even with the window down, which is absurd because," Torrie lowered her voice and leaned her sharp chin closer, "she used to be a pack-a-day girl. I know she wants a cigarette, but she's too terrified of wrinkles to take it up again." She took another drag. "Hibbert is here?"

"Inside, putting away luggage." I looked to the second SUV. Another man climbed down from the driver's side, but I didn't see anyone else.

"Surely, this isn't a second decoy?" I asked.

"No." Torrie waved her hand with the cigarette. "She's on the phone. She'll be along in a minute."

The man from the driver's seat went to the back of the SUV and a few seconds later walked toward us, toting several more pieces of Louis Vuitton luggage. I did a double take. He looked *exactly* like Chester.

He wore the same dark suit and white shirt with an open collar, but the resemblance didn't stop there. His head was shaved, and his face was a carbon copy of Chester's with the same dark eyes, dark brows, and trace of stubble. He even had the same crook in his nose. He nodded to me as he passed us. I turned and looked after him, then at Torrie. "That wasn't Chester, was it? I thought he was inside."

"I have no idea." She tapped her cigarette, and the ash from it fell onto a row of rocks that lined the drive.

How can you not know your security people? That's got to be one of the most basic things when it comes to security. My confusion must have shown on my face because Torrie said, "It might have been Chester, or it could have been his cousin…um, Sylvester, I think it is. I can't tell them apart. Just call them Hibbert. They both answer to it."

I turned to look at the man who'd come out of the house to retrieve more of the luggage. He did look like the man I'd given the code word to. I wasn't sure which man it was, but then he turned after picking up two suitcases, and I saw that he didn't have a silver hoop in his ear…so he must be Chester's cousin.

Torrie cleared her throat. I switched my attention back to her. "Sorry. That must be very confusing. Does Chester always wear the hoop earring?"

"No idea." She looked at the bundle of keys and gate remotes that I held and raised her eyebrows, clearly moving on from the subject of the unusual security set up.

"Right, okay. Here are the remotes for the gate and the keys to the front and back doors. The gate can be opened from inside the house as well. I'll show you."

"No need. I have the instructions on that and the super hi-tech lighting and things. I got the email."

"Okay, good. Then I guess the only other thing you need to know about is the lighting in the back. It's not on the same system as the house. You have to turn it on and off separately."

"How old-fashioned."

"I'll show you. It's just around this corner here." I followed the same route that Chester had taken during his survey of the grounds, keeping to the narrow lane of lawn that ringed the house. Torrie followed me, and I was glad to get in front of the smoke filling the air around her. We turned the corner, and the grassy area widened, running from the curved turret of the house to the enclosing tree line. "Nice," Torrie said as we passed the iron table where Claire and I had worked out the details of the house rental. I rounded the next corner of the house and stepped up onto the flagstone terrace. I'd gone a few steps when I realized Torrie wasn't behind me. She'd halted at the edge of the terrace.

"It's quite a sight, isn't it?" I said.

"Yeah, but I can't go out there. The paperwork didn't say anything about a garden."

"That's true," I said, mentally reviewing the pages that had been sent back and forth. They had described the house, the woods, and the gate, but nothing about the garden. "Is something wrong?" Was the rental situation going to fall apart before the bags were even unpacked? There really wasn't another option in the area for Arabella and her entourage. I'd done a little more checking after my initial meeting with Claire, in case Arabella didn't like something about Tate House. This was the only viable location in the area.

"It's the pollen." She gestured to the carpet of flowers tumbling down the hillside. "I'm highly allergic. It sends me into sneezing fits. And then there are the bees. Highly allergic there, too. I nearly died after a bee sting when I was a kid." She patted her purse on her hip. "I keep an EpiPen with me all the time—just in case, you know."

She backed off the terrace and stepped onto the grass. "I know there's been all that stuff in the news about the decline of honeybees in Britain, but they're not gone. Especially in a place like this."

"I'm sorry about this. I had no idea. It wasn't mentioned—"

She waved her hand with the still-smoldering cigarette, sending a trail of smoke toward me. "Don't look so worried. I'm just the help." She sent me a brief, bitter smile. "My concerns don't come into it. I'll stay inside or," she motioned with her shoulder back the way we'd come, "use that little lawn area that looks so fairy-tale-ish." She looked toward the garden and the cascade of color. "Arabella will like it, though. She prefers to do her yoga outside, if she can. She'll be down there, on one of those little stone landing things on the stairs, I bet."

"Oh, that will work out well," I said, relieved.

She grinned at me then, a genuine smile breaking across her face as she snuck a glance back over her shoulder. "And it means I won't have to be part of the torture."

"What?"

"Arabella's workout. She calls it yoga, but it's more like an hour-and-a-half drill for…I don't know…the Special Forces, I guess. Her fitness coach was in the SAS. Her workout involves a lot more than stretching and inner peace. She likes to have a workout partner, and since her fitness coach couldn't come with her, I thought I was in for it. But this," she tilted her pointed chin at the garden steps, "may not be so bad after all." She turned back toward the drive.

"Oh, wait." I halted. "Let me show you the switch for the garden lights. It's over there by the door to the kitchen." I crossed the terrace and flicked on a light switch located on the exterior wall of the house. Landscape lighting around the terrace glowed. "You probably can't see it from where you are, but there are lights on each side of the steps all the way down and more landscape lighting in the garden."

"Right. Got it. I'll let Hibbert know. Odd that the switch is out here. They made such a big deal about this being a smart house—everything automated and able to be controlled digitally. Arabella liked that."

The same thing had occurred to me, and I'd asked Claire about it. "The garden lighting and the pump for the pond are on a different circuit than the house. They run through the potting shed. See the roof of the little building about halfway down the hill?" A tall hedge enclosed the square stone building.

"Ah—no, I'll take your word for it."

It was obvious that she took the threat of a bee sting very seriously and wouldn't venture more than a step or two into the area around the garden. I could see that there was no way I could convince her to cross the terrace and go in the house through either the door to the kitchen or one of the glass sliders in the dining room, so I turned off the outdoor lights and retraced my steps across the terrace.

As we entered the shade of the trees on the way back to the drive, she stifled a sneeze. "See, there I go. Can't do a thing about it except stay indoors. I have medicine for it but, honestly, it doesn't do much good."

We reached the front of the house, and Torrie took another long drag on the now stubby cigarette. The back door of the SUV popped open, and Arabella emerged. At least, I assumed it was Arabella.

A long gray raincoat was belted around the woman's tiny waist and even with the layer of the coat, she looked as if a strong gust of wind would topple her willowy form. Under the slouchy brim of a woven summer hat, dark sunglasses covered half her face. The fringe of a pale pink scarf fluttered around her neck as she glided toward us. She wore black leggings that stopped at her calves and athletic shoes with bright pink accents.

A charm bracelet jangled as she reached up to pull her sunglasses down an inch, revealing makeup-free and close-set brown eyes with stubby lashes. Dark half circles shadowed her eyes, standing out sharply against her porcelain skin. Her dark gaze focused on the cigarette, and her shapely eyebrows lowered into a frown. "No smoking in the house, Torrie. You know I can't stand the smell." Her tone was understated, but Torrie quickly stubbed out the cigarette. Arabella surveyed the front of Tate House then she wheeled around and looked at the woods.

She gave a tiny nod. "This will do," she said in the same restrained tone. She glanced pointedly at the stack of luggage that remained on the drive. "Get that inside. Have Hibbert bring the trunk in next. It goes in my room."

"Of course." Torrie dropped the cigarette butt on the tarmac drive and hurried to meet one of the security guards who had just come out the front door. Arabella sent a vague smile in my direction, then drifted into the house.

CHAPTER 4

"*B*UT WHY INSIST I BE here, and then barely talk to me?" I tugged the hood of my windbreaker lower over my forehead. Drizzle had set in the day after Arabella arrived and had continued for two days, layering the countryside with a continuous fine spray of moisture. Fortunately, we were doing several interviews during the time and hadn't had to do too much shifting of the schedule since we were indoors for most of the time already.

Since Arabella had requested me by name, Elise had insisted that I check in with Arabella in-person each day, which meant I'd spent the last two days shuttling between Tate House and Parkview Hall, where we were shooting the expert interviews. I'd dropped in at Tate House on my way home from the day's filming. Torrie had reported everything was fine. Arabella was not in sight. Alex had called while I was there, so I'd stepped outside to take the call in the garden.

"No idea," Alex said.

"Easy for you to say that in such a relaxed way. Arabella Emsley hasn't put your schedule in disarray." I stopped at the potting shed and looked in the window. Gardening tools and empty pots were strewn across a small wooden table almost completely obscuring it, and sagging bags of dirt and fertilizer were stacked haphazardly around the floor.

"That's true," Alex conceded.

I turned away from the shed and meandered down the grassy pathway of the yew walk that ran in a straight line. Cone-shaped shrubs that towered above my head bordered each side of the path. They were interspersed with banks of plants with silvery-green leaves that came up to hip level. "But if it *had* happened to you," I said, "you'd probably like having your schedule shredded and turned into confetti." Alex was much better at rolling with the punches than I was.

"Comes from being a Foreign Service brat," Alex said. "You learn not to get too settled with anything." Alex's father was still in the diplomatic service. Alex was American, but had grown up moving from one diplomatic post to another around the world. "Routine is so boring. Nothing wrong with shaking things up a bit," he said. "But I do understand that it's frustrating."

I glanced at the stone stairs that climbed to the terrace, but they remained deserted. I had the garden to myself and could speak without worrying someone would overhear my complaining. "It's just so…inefficient, going back and forth between Parkview Hall and Tate House. Elise insisted I stay close and check in, but I don't think Arabella wants me around. Torrie runs interference for her on everything. I haven't even seen Arabella. Well, that's not true," I amended. "She's been invisible every time I've stopped by Tate House, but I've seen her on the footpath behind the cottages walking down to the village a couple of times."

Each time, an umbrella shielded her face, but I recognized the gray raincoat. If that detail hadn't been enough to know who she was, the real giveaway was her companion, a broad-shouldered man with a shaved head, a crooked nose, and a layer of stubble.

"Slink and I met them last night on the path when we were leaving for our walk."

Slink was Alex's greyhound, and I was taking care of her until Alex returned. Slink had been quivering with excitement to get out for what was really more of a run than a walk, and she'd shot out the back gate. I'd been focused on latching the gate and hadn't realized Arabella and one of the Hibberts were on the path. At the sight of Slink, Arabella had hugged a large flat box to her chest and shied away, pressing herself up against the stacked stone wall.

I'd said, "Don't worry, she's sweet." I tugged the leash and Slink, who was only in the middle of the path, had pranced back to me, her long tail whipping back and forth.

Arabella had half smiled. "I'm sure she is," she said in her quiet tone, then tilted her head at her companion, indicating they should move on. I had hung back, deliberately setting a slow pace, watching as Arabella's umbrella bobbed down the path away from us. Once in the village, she had turned and headed for the red postbox while Slink and I continued to the river and the wide-open stretch of meadow beyond it where Slink could run at top speed.

I ambled by the garden's pond with the lily pads and said to Alex, "Arabella reminds me of my fifth grade English teacher, Mrs. Walthrop, who never raised her voice. She controlled the class with a look or the lift of an eyebrow. It's really quite amazing, now that I think about it. She had an air of authority. She knew we'd do what she said. She never doubted it...and we did. Arabella has that same aura of command."

"Money and fame do that for you," Alex said.

"I suppose so. I had lunch at the pub, and Louise said Arabella's been in town a couple of times every day. She causes a stir each time. She always has one of the Hibberts with her, and he scowls at anyone who gets close. But there's something about

Arabella, too, a detachment or reserve that keeps people from approaching her. Louise says no one has been brave enough to ask for an autograph or to even attempt a selfie with her." I paused to admire some yellow flowers that I thought I remembered Louise calling cowslips. "Arabella seems perfectly set up here with Torrie and the security guys. She never wants to speak to me when I come by. Why does she want me checking in on them?"

"Who knows why the talent makes the requests that they do? Don't try to figure it out—you'll only drive yourself crazy. That movie I worked on last summer, one of the stars had to have fresh flowers in her trailer that matched whatever costume she was in that day. Another guy insisted that no one was allowed to speak directly to him on-set except the director—said it broke his concentration."

"I suppose you're right." I watched several beads of water gather on a leaf until their weight bent the leaf, and the water drained away. I should be like the leaf and let the stress roll off me. I rotated my shoulders in an effort to relax. "Everything is getting done. Although, I'm relying on Freya more than I usually do. I shouldn't complain. How's it going where you are?"

"Weather," he said.

"I'm sorry."

"We're waiting for the rain to stop. You're at the edge of the storm. We're getting the full brunt of it. We've done everything inside we can. It's supposed to clear tomorrow, so maybe we can finish up here the next day."

"That would be great. You could be back by the weekend."

After a tiny pause, he said, "I have an appointment Saturday."

"Are you stopping off in London?"

"No. I'm not sure how long it will take."

"Oh." He didn't fill the silence with details, only said, "I'll let you know when I'm on my way back."

His voice said the subject was closed, and I felt as if a cold finger had touched my spine. It wasn't like Alex to keep things back. He was one of the most open people I knew...except lately he'd been a little secretive. Especially when it came to his laptop. Anytime I came near him while he was working on it, he'd minimize the window he was working in or shut the laptop altogether. I hadn't thought much of it at first, but it had been going on for several weeks, and it was at the point where even I— someone who liked to avoid confrontation—was beginning to think I should mention it.

"Okay," I said, but things didn't feel okay. How can one short sentence throw off everything? I'd looped back to the yew walk and frowned at the symmetry of the plantings, wishing I could line up everything so neatly in my life.

"So, any sightings of the bodyguards today?" Alex asked in his normal tones as if he hadn't just strong-armed me off the topic of when he'd return.

I wasn't good at relationship stuff—I shied away from discussing "us." I knew I overanalyzed things, so I'd tried not to do that with our relationship. Every time Alex brought it up, I put him off. It would seem hypocritical to insist he share with me, when I'd refused to do that in the past. I tried to backtrack to our previous conversation and ignore the flutter of uneasiness I felt. "No, not a peep from them. I suppose they're still here—"

One of the yews in the line shivered, raining water onto the grass.

"Sorry, you broke up," Alex said. "What did you say?"

"It's not the connection. I stopped talking." I watched as the yew trembled again, releasing another shower of droplets, smaller this time. Unlike the first time I saw the garden, when the wind was strong, today was completely still. I took a few slow steps forward.

"Why are you whispering?" Alex asked, his voice matching my quiet tone.

"I'm in the garden. I thought I was alone, but now I think there's someone else here."

"Why shouldn't there be someone else there?" he asked, his voice returning to its normal level. "Is it closed or off-limits or something?"

"No, but it's dreary and not a day for strolling in the gardens."

"But you're strolling in a garden on a soggy day. It's not unheard of in England."

"I know, but I could see the whole garden from the terrace when I came down. No one else was down here then. Where did they come from? I've been within sight of the stairs the whole time." It was too damp to wander off the main paths. "If someone else came down from the house I would have seen them." While I spoke, I'd stood still and kept my gaze on the yew, but it didn't move again. "Must have been an animal or...something."

I turned to head back to the stone stairs, but a blur of motion caught my eye. A figure appeared from behind the yew then ducked out of sight. The silver-green leaves rustled and shook, and water drops sprayed.

The person—a man, I thought—with dark hair hunched down behind the garden plants and stayed out of sight as he moved away from me. I headed for the stairs, but before I'd gone even two steps, the figure reached the point where the landscape of the garden gave way to the edging of beech trees. He disappeared into the deep shadows under the trees. Faintly, I heard the sound of someone squelching through the fallen leaves, then the garden was quiet again, except for the *plink* of water dripping off leaves.

A thin voice called my name, and I put the phone back to my ear. "Kate? Are you there?"

"Yes, I'm here. There *was* someone in the garden with me. He

—or it could have been a she, I guess—ran when they realized I'd noticed them." I went back to the yew walk.

"Ran away?"

"Yes, all bent over so that I couldn't see them." A few low branches on the beech trees swayed where the figure had pushed through. It was easy to follow the path the person had taken, a trail of flattened silvery-green leaves and broken stems ran in a straight line from the yew to the garden's edge.

"Could it have been someone from the house?" Alex asked. "Maybe one of the security guards sneaking out for a smoke?"

I'd told Alex about the no-smoking-in-the-house rule that Arabella had implemented. I looked back at the yew, trying to remember. "No, it couldn't have been one of them. There was a second before he ducked behind the plants, and this guy had longish dark hair. Well, I suppose it could have been a woman with dark hair cut in a bob..." I trailed off. It couldn't have been Torrie. She had dark hair, but she had an abundance of gold highlights. I was sure the person who had been in the garden didn't have highlights.

"Could it have been Arabella?" Alex asked. "She's got short dark hair in one of those cuts—what did you call it?"

"A bob. No, it couldn't have been her. She has light brown hair, not dark brown. Actually," I said more slowly, "I suppose it could have been her. The only time I've seen her, she was wearing a big hat, and I couldn't see her hair. I haven't spoken to her or seen her up close since they arrived, except on the path that time. Her umbrella was one of those with the steep curved sides, and she held it down almost covering her face. I couldn't see her hair then. In the photo I'd seen on the tabloid front page she'd had brown hair, but it could be any shade." Different roles required different looks so her hair could be a different shade, depending on what role she'd just finished, or she could have changed her hair color herself. "But why would she run away from me?"

"You said Torrie told you that Arabella gave up smoking. Maybe Arabella wanted a cigarette, but didn't want anyone to know. Maybe she was embarrassed to be caught smoking."

I sniffed. "I don't smell any smoke." But a fruity smell that I couldn't place immediately lingered in the air. The wet turf around the yew was flattened on the side of the shrub that had been opposite of me. "No cigarette butts anywhere." My gaze ran up the shrub from the wide base to the narrow top. It was certainly big enough for someone to hide behind. The top of it reached several inches above my head. I noticed something white below the prickly branches and picked it up.

I smoothed the tiny rectangle of paper, a balled up gum wrapper. I wasn't familiar with the brand name, which was printed diagonally across one side. I sniffed the inside of the wrapper. Banana.

"Did you know there is a gum that's banana flavored?" I asked.

"Now that's random."

"I found a bit of paper—a gum wrapper—under the tree. Banana flavored."

"Do you think the person dropped it, or maybe it fell out of their pocket?"

"Could be, or it could have been here for days...but it's not wet." I scanned the rest of the yew and the ground. "Oh, wait. There's a footprint." A clear indentation of a shoe print showed in the flowerbed beside the yew. I poised my foot over the muddy imprint, but didn't touch the ground. "Nope, I bet it was a man. The footprint is quite a bit larger than mine. Some sort of work shoe, I think from the treads. I should go and let one of the Hibbert cousins know someone got inside the gate." I blew out a sigh. "Arabella and company won't be happy with this."

CHAPTER 5

I FOUND TORRIE IN THE kitchen, making tea. One of the Hibberts sat at the long table. I guessed it was Sylvester because he wasn't wearing a silver hoop in his earlobe. He nodded to me and went back to his game of what I thought looked like Solitaire, but what I'd learned the Brits called Patience. I pushed back the hood of my raincoat, staying on the mat so I didn't drip water. "There was someone in the garden when I was down there. A man, I think."

Torrie and Sylvester exchanged a look. I'd thought I'd have to convince them, but there was no question they both believed me. Some unspoken communication flickered between them. Torrie's gaze darted to the row of windows overlooking the terrace. She put down a package of tea bags. "I'll tell Arabella." She darted out of the kitchen.

"Are you sure it was a man?" Sylvester—or maybe Chester—put down the stack of playing cards.

"Pretty sure. He left a footprint in the mud in the yew walk. I think it's too big to be a woman's footprint. As soon as he realized I was there, he took off. He ran through the garden and disappeared into the woods." I didn't say anything about the gum wrapper that was now tucked away in my pocket. It could have been there a long time. Maybe the branches sheltered it from the drizzle, and that's why it was dry.

"Wait here," he said. "I'll check." He didn't bother to get a jacket, just went directly outside.

I scraped my feet on the mat and shook out my jacket then stepped into the kitchen, my gaze running over the card game as I waited for Torrie to come back. He was near the end of the game. Long rows of cards trailed across the table with a few of them bumping up against a stack of mail.

"...it could have been Violet," Torrie was saying as she and Arabella came down the hall into the kitchen. "She came by earlier today."

Arabella's stride checked in the doorway. "Violet? Here?" She sighed. "I suppose she's still going on about her ridiculous little school?"

"I don't know," Torrie said. "Probably. She didn't say why she'd come. I talked to her through the intercom. She said she was in the area and wanted to see you."

"And what did you tell her?"

Torrie said, "That it wasn't a good time—like I always do."

"Good. Although, I'm sure she'll be back later. Don't let her in. I suppose I'll have to speak to her. I'll call her later," Arabella said in a vague tone of voice, then she spotted me. "Kate, darling, was it terrible?" Her hair was wrapped up in a towel, and she wore a long green silk kimono that fluttered around her ankles as she crossed the kitchen, giving the impression she was floating. She gripped my hand, and her charm bracelet jangled with the movement. "He didn't hurt you, did he?"

Surprised by her physical presence, and the intensity of her dark gaze as she studied every inch of my face, I leaned back. "No, I'm fine. He ran away."

"There," Torrie said with satisfaction. "You see, it couldn't have been Stevie. He'd never run away."

A frown creased the skin between Arabella's perfectly shaped brows. "No, you're right. He wouldn't do that. But I don't think— Violet wouldn't...no, she's never been brave enough to even *try* to get inside grounds that are gated and walled."

Stevie Lund's photo had also been on the cover of the tabloid when they ran the story about Arabella and Stevie's break-up. The inset photo of him had been much smaller, but I did remember he had dark hair and a prominent brow over small, close-set eyes. Had it been Stevie in the garden? I hadn't seen enough of the man to say, so I didn't mention it. Instead, I asked, "Who's Violet?"

Arabella's expressive eyes went to the ceiling as her shoulders dropped. "My sister. So trying. Always sniveling and going on and on about her painting." She still gripped my hands and pulled them out a few inches to look me over, head to toe. "You're sure you're okay?"

"Yes. Fine."

"Good." She squeezed my hands then dropped them.

"One of the Hibberts is out there now," Torrie said.

Arabella folded herself into a seat at the table, casually sweeping the rows of cards out of her way. "Where is that tea? I'm parched."

Arabella missed the flat line that Torrie's lips compressed into as she picked up the kettle. The other security guy came into the room, shrugging into a jacket. He turned his head as he pulled his collar free, and I saw he had on a silver earring so it must be Chester. Arabella stared at him. "Where are you going?"

"To help—"

"No. You stay here, in the house."

He opened his mouth to protest, but Arabella said, "You go back to watching the gate on the monitor. Let me know if anyone approaches." She sent Torrie a look. "*Anyone.*"

I felt as if I'd walked into the middle of a play's second act. Unspoken messages were thick in the air at Tate House, and I was completely lost. Chester left the room, and I said, "It does seem that the person in the garden wasn't interested in the house or being caught or even seen. As soon as I realized he was there, he ran."

"Yes, I'm sure you're right. Probably just a nosy fan." She turned the full wattage of her smile on me, but despite her relaxed pose in the chair with her leg crossed and one foot bobbing in the air, I didn't quite believe she was so unconcerned. "I'll have the Hibberts patrol the grounds. That should take care of it." She adjusted the position of the charms falling across her wrist, carefully separating a key from a sandal encrusted with diamonds.

The door opened, and Sylvester came in. "No one out there now, but you're right about the footprint," he said. "It was a man. He didn't leave a trail in the woods because of the leaves." He frowned as he took in the jumble of cards that Arabella had pushed up against the mail.

The whistle of the kettle cut through the air. Torrie removed it from the stove and flicked off the burner. I asked, "How did the man get in, though? It couldn't have been through the gate, if... um...Chester?...is watching the monitors."

"Probably came over the wall," Sylvester said. "If someone was determined, they could climb it."

"Well, Stevie would never do that—it might ruin one of his precious suits," Arabella said as she fingered one of the larger charms, a square in the shape of a handbag with the imprint of the word *Cartier* across it. "What did the footprint look like? What sort of shoe was it?" Arabella asked still examining her bracelet. Her posture was casual, but the tension was there again, underlining her words.

Sylvester handed his phone to Arabella. She frowned for a

moment, then laughed, and turned the phone so that Torrie could see it. The flash had highlighted the thick treads and showed deep grooves in the dirt.

Torrie set down a mug in front of Arabella and took the phone. "That must be…what? A work boot or hiking boot?"

Arabella picked up her tea. "And that is how I know it wasn't Stevie. He never lets anything except Italian leather cover his feet. He wouldn't even pick up something as…well, crude and workmanlike as that. I'm sure it was just some fan." She sighed, all trace of anxiety gone now. "I can't tell you how tedious it is to be in the limelight. I can't go *anywhere*, do anything, without people staring. And now I have people climbing over walls to get close to me."

She sighed again before she sipped her tea. She didn't sound all that upset—more like she was secretly delighted with the situation. "Torrie, how rude," Arabella said suddenly. "You didn't offer tea to our visitor."

Torrie's lips flattened again as I said, "Oh, no, that's fine. I'm on my way out. As long as everything is under control, I'll get out of your way."

"Yes, this sort of thing is nothing new, unfortunately. I've never had anyone scaling walls to get to me, but there were those awful people in Brighton. Remember that, Torrie? The ones who —" She shifted in her chair and her elbow connected with the stack of mail and pile of playing cards, sending everything sliding across the table. I caught a thin flat box before it hit the floor, and Sylvester bent to gather up some letters and playing cards. "Hibbert, don't leave your things out. Always tidy up."

"Yes, ma'am," Sylvester said. I felt myself coloring in embarrassment for him. After all, he'd left the cards neatly arranged on the table and gone to check the garden to protect Arabella, but I knew better than to point this out. My first location scouting boss had a saying, *When working with the talent, keep your thoughts to yourself.* I bit my tongue and picked up the last pieces of mail, which included several more flat boxes. They were addressed and pre-stamped with the customs form filled in, ready to go to New Jersey. "Would you like me to drop these in the postbox?" I asked to break the uncomfortable silence.

Arabella, who had been sipping her tea while watching us pick up the playing cards and mail off the floor, put her mug down with a firm thud and reached for the stack. "Oh, no. I couldn't ask you to do that."

"It's no trouble," I said as Sylvester stood and tapped the playing cards into a neat stack, then handed the rest of the mail to Arabella. "I'll go right by there tonight."

She positioned the boxes on the table and rested both hands on them. "No, this is business correspondence. Contracts, you know, along with some replies to fan mail—signed photos. I like to send them off myself. It gives me a bit of exercise."

"Okay, great. Well, big day tomorrow. If there's nothing else you need…"

Arabella shook her head. "No. You run along. Thank you for your concern…er—" She paused uncertainly. Torrie breathed my name, and Arabella belatedly said, "…Kate. Oh, one other thing, Kate. I expect you to keep this incident about the intruder to yourself. No spreading it around the village."

"No, of course not," I said, feeling sure that she wanted to be the one to spread the story. "See you tomorrow, bright and early."

A tiny line marred the skin between Arabella's eyebrows. Torrie said, "Arabella's looking forward to the interview," with a slight emphasis on the last word.

Arabella's face cleared. "Oh, right. Yes, delighted to be involved in your little production. Torrie and Hibbert went over to Parkview this morning playing tourist. They said it was quite pretty. I'm so looking forward to it."

I left, thinking that I shouldn't believe a word Arabella said.

CHAPTER 6

I HEARD MY NAME AND looked up from raking the gravel on one of the paths that surrounded Parkview Hall to see Melissa coming my way. She carried a large box propped on her hip. "Can you believe how gorgeous it is today?"

I leaned on the rake. "We should be so lucky every day we shoot outside." Not a single cloud interrupted the continuous arc of cobalt blue. With the huge oak and beech trees that were spaced across the rolling green lawn, their emerald leaves flickering in the light breeze, it was hard to believe that the whole landscape had been coated in a gray mist for the last few days.

The forecast predicted another band of rain coming our way later in the day tomorrow, so we had to take advantage of the nice weather. We'd switched Arabella's interview, which would take place indoors, to tomorrow. Fortunately, I didn't have to do much to get the outside of Parkview Hall ready. The trashcans had been removed, and the fixed landscape lighting that lit the walls of the stately home in the evening had been hidden with some artfully placed plants.

Melissa shifted the box higher. "At least it's nice today. I was beginning to worry we'd never get these last scenes done." Melissa had recently moved to Costume. She was in her element, working with clothes. Her own style was eclectic, and I never knew what she'd wear. One day she'd have on a gauzy shabby chic outfit, then the next day she'd wear a punk style of spandex and leather. Today she was clearly channeling a preppy look with a knee-length skirt, dark tights, and a white button-down shirt.

"So Arabella is here?" I asked.

Melissa frowned. "Yes, she's in Makeup right now."

"That's good."

"Why? Were you worried? She's been in Nether Woodsmoor for days, right?"

"Yes, but I don't think we're her top priority."

Melissa grinned. "We're certainly not on the same level as a feature film. And she doesn't have any lines to remember here. In fact, today she doesn't have to speak at all. It should suit her just fine now that she's gone all superior. Not that she'd need to speak to me. She made sure that wouldn't happen."

"What do you mean?"

"Didn't I tell you? I knew her eons ago. Arabella, Torrie, and I were all in a production together, but she doesn't even want to cross paths with me now. She had another requirement besides working with you. She *didn't* want to work with me. It was in that last email Torrie sent. Paul didn't read that part out to you and everyone else, but he told me about it later. But that's fine by me. I don't want to see her either." Melissa squinted up at the sun, which was shining down, warming the path and the golden stone of Parkview. "I better get back with these parasols. The women will need them today."

A voice called Melissa's name, and we both turned to see Paul cutting across the grass to us. He said, "Going back to the trailers?"

Melissa nodded.

"I'll go with you."

I went back to raking. I knew neither one of them would hear another word I said. Since our last scouting trip to Bath, Paul and Melissa had trouble concentrating on anyone else when the two of them were together. It was like they were in a rosy little bubble of their own, separated from everyone else.

I finished smoothing out the low spots in the path then stepped back and took in the whole scene. The pale path contrasted sharply with the deep green of the grass and hedges that bounded it on one side. On the other, the golden stones of Parkview soared up with its rows of windows glinting in the sun. The massive stone urns and finials that lined the roof stood out sharply against the deep blue of the sky.

Beatrice, more formally known as Lady Stone, would be pleased at how good Parkview looked, I thought. She and Sir Harold still lived in Parkview Hall, but they were currently away meeting their new granddaughter who had arrived a few days ago. Beatrice and Sir Harold did their best to balance actually living in Parkview while also opening it to let visitors tour it and have celebrations like weddings and parties.

Its use as a filming location was another boost to Parkview's bottom line. This side of the exterior of Parkview Hall glowed a buttery golden color after the scrubbing it had received during the winter when it was closed to visitors. Each side of the building was being cleaned and restored, removing layers of grime. It was a labor-intensive, not to mention costly, job and the most that could be managed was one side each year. I'd heard some grumbling from visitors, who complained that the enormous square of draped scaffolding ruined the tour of Parkview for them, but Beatrice had added a new section to the tour that let visitors see the work in progress. I'd seen several selfies with people posing beside the nearly life-size urns.

Thankfully, the side that was being worked on now was at the back of the house and out of sight of our cameras. Scaffolding covered the back of the house, which in turn, was covered in a white draping. The whole area was barricaded off as it contained not only some of the now-silent equipment used to clean and repair the surface, but also the stone decorations of urns, the smaller finials, and even two life-size statues from the roofline at the back of the house, which would be cleaned then replaced.

I'd checked the space this morning to make sure the workman indeed had the day off because we couldn't have the noise of the restoration interfering with our filming. Even though our scenes would have a voice-over or music over them in the final version, it was better to have the area cleared of workmen during filming. The rumble of equipment could be distracting to the actors, not to mention the complication of wrangling additional people near the set.

I double checked now to make sure that none of the scaffolding or rows of statuary were visible from where I stood. Everything looked fine. From this point, no one would suspect that the back of Parkview Hall was swathed in white drape and surrounded by what looked like an open-air lawn-and-garden center with rows of urns, finials, and statues waiting to be cleaned.

I put the rake away and went to check the garden, which was ready as well. It helped that we had agreed that we wouldn't alter the gardens, which meant no trimming or replanting.

My walkie-talkie crackled. "Kate, Trent here. You're needed at the parking area."

I unclipped the walkie-talkie from my hip and hit the button to talk. "On my way."

Parkview's grounds were extensive so it took me several minutes to get to what the Brits on the crew called the car park, which we'd taken over for the day. Usually the parking area was filled with cars disgorging families and tour buses dropping off day-trippers, but now it was sectioned off into areas for crew parking and trailers for Costume, Makeup, and Catering. Another area was marked off for the trucks that had brought our cameras, lights, and electrical equipment. The least glamorous area was the row of Portaloos.

I spotted Trent in his typical workday uniform, a black shirt and brown cargo pants. With his toned arms, he could have given the Hibberts a run for their money in a shoulder-width competition. Trent was one of the security guys who kept out the people who shouldn't be on set. It was my job to run interference when neighbors got upset or frustrated, but we'd filmed in Nether Woodsmoor several times and, for the most part, the villagers were used to us. We weren't quite the novelty we had been in the beginning.

Trent had his hand wrapped firmly around the upper arm of a young man with large, deep-set brown eyes and dark hair that fell over the collar of his jacket. Despite the rising temperature and sunny day, he wore a black windbreaker with a brown-and-white plaid scarf around his neck. His jaw was working as he chewed a piece of gum.

"...just want to cut through. No problem, mate."

Trent nodded in a noncommittal way then tilted his head to me. "She's who you have to make your case to." To me, he said, "Let me know if you need me." Trent stepped back and crossed his arms over his chest, staying nearby in case I needed him.

I raised my eyebrows at the man.

"So you're the lady in charge," he said, one corner of his mouth curving up. "You are...?"

"How can I help you?"

He fixed his deep-set brown eyes on me, doing his best imitation of a puppy dog. "Don't want to do formal introductions, yeah? We'll keep it casual then. I'm Gil, by the way. I live over there," he pointed vaguely across Parkview's grounds. The motion caused his lightweight jacket to gap, and I saw black plastic under the scarf.

"You live around here?" I asked. "You don't look familiar."

"Of course, I live here," he said around chomps on the gum. "In Rose Cottage."

I smiled and leaned forward as if I were about to share a secret. "Did you know that is the most common name for cottage name plates in England?" I caught a definite whiff of banana.

Gil smiled again, this time with his whole mouth, but continued to work the gum with his mouth half open. "Interesting. But that's where I live."

"Hmm. I know that detail about how popular the name Rose Cottage is because *I* live in a cottage. I needed to order a new nameplate. Honeysuckle Cottage is not nearly as popular as Rose Cottage—the website listed the top names."

"That's fascinating—really, it is. I'd love to stay and chat about home names, but I must get moving. An appointment, you see." He shifted slightly and raised his chin in an effort to see over the hedge that separated the parking area from the grounds. "What's going on here? I've never known the paths to be closed."

"We're filming."

His eyes widened. "A movie?"

"No, a documentary, but I think you already know that." I made eye contact with Trent. "Gil is not allowed in. And he doesn't live in Nether Woodsmoor. Keep him off the grounds."

Trent nodded. "Yes, ma'am." He fastened his hand around the guy's upper arm again and practically levitated Gil as he pulled him back toward the main road.

"Hey," Gil shouted, "I do live here. You can't call me a liar."

"I live here, and I've never seen you around." I took my phone out and snapped a picture of him as Trent propelled him backward to a white Ford Fiesta with a large dent near the front wheel well. "You should do a better job of keeping your camera hidden when you're trying to sneak onto a set," I added.

I checked the photo and nodded. I'd managed to snap a full-length shot that included the hiking boots he wore.

CHAPTER 7

"**Y**OU DIDN'T FIND HER?" TORRIE asked as she rushed up to me.

"No. And I checked all the trailers," I said.

Everything had been going so well. The first part of the day had passed uneventfully with the filming in the garden going smoothly. Arabella, dressed in a high-waisted gown with her parasol shading her face, moved through the garden alone, then with other actors, including a stand-in for Mr. Knightly. Since he wasn't the same actor who would appear in the movie version of *Emma*, the imitation Mr. Knightly was positioned so that he was turned away from the camera, or he was in the area of the shot that Ren said would be slightly out of focus.

The only problems were Arabella's complaints about her wig, and the fact that I had to stop an enthusiastic crewmember from cutting some flowers that were in the frame.

Ren had given the talent a break while the crew transferred to the gravel path beside Parkview, but when the production assistant went to call Arabella, she wasn't around. "You're sure she's not strolling around Parkview? You checked the other side of the house?" I asked Torrie.

"She wouldn't stay outside in the sun during a break—her skin, you know," Torrie said, a trace of sarcastic bite coming through her worry.

"What about the Hibberts? Isn't one of them with her?" I hadn't thought to ask about the bodyguards when the alarm was raised a few minutes ago.

"One of them came with us, and one of them stayed at Tate House. But Arabella said she didn't need someone with her every moment on the set, and sent Hibbert into town to pick up a salad for her."

I nodded, realizing that Arabella had assumed that she was safe at Parkview. Film crews did tend to create their own self-enclosed world, which gave the location the feeling of a sealed off ecosystem, a place where the real world couldn't intrude.

Unfortunately, I knew the invisible barriers surrounding this location were flimsy and could be easily penetrated. Parkview had miles of grounds, most of them open. We did have security at the gate and people patrolling the area that ran along the road to make sure no one slipped in there, but the property was too extensive to monitor every inch.

Elise—outfitted head-to-toe in black as always—swept across the lawn, and descended on us like a crow attacking a scrap of food. "Well?" she asked, eyebrows raised. I shook my head. "Arabella can't have disappeared," Elise said, exasperated. "We still have the scene by the house to do."

Paul trotted up, his pencil falling from his ear. He caught it in midair and said in a low voice to Elise, "Ren says if we don't find her soon, we need to call the police."

"Nonsense," Elise said quickly, and I knew she was thinking that calling the police would effectively shut us down for the day, which would affect the budget and the schedule. "She's probably wandered off on her own. The grounds are massive. We shouldn't do anything until we've looked everywhere."

Elise waved Paul in the direction of the long tree-lined drive. "Check to make sure she's not at the end of the drive. I don't know why she would go there, but check anyway."

I asked, "Did anyone look in the greenhouses?"

No one replied. "I'll do that," I said, remembering Torrie's aversion to being around any type of flowering plant. She had stayed clear of the gardens this morning, and I doubted that even searching for her missing employer would induce her to enter the gardens. Torrie said she'd check the parking area and trailers again.

I crossed the lawn, rounded the manor house, then hurried down the flight of steps to the garden, pausing to run my gaze over the immediate area. But the only people I saw were in modern clothes, not Regency gowns. I reached the first green-house and entered the steamy atmosphere, which was heady with the scent of damp earth and flowers. It appeared empty, but I walked the length of it then left through the door at the opposite end. Several narrow greenhouses were situated end-to-end, and I walked through the chain of glass enclosures, passing fruit trees and flowering shrubs.

They were built on a steady rise of land. Between each green-house I trotted up a set of steps. When I reached the last one, the view out the steamy windows overlooked the formal gardens and the rolling countryside. You could even see the sparkling gray ribbon of the river that bounded one side of Parkview. I didn't pause to take in the scene, but hurried through the last green-house because I'd caught a glimpse of a figure in white outside the building. Ducking under tropical plants with mammoth drooping leaves, I pushed through the door at the far end and stepped into the cooler air outside. Arabella stood in the shade of a magnificent old oak, her parasol propped against the trunk, and her gloves and reticule tossed on the grass.

She faced away from me toward the view, but she heard my approach and turned.

"Everyone is looking for you," I said.

"Are they?" She sounded completely unconcerned as she lifted what was left of a cigarette to her lips, drew in a breath, then blew out smoke with a sigh of satisfaction.

If Melissa were here, I knew she'd have heart palpitations at the sight of the cigarette. Many of the costumes were borrowed from Parkview Hall and were actually from the Regency era. At least Arabella had removed the long white gloves that were part of the ensemble.

"They can't start without me, can they?" She studied the end of the cigarette. "My guilty secret. I've been so good for so long, but sometimes I simply *must* have one."

I unclipped the walkie-talkie. "I'll let them know we're on our way back."

"Yes, do that. Is Torrie having one of her panic attacks?" Her tone was disinterested as she looked back to the grounds.

"She was worried about you. We all were."

"Hmm. She should be—worried, that is." Arabella dropped the cigarette and ground it into the turf with the toe of her satin slipper. "Someone is trying to kill me."

CHAPTER 8

*H*AD I HEARD HER RIGHT? "Did you say someone is trying to kill you?" I let go of the TALK button on the walkie-talkie.

"Yes." She nodded. "I got another threat this morning. Nasty thing." She closed her eyes briefly, and her affected manner dropped away. "I destroyed it, of course, but I'm sure Torrie has the others. She's like that—she would keep them."

"The others?"

"Yes, they've been arriving quite regularly, words clipped from magazines—rather juvenile, you know—like some child's art project, telling me my days are numbered—that sort of thing."

I blinked then spoke into the walkie-talkie. I let Paul know I'd found Arabella and that we'd be back shortly, then focused on Arabella. "You let the police know about the threats, right?" I asked while my mind raced. Death threats were definitely something that should have been mentioned to us.

"No. I know it's Stevie. And the police can't touch him. Stevie always makes certain of that, after what happened to his uncle. Who else could it be?"

"Perhaps this guy." I took out my phone and pulled up the

photo I'd taken earlier of the dark-haired man as Trent was escorting him away. "He tried to get through security today. He has a nasally voice and lied about living in the village." I wouldn't have pegged him as a serious threat. "He seemed more of a self-absorbed guy out to get what he could for himself, but..."

She looked at me sharply, her face worried as she yanked the phone out of my hand then her expression cleared as she laughed. "Gil? He's not a threat. He's a gnat. Pesky and irritating, but not threatening."

"He did say his name was Gil. Who is he?"

She shoved the phone back at me then bent to pick up her gloves, parasol, and reticule. "Gil Brayden, a low-rung paparazzi. He's decided I'm his ticket to the big time. He's followed me everywhere lately."

The drawstring mouth of the reticule gapped open as she picked it up, and a cloth pouch spilled halfway out. She shoved it back inside as I said, "That doesn't mean he's not the one sending you the notes. It could be him. How are you getting the notes?"

"The first were through the post, but I threw those away. Lately, Stevie has gotten more inventive. This morning it was in the card that came with a flower delivery. They were orchids," she said as if I couldn't argue with that statement.

"I'm sorry I don't see what that has to do—"

"Stevie *always* sent me orchids," she said impatiently. "It was our thing."

"Hmm." That didn't seem conclusive to me, but I only asked, "How else have the notes been delivered?"

She swished the furled parasol idly through the air, but her eyes sparkled. "He's been quite creative, I'll give him that. If he wasn't talking about my death, it would be almost...entertaining."

She was enjoying the whole situation, and I couldn't help but wonder if she was exaggerating things. It wouldn't be the first time a celebrity had a skewed picture of reality.

"Let's see," she said, her gaze roving up the tree branches. "One showed up in my menu at dinner about a week ago, another was left under the wiper on my car, and—oh, yes—one came with a Chinese food delivery."

"Have you received any at Tate House?"

"No. I thought maybe it was over—that he'd lost interest—but I should have known better. He's not one to give up."

"Give up on what?"

"Getting me out of the way, of course. It's the flat in London. He loves it. It was…" She shrugged. "…I don't know—a symbol, I suppose, that he'd arrived. And I'm going to take it away from him." Her mouth curved up into the first true smile I'd seen on her face. She tilted her head to the side as she studied me. "I can see you're not convinced. Stevie is quite ruthless and rather simple, poor thing. He sees what I'll do to him, and he's trying to get me out of the way."

"But surely if he were going to…attempt to harm you, he wouldn't announce it. If something happened to you, he would be the first suspect."

"Yes, but as I said, he wouldn't do it himself." Her tone was patronizing as if she were explaining something to a child. "He'll assign it to someone, someone who doesn't connect to him. But I don't have to worry about it. That's why I have the Hibberts with me. And I'm leaving on a long holiday far away from England as soon as we're done here. In a few days, Stevie will have absolutely no idea where I am."

She pulled on her gloves. "You still don't believe me, do you? Ask Torrie. It's not all in my head, I assure you." She smoothed the fabric up to her elbows. "Now, let's get back so we can shoot this last scene, and I can get out of this horrible corset. I swear, I'm never doing anything remotely historical ever again. The clothes are murder."

60

She walked by me, swinging the parasol. I picked up the cigarette butt from between the tree roots and followed her.

THE CREW BREATHED a collective sigh of relief when Arabella appeared, except for Elise. She looked thunderous. Arabella didn't seem to notice as she drifted down the gravel path to Ren. She put a hand on his arm. "I'm so sorry. I didn't realize about the time or that I'd wandered so far away. It's so gorgeous here..."

Ren smiled politely and went on to discuss what we were filming next, but there was a frosty politeness in his manner that was unusual. I glanced around and saw Torrie. I motioned for her to join me a little away from everyone.

"Arabella told me about the threats." I kept my voice low.

Her eyes widened then a blush flooded her cheeks. "Of course she did. Couldn't keep it to herself, could she? It was too good. Too juicy. I suppose there was one minute when she wasn't the center of attention."

"Do you have the threatening notes?" I asked, trying to stay focused. "She said you would have kept them."

"Yes," she said, sulkily. "I have them back at Tate House."

"We have to call the police. The production needed to know as well. We should have been informed of the issue before you arrived."

Torrie's shoulder twitched. "You know as well as I do that something like that is almost impossible to keep under wraps once you start telling people."

I let that argument slide. We were past that now. "We need to reassess everything, especially security. I'll contact the local constable. I'm sure he'll pass it along to the appropriate person to investigate it. They will want to see the notes." I'd become acquainted with Constable Albertson over the last year. This wasn't the first time we'd had trouble associated with filming, but hopefully this wouldn't be as serious as the incidents in the past.

Torrie's gaze connected with someone behind me. I turned and saw it was one of the Hibberts, dressed in khaki pants and a knit shirt today, striding across the lawn. His path took him in a wide circumference of the house. I narrowed my eyes and didn't see the silver hoop earring, so I assumed it was Sylvester. To head off any trouble, I said, "You let Sylvester know we located Ms. Emsley, right?" I looked back at Torrie and saw she was giving him a slight nod with her pointed chin. He gave me a hard stare, but didn't break his stride as he continued on his circular track around the house.

She focused back on me. "What?"

"He knows that Arabella has been found?" I repeated. With the mass of the crew, the shrubs, and the side of the house blocking the scene, Arabella was barely visible.

"Oh, that. Yes. I sent him a text."

I watched his barrel-chested figure until a raised bed of lupines in the garden blocked him from view. Torrie must have noticed my interest and said, "I told him to do a sweep of the entire area. Just to be on the safe side."

"Yes, I suppose that's a good idea. We did have someone try to get on the set earlier today." I brought up the picture of Gil Brayden on my phone and handed it to her. "Ms. Emsley recognized him. Said he was paparazzi."

Her eyes narrowed. "He's nothing but trouble."

"Arabella wasn't too concerned about him. She seemed to see him as a nuisance more than anything else."

She shoved my phone back. "Arabella is not as smart as she thinks she is. She *should* be concerned." From her clipped words and the set line of her mouth, I realized Torrie was angry.

There it was again, an undercurrent of emotion that I couldn't sort out. I sighed internally, thinking that Elise might be right. Working with "stars" was more trouble than it was worth.

Torrie's angry gaze focused on the huddle of people moving along the side of the house. As the call went out for silence, I wondered why Torrie would be upset with Arabella. Surely unwanted photographers were a run-of-the-mill occurrence that they had to handle frequently. Arabella had certainly taken that attitude yesterday, indicating that strangers appearing in the garden were no big deal.

I whispered to Torrie that I would be in touch with her at the end of the day. I left her with arms crossed, scowling at the façade of Parkview.

I tiptoed to the grass and carefully moved away so that I could make my phone call to Constable Albertson a safe distance away. He wasn't in, so I left a message then quietly returned to the area near the gravel walk, but remained on the outskirts of the crew.

Arabella, her parasol open, walked toward the camera, which was being rolled backward. A bird swooped from the line of shrubbery into the shot and Arabella flinched. Ren called, "Cut," and Arabella turned and walked back to her mark, her stride quite a bit less graceful and ambling than a moment ago. Everyone repositioned then Arabella strolled forward again when Ren called for action. Almost immediately, Ren's voice rang out, halting Arabella. "The parasol, it's too low. We can't see your face."

Arabella stepped back to her mark and shifted the parasol. It was amazing how difficult and time-consuming even a simple shot could be. I scanned the crew as everyone inched forward again synched with Arabella as if she was a cog that set a huge machine in motion. Arabella was about halfway along the side of the house, when a dark shape plummeted from the roof.

It happened so quickly that the thing had already hit the ground a yard or so behind Arabella and shattered into pieces before anyone reacted. A ripple of astonishment went through the crew, and I started forward, my heart accelerating.

What had fallen? I scanned the roofline as I ran. Everything looked exactly as it had earlier. All the stone decorations were in place, but when I pushed my way into the group that had closed around Arabella, I saw bits and pieces of stone scattered across the gravel. I recognized the graceful curves carved into the stone. The impact had broken it into several pieces, but I could tell it was a roof finial.

Through the babble of talk around us, Arabella, her hand pressed to her heart, stared at the bits of shattered stone. She looked at me, and her face transitioned as she raised an eyebrow. She was an actress and could convey so much with a look. It was as if she'd spoken aloud saying, "See, I told you someone wants to kill me."

CHAPTER 9

"HOW COULD A PIECE OF stone fall off Parkview?" Alex asked.

I switched the phone to my other ear and wished he were here with me, instead of miles away. "I'm not explaining this very well. It was a finial—one of the stone decorations from the roofline. You know, the smaller ones, not the big urns—and I don't think it fell. Nothing is missing from the stone decorations directly above the gravel walk. They're evenly spaced so it's easy to see that they're all there."

I slowed as I reached the stone bridge that arched over the river. It had been a chaotic scene on the gravel walk, and now that I was on my way home, I wanted a little time in the quiet of the countryside.

"Then where did the finial come from?" Alex asked, still sounding as bewildered as I felt.

I blew out a sigh. "The official line is that it must have been a piece that was removed from the other section of the roof that's under renovation. The theory is that it was somehow overlooked, left in a precarious position, and finally just happened to slip off and fall today, almost hitting Arabella."

After a few seconds of silence, Alex said, "That sounds doubtful."

"I agree." I let my tote bag, heavy with my camera, slide off my shoulder. I set it on the ground, then I leaned on the bridge's parapet and watched the water sweep by below me. After all the rain, the current was fast and water was high on the banks, drenching the long grass and stones that edged the river. Farther out from the bridge, the water smoothed out and reflected the overhanging branches.

Parkview Hall was a short walk away from my cottage, and on days like today when the weather was nice, I walked to work instead of driving. The wind had picked up in the afternoon, and I thought it probably wouldn't be so nice tomorrow. "I don't think that anyone else really believes it either. And the media are happy to play up the drama of it. A photo of Arabella leaving Parkview is already online at all the celebrity sites with the news that she had a near miss. Freya showed it to me."

I transferred my gaze to the water directly below the bridge. A murky reflection of my face framed with dark hair dangling on either side of it undulated in the current. "Some of the crew swear that they saw movement on the roof right after the finial hit the ground."

"But that would mean it would have to be someone from Parkview. You'd have to be familiar with the layout of the house and know how to get through the attic to the roof. I mean, I assume, access to the roof is through the attic?"

"I have no idea how someone would get up there. I don't think even the tour guides know details like that."

"And why would someone do that?" Alex asked. "Does someone have a grudge against the documentary?"

"No, I don't think so. For one thing, it's a little late for that, isn't it? We've filmed there before without problems, and we're almost done now. No, I don't think it was anyone from Parkview."

"But how would someone get up there? They couldn't just drag a ladder into place."

"No, but there is scaffolding." The bridge was constructed of the same buttery golden stone as Parkview and was hot under my arms so I shifted position, leaning back a bit.

"Ah, yes. I'd forgotten about the renovation," Alex said. "How far up does the scaffolding go?"

"All the way to the roof. And the stone roof decorations are sitting in rows in the same area on the ground, waiting to be cleaned. The area is cordoned off, but it wouldn't be hard for someone to get inside, pick up a finial, and climb the scaffolding. Once they were behind the drape that covers the scaffolding, no one would know they were there. The finial shattered when it hit the ground, but I saw the pieces. It was covered with a dark layer of grime."

"How big are the finials?"

"Much bigger than I thought. About two feet tall. They look enormous when they're lined up on the ground, like one of those oversized outdoor chess games. Of course, the urns are twice as big and must be massively heavy. There's no way one person could haul an urn from the ground to the roof without a crane or pulley. But I think the finial wouldn't be impossible to move. Slightly awkward, but doable, especially for someone strong."

"I don't like that I'm stuck here when something like that is going on." A gusty sigh came over the line. "I can't get away. We still have at least one more day here."

"I'm fine. I wasn't anywhere near it," I said, wanting to acknowledge the uneasiness I heard in his voice, but as always, my mind was a total blank. "Um, thanks for—ah—being concerned." *Lame.* Why was I so bad at this relationship thing?

Why did I sound so stilted? Alex seemed to be able to put exactly what he felt into words. Why couldn't I do that?

"Of course I'm concerned. I know how curious you are about, well, everything. And it sounds like you're already in the middle of this mess with Arabella. The whole situation worries me. Do you think it has anything to do with that paparazzi guy? Could he have set it up to get photos and a dramatic story?"

I'd already told Alex about the confrontation with Gil Brayden. I pushed away from the bridge's parapet, picked up my tote bag, and ambled along the shadowed footpath that ran back to the village. "I don't think so. For one thing, I didn't see anyone taking pictures. I suppose he could have slipped onto the grounds and been hiding behind some of the shrubbery, but he'd need an accomplice, someone to drop the finial. I got the feeling that he wasn't a team player."

"More of a one-man-show type?"

"Yes, with the man he was most concerned about being himself."

"And if Arabella had been hurt, he wouldn't have a chance to get additional photos, not if she was in the hospital."

"Right," I agreed. "So that leaves Arabella's ex. She has been getting threats that she's sure are from him." I recounted what Arabella had said about the notes. The path wound through a thicket then ran along an open stretch, giving a view of the treed hill ahead where the gables of Tate House were visible. I couldn't see my cottage because it was on the other side of the hill. "Constable Albertson has the notes now."

I crossed the meadow then lengthened my stride as the path climbed up the rise of the hill. "He sent someone with Torrie to get them from Tate House while he interviewed everyone at Parkview. He told me a detective chief inspector would be in touch."

"With something like this—a case that involves a celebrity—it's not surprising it's been passed up the chain."

The path flattened again. On my left was the dry-stone wall that enclosed Tate House while on my right dense woods ran right up to the path. I paused to catch my breath. "Yes, I suppose it had to be, no matter how…odd…the situation is."

"What do you mean?" Alex asked.

"Well, it's such a strange way to hurt someone. Kind of showy, but not what I'd call highly effective. The finial didn't actually hit that close to her. It was several feet behind her. Arabella hinted that Stevie Lund would—okay, I feel weird just saying this aloud—but I'm pretty sure that she was trying to tell me that he'd hire a hit man to hurt her. But I don't think many hit men use rocks dropped from a height, you know?"

"It certainly wouldn't have the same advantage as a gun or something like that," Alex said, and I could hear the grin in his voice, then he turned serious. "So what are you saying? You think the whole thing was a stunt?"

"I don't know." I walked slowly, my pace matching my words. "Arabella *is* afraid. Yesterday, she was scared when she first found out about the man in the garden. And she does have two security people working for her—"

I moved the phone away from my ear and listened. Yes, I'd definitely heard someone shouting, and it was coming from Tate House.

CHAPTER 10

I PUT MY PHONE IN my pocket as I backtracked along the path. I'd told Alex I would call him back after I checked in at Tate House. Wrangling Arabella and her entourage still fell to me, and I knew Elise would hold me personally responsible if something went wrong. I had to at least check that everything was okay.

Ren had dismissed most of the crew and cast once the police had said we could leave. I knew Arabella and Torrie had to stay longer, but Constable Albertson talked to them relatively early, and I'd seen them leave Parkview before I did. Even though we'd stopped filming for the day, I still had my normal end of day wrap-up to see to, and I was one of the last of the crew to leave Parkview.

As I got closer to Tate House's drive, I could hear a few words and raised my eyebrows at the vicious tone. The voice was too deep to be a woman. Had Gil returned? If he was making all that noise, he was persistent. But I didn't think he'd get inside the gate using that kind of language. The drive to Tate House curved sharply into the trees at a steep incline. I took a few steps up the drive. A yellow Ferrari with one door hanging open sat in front of the closed wrought iron gate.

It wasn't Gil. A man paced back and forth in front of the gate like a restless animal at a zoo, his suit jacket flapping with his jerky movements. He kicked the bars a few times, the metallic clang filling the air as the gates gave an inch then resettled into position. He stalked back to the intercom box. He leaned close to it, giving me a profile view of his bulging brow. I realized he was Stevie Lund as he said, "I know you're in there Arabella. Do you hear me? I found you." His voice, which had been rough and loud, went soft. "And I want what's mine." The quieter more controlled tone made the words more frightening than if he'd shouted them.

I swallowed and backed away a few steps, using the dry-stone wall to shield me. This situation was not something that I could handle. I inched forward enough that I could see the gate again. Lund looked at the gate, hands on hips. Then, in a burst of speed, he moved quickly. Striding around the open car door, he leaned in, shut off the engine, and slammed the door.

He took a few steps back and ran toward the gate. He leapt about halfway up the stone pillar that served as the gatepost. Using the grooves in the mortar between the stones, he climbed to the top, grabbed the stone orb that crowned the post, and levered himself over, landing lightly on his feet on the other side of the gate.

So much for the security of the wall and gate. The man pulled his cuffs straight, ran his hands down the lapels of his jacket, then strode up the drive as if he owned the place. As his figure disappeared into the trees, I took out my phone and dialed Torrie's number. Wasn't one of the Hibbert cousins watching the security monitors? But I didn't hear a shout or the thud of feet coming from the house, only the rustle of leaves and some birdsong.

I listened to the line ring several times then hung up and scrolled to Arabella's number. I'd never called her directly, but I'd entered her number in my phone when Elise insisted I take on the role of liaison between her and the production.

I kept an eye on the gate in case Stevie Lund returned while I listened for Arabella to answer. When the call switched to voicemail, I hung up. Briefly, I considered calling the police, but decided to continue through my contact list. Even in a small village like Nether Woodsmoor, it would take a while to explain what had happened and send someone here. I called Sylvester's number first since he had been the one with Arabella today at Parkview. He answered before the first ring ended. "Yeah?"

"Sylvester, this is Kate Sharp. Are you at Tate House?"

"No. Upper Benning."

"Is Torrie at the house?" I asked.

"No, she's with me."

"Where is Arabella? Is she with you, too?"

"She's back at the house with Chester."

"Okay. Stevie Lund just climbed the gatepost and got into the grounds—" The drone of the dial tone cut into my sentence. I pulled the phone away from my ear and looked at the screen. "He hung up on me," I muttered as I found Chester's number and called him.

He answered immediately. Before I could say more than my name, he interrupted. "I'm on it."

A dial tone buzzed in my ear. "Well, you're welcome." I ended the call then stood there a moment, my thumb hovering over the numbers. Should I go ahead and call the police or wait? Arabella had not been happy that she'd had to speak to Constable Albertson today. She'd been even more upset when Torrie told her the police wanted the threatening notes.

Leaves rustled and branches snapped behind me. I spun around, but the path was empty in both directions as far as I could see. Then several dull thuds sounded. The noise had come from the direction of the village. The curve of the path meant that I couldn't see more than a few yards. I wondered if Stevie Lund had decided to leave Tate House a different way than the gate.

I stepped away from the stone wall, crossed the path, and merged into the trees on the other side. I waited, tense and ready to step deeper into the woods, but the only thing that moved were the treetops as they swayed in the wind, which had picked up as the day went on.

I waited a minute or two more, then left the trees and walked along the path in the direction that the sound had come from. As I moved around the curve, a pile of tumbled stone came into view. The dry-stone walls of Derbyshire were made without mortar. The flat stones were stacked horizontally one on top of another, except for the top row where the flat stones were positioned vertically like a row of books standing on a shelf. A gap on the top row of the stone wall looked like a missing tooth.

The stone walls of the countryside were ancient and crumbling in some places, but this wall was normally in good shape. A group of volunteers had even repaired some breaks in it not long ago. The thuds I heard must have been the stones as they landed on the path. I glanced up and down the section of the path that was in my view, but I only saw a few cyclists in the distance.

I turned and headed back to the gate to tell Chester that Stevie Lund had gotten away over a different section of the wall. The sound of pounding feet filled the air as I reached the drive. A clang of metal, the same sound that I'd heard when Stevie hit the gates in frustration, rang out. I slowed and peered around the curve of the wall up the drive.

I was in time to see Stevie scale the gate and throw his leg over the top of it—he hadn't bothered using the gatepost this time, but had gone straight for the gate, using the ornate iron swirls for footholds. He dropped to the ground just as nimbly as he had before then sprinted to the yellow sports car. He slid inside and closed the door with one smooth motion. The growl of the engine filled the air as Chester rushed the gate, a handgun angled toward the sky as he ran. The rumble of the engine intensified. The car shot backward, red brakes flared, and I caught another glimpse of him in the side view mirror. He looked thrilled, a smirk on his face. Our gazes connected for a second, then the engine roared, and the car accelerated away, sending bits of leaves spinning in its wake.

When I looked back at Chester, the gun was out of sight. He was breathing a little hard as he shook the gate with one hand. I went up the incline and spoke to him through the bars. "Didn't you see him on the monitor?"

He fiddled with the silver hoop in his earlobe as he looked at me out of the corner of his eye. "I was in the loo." He paced away in a small circle. The gate clanged as he came back and gave it another shove. I decided not to ask any more questions about the security arrangements...or about the gun. I knew gun ownership in the UK was more limited than in the States, but I supposed he could be authorized to carry a gun since he was a security guard.

"Arabella's okay?"

He nodded. "She's in the garden." His gaze cut back to the road where Lund had disappeared. "He didn't get to the back of the house. I spotted him as he came up the drive to the front door."

"I better speak to Arabella," I said, thinking of damage control. I wanted to make sure Arabella was okay and see if she was thinking of complaining to Elise about the security arrangements at Tate House—although it's hard to defend against an aggressive man willing to climb over gates. "If nothing else, Torrie's probably called her," I added. I had the code and could let myself in, but I waited. He reluctantly punched the code into the keypad on his side of the gate. It slowly swung open, and he went to the end of the drive, his gaze fixed on the road where the Ferrari had disappeared.

I left him there and went around the house through the quiet grassy alcove with the iron table to the terrace. I crossed to the edge and spotted Arabella on a landing about halfway down the staircase. I thought she was doing some sort of stretching pose that I'd never seen before. I dropped my tote bag at the top of the stairs and started down.

"Arabella," I called. "We had some excitement at the gate, but everything is okay..." She didn't move. Then I realized that her feet were dangling off the landing, and something about the position was all wrong. The human body, even in the contortions of yoga, wouldn't normally twist like that. With a sick feeling in my stomach, I surged down the stairs.

CHAPTER 11

*A*S I HURRIED DOWN THE steps with my gaze fixed on Arabella's unmoving body, I slipped. I windmilled an arm, recovered my balance, and slowed to a more careful pace.

My heartbeat thudding, I jogged down the steps and across the wider landings until I reached her. She was near the base of the stairs, but not at the very bottom.

She was in workout clothes, yoga pants and a spandex sports top. Her hair—solid dark brown without the bold gold highlights that Torrie favored, I was finally able to see—was pulled back in a low, short ponytail. Her head was turned away from me, but now that I was closer, I could see the unnatural bend in the angle of her neck. I swallowed and looked away, drawing in a deep breath before I moved carefully around her to the step below her.

Her face was whiter than the blooms on the lily of the valley plants that lined the stairs, and her eyes were wide open and fixed. A gust of wind whipped around me. Leaves and a scrap of paper danced across the step above her. The wind stirred her hair, and a few strands fell across the lashes of her blank eyes. I suddenly felt sick and dizzy. If she were alive, she would have reached up to brush the hairs away or tossed her head to shake them free, but she would never move again.

I sat down on the nearest stair, and looked away, focusing on the flowers as the wind tossed the drooping heads of the lily of the valley. The scrap of paper had caught in the leaves. One corner of the paper flickered in the wind, and I saw print running diagonally across it before another gust of wind waved the leaves, releasing the paper. The breeze whipped it away downhill.

I heard a voice and turned. Chester's bulky figure was descending the stairs at a fast clip, but he checked as his foot slipped. The stumble barely slowed him down, and he was directly above me almost before I could rise unsteadily to my feet. I held up a hand. "Don't move her. She's…it's not good," I said.

Chester stepped around Arabella and joined me on the lower step. His face changed as soon as he saw her face, his skin going almost as white as Arabella's. He ran his hand over his mouth and jaw then shook his head. "I'll call 999." He took out his cell phone and faced the garden, his back to me. With one hand on his hip, his suit jacket flared and moved with the wind, making him look wider than his already substantial width as he spoke quietly into the phone.

I looked back at Arabella, almost unable to believe that she was dead. But she remained unmoving, her head at that awful angle, her arms splayed, and her feet with her toenails painted seashell pink dangling off the step. She had tiny, delicate feet. The sunlight glittered on her toe ring and a thin gold ankle bracelet. Above the line of the gold chain, her toned calf muscles showed how seriously she worked out. In her form-fitting workout clothes, she looked more like an Olympic athlete, lean and toned, than a film star.

But it didn't look like she'd even started her workout today. I twisted around and looked up the stairs. She must have slipped on the way down, like I'd slipped on the step near the top. I could have ended up at the bottom of the steps just like Arabella. I felt a bit light-headed at the thought, and forced myself to keep looking around to keep my mind off that track.

A yoga mat, still fastened into its tight roll, rested in the flowers at the side of the stairs. A full water bottle had rolled up against one of the landscape lights.

I fingered my phone, and considered calling Elise. She needed to know what had happened, but I decided to wait until after the police arrived. I didn't want to think about what Arabella's death would mean to the filming schedule and the episode that was to feature her, not to mention what Elise's reaction would be to the news that an up-and-coming star had died while working with us. The wind flung my hair over my eyes, and I pushed it back. I hoped Elise had seen to the insurance.

Chester's mention of my name drew my attention back to him as he said, "Yes, Kate is here with me..." His tone turned sharp. "No, I'll not wait in the house." He ended the call. "Like the house needs guarding right now," he muttered as he turned toward me.

"Torrie and Sylvester are on their way back. They turned back when they got your call, so they should arrive within a few minutes. The ambulance...or police, or both, I suppose, will be here soon, too," he said.

I nodded and took a deep breath. I was relieved that I didn't feel as shaky as I had a few moments ago. I was still trembling, but didn't feel light-headed anymore. "When did she come out here?" I asked.

He rubbed his hand across his chin again, his fingers brushing against the silver hoop earring. "About half an hour ago, maybe more," he said. "She told me to stay inside. She wanted to be alone."

He looked so upset that I said, "I don't know if you could have done anything. She must have slipped...even if you were out here, you couldn't have prevented this..." I shrugged. Unless he'd been in front of her and managed to break her fall, there was no way he could have saved her. "I nearly fell, too, on my way down. It could have happened to anyone."

Chester's heavy brow knit together. "My foot skidded, too."

"Yes, it did." I'd seen him struggle to get his balance, but with the shock of finding Arabella, my mind was moving slowly. I'm sure my face reflected his troubled look. We both moved carefully around Arabella and headed up the steps, slowing as we neared the top.

Four steps from the terrace, I pointed to a shallow dip in the step where a puddle of water reflected the sky. "I think I slipped here. It's just a little bit of water." A ground cover with small purple flowers edged the stairs on each side, the splash of color spilling over onto the steps and filling in around the landscape lights.

"Or maybe here." Chester studied the step above it where another pool of water shimmered in a low-lying area.

A door at the back of the house opened. I was high enough on the steps that my head was level with the terrace, and I could see Sylvester come out the door from the kitchen. He crossed the terrace in a rapid stride. Torrie stopped in the doorway and braced herself, her hand against the doorframe, as she scanned the terrace. I was surprised that she didn't follow Sylvester outside, but then I remembered her allergies and her fear of bee stings.

Chester threw up an arm. "Don't come down. It's dangerous." He went up the steps, giving the water puddles a wide berth. I was doing the same thing when Sylvester tried to push by Chester.

Chester gripped his cousin's arm and jerked him back. "It's dangerous, I said. She slipped at the top and fell."

Sylvester surveyed the steps, his gaze going from the puddles to Arabella below us. "You're sure she's dead?" he asked, looking from Chester to me. "There's nothing we can do?"

"No, not a thing," Chester said.

Sylvester stepped back to the terrace and gave Torrie a little nod. "It's true. Arabella is dead." Torrie raised a hand to her mouth, but wasn't able to stifle her sob. She spun away from us and ran directly into the brown-suited form of Detective Chief Inspector Quimby.

CHAPTER 12

I WOULDN'T HAVE THOUGHT TORRIE would be the type of person to cry, even at the news of the death of a friend, but I pressed another tissue into her hand and wondered if I should call one of the emergency people in to give her a sedative. That sounded very antiquated, giving the crying woman something to knock her out, but Torrie was weeping in a way that worried me. It was full-blown sobbing, and she only paused for a second to gulp in air so she could continue sobbing. Her eyelids were puffy and red, and she couldn't breathe through her nose. I seriously wondered if she'd be able to stop crying. I frowned. Maybe it would be better to have someone get Quimby. He had asked me to take Torrie inside and stay with her.

I'd met DCI Quimby when I'd first arrived in Nether Woodsmoor. I hadn't been a big fan of him last year—he had placed me on his list of suspects, after all—but I now knew that he was methodical and diligent and also carried tissues because his job often brought him into contact with people who were devastated.

I had wanted to ask Quimby why he was at Tate House, but I

decided that since everything was so chaotic, I'd hold my question until later and do as he asked. The small pack of tissues he'd handed me from inside his jacket pocket didn't last more than a minute after I got Torrie inside.

I managed to get her into the morning room at the front corner of the house away from the windows that overlooked the terrace. I didn't want her to see the body bag, which I knew would have to come up the stairs at some point.

"Torrie," I said in the firm voice I used to get interns to pay attention, "you've got to get a grip on yourself and calm down." She was halfway through the box of tissues I'd found in the hall bathroom upstairs. "You'll be no help at all if you can't talk to the police." She nodded and sucked in several shaky breaths. "I'll try," she said through her tears.

"What you need is a strong cup of tea." I sounded like Louise, whose recommendation for any problem always included either food or drink. I was still more of a coffee girl, but there was something comforting about ritual and routine, and I figured tea would be what Torrie would want.

Torrie nodded and pressed a tissue to her eyes. "Yes, I suppose so."

I found an unopened box of tea bags on the counter in the kitchen beside my tote bag. Someone, probably Constable Albertson, must have brought it inside for me. I waited for the water to boil, relieved that I didn't hear more audible crying from the front of the house. I returned with the steaming cup of berry-flavored tea, hoping that in the time it had taken for the water to boil that Torrie had pulled herself together, but the morning room was empty. Had she gone back outside? She hadn't passed through the kitchen, but other doors opened onto the terrace, too. I checked in the dining room and the study, but they were both empty.

Still holding the saucer and tea cup, I climbed the glass staircase, its suspension wires shifting slightly with my weight. I paused at the top of the stairs. "Torrie?"

On either side of the carpet runner, the shiny pale oak flooring of the hallway extended to the left and right of the stairs. I took a few steps to the nearest doorway on the left and bumped my shin on a decorative trunk. Framed pictures on top of a crocheted tablecloth rocked, but didn't fall over. I peeked in the doorway of the first bedroom. The large sitting room in shades of pale blue and yellow would have been charming—if you could see it without the veneer of clothes and shoes scattered around the room. A large designer handbag sat barely inside the doorframe, a pink scarf tied to the strap and a slim mailing box poking out of the drawstring top.

Several empty Louis Vuitton suitcases in the middle of the room signaled that this was Arabella's room. Clothes were draped over the chairs, piled on the ironing board, and puddled on the floor. "That doesn't look safe," I muttered, seeing the green kimono balled up next to the iron, but then I saw the cord of the iron was unplugged and twisted in the folds of silk. At least someone—probably Torrie—had the foresight to unplug the iron. Shoes, many of them with red soles, dotted the floor at random intervals where they'd been kicked off.

I thought of Arabella's lifeless body on the stairs. She'd never again kick off her shoes and walk barefoot across the carpet, probably trampling on silk and linen and cashmere without a thought.

I turned away, shaking my head over parallel scratches in the wood floor. The flooring had been pristine throughout the house when I'd completed the walk-through before Arabella arrived. Someone had dragged a suitcase down the hall and marred the floor in the process. I was sure we'd have to pay for the scrapes, but move-out damages were the least of my worries now.

I was about to tap on the door across the hall when I heard

the sound of a toilet flushing from behind the closed door of the hall bath.

I retreated down the stairs, reheated the tea, and came back into the sitting room where the suspended staircase quivered. Torrie trotted down, her ballet shoes making no sound on the frosted glass steps. She was no longer sobbing, only patting at her eyes with a wilted tissue.

She reached the bottom step and started as if I'd jumped out from behind a door. "Oh, Kate, you surprised me." She patted her chest. "I went upstairs to wash my face."

"I'm sorry. I didn't mean to frighten you. Here's your tea."

She wadded the tissue into a ball in her hand, then took the cup and saucer and dropped down into an armchair, looking limp and spent. She took a long sip of the tea, and smiled sadly. "Berry-infused."

"I'm sorry?"

She lifted the cup and saucer. "The tea. It's a special kind, Arabella's current favorite—was, I mean—her current favorite." I was afraid the tears would well up again, but she swallowed and went on. "You can't find it here in Nether Woodsmoor. Arabella sent me and Sylvester to Upper Benning to get some for her."

"The box was on the counter in the kitchen, and I didn't realize. Would you like something else?"

"No, it's fine." She took another sip then shook her head. "I do wonder, though, if I hadn't left…if I'd been here, then maybe she wouldn't have gone out into the garden. Maybe it wouldn't have happened." She stared into her cup.

I didn't have an answer for that so I stayed silent. She took a slow sip of tea, and I decided I didn't need to get the tissue box. She rested the cup and saucer on her leg and let her head fall to the back of the chair. She looked exhausted from her crying jag. Above the point of her chin, the skin around her eyes and nose was still pink.

I perched on another chair and wondered what was going on in the garden. A row of official vehicles now filled the driveway, but I hadn't seen anyone, except for Constable Albertson. He had poked his head into the morning room earlier, taken one look at Torrie's shoulders, which were shaking with her sobs, and said, "Right, looks like you have everything under control," before disappearing. As far as I knew, no one from the police or emergency services had entered the house.

Torrie opened her eyes and took another long sip. "Thanks for this."

"Sure, it was no problem. Is there someone you'd like for me to call?"

"No." She straightened, sitting up in the chair as she placed the empty cup and saucer on a side table. "I'm okay now. Sorry I fell apart. It was just so…shocking. I don't quite know what came over me."

"She was your friend. It's totally understandable," I said, but then I remembered Torrie's tight lips when Arabella ordered her around in the kitchen.

"We were friends." Torrie put a slight emphasis on the verb. "I suppose that's why I cried. We were best friends…once. That all changed after *The Red Poppy*. She was *famous* after that." She widened her eyes and lifted one shoulder in a what-can-you-expect motion. "Lately, she saw me as more of an employee than a friend, but that doesn't erase the past, does it? All those years sharing a tiny apartment and scrimping to get by. We kept the heat so low that when we got home from waitressing and auditions we actually put *on* more layers." She toyed with the empty tea cup, tilting it one way then another as a smile softened the sharp angles of her face. "And the food—beans on toast, for days on end. If one of us were flush with cash, we'd get fish and chips. Now, it's lobster or nothing. Nothing but the best for Arabella. Or it was." She set the cup down with a click. "Who's back there now?" she asked with a tilt of her head toward the garden.

"I'm not sure, but I did see the local constable and, of course, the DCI. He's the man in the brown suit."

Her head swiveled toward me sharply. "A DCI? Why?"

Now it was my turn to lift a shoulder. I'd wondered why Quimby had shown up so quickly, too. "Well, she'd had death threats so—"

"But it was an accident. She slipped and fell."

"I'm sure they have to...check everything," I said, but it did seem like they'd been out there a long time. "I think that's always the case when someone dies suddenly."

"But why would a DCI be here *now*? Don't those things take time? The local people first—the constable—and then later the detectives? The police force here in Nether Woodsmoor is small, isn't it?"

The same question had crossed my mind, and my thoughts flashed back to that shiny puddle on the stone steps, but I wasn't about to go into that here with her, not when the tears had finally stopped. "No, it's quite a small village—"

"Then why is there a DCI here so soon?" She pushed her hair behind one ear with quivering fingers. "I don't think I can talk to a detective...all those questions. It wasn't too bad talking to the constable about the notes—he was only a local bloke, but I don't know that I can face more questions today. And why is it taking so long? What are they *doing* out there?"

Her voice rose with each question. Trying to prevent another crying jag, I said, "I'm sure it will be okay—"

"You don't think it means that they think something else happened, do you?" Torrie clearly hadn't even realized I was speaking. "That it wasn't an accident?" She leaned forward, her posture intense. "Because that's what Chester said. She'd fallen.

It's one of those horrible, tragic accidents. I mean, yes, she got nasty notes, but no one would ever actually *do* anything. That's what she always said."

"But Arabella did seem worried. The day I saw the man in the garden, she was afraid at first. And then with the finial falling…"

Torrie swished a hand through the air, brushing away my questions. "Arabella was an actress. She loved the attention. And once she was the center of attention, she'd milk it for all it was worth. She couldn't help it. That's just the way she was."

"But yesterday, you both seemed to be worried about those notes."

Torrie glanced at the door to the hallway then leaned another inch closer. "Arabella thought she could play up the whole situation—the notes and having a stalker." Torrie made finger quotes as she said the last word. "She thought a few stories in the press about things like that would give her an edge when it came to *The Darkness*. It is a psychological thriller, you know."

"Yes, I've heard of it." I didn't know how anyone could have *not* heard of it. An updated take on *Gaslight*, but with a shocking twist—didn't all thrillers have to have a shocking twist?—it had been a best-selling book and now a feature film based on the book was in preproduction. "But there really was someone in the garden." I was sure of that. "And she did receive notes, right? She didn't make those up. You gave them to Constable Albertson."

"Of course the notes were real, but it was the degree of the thing. Once we realized it wasn't Stevie in the garden, then we both knew there was nothing to worry about. With the Hibberts here, Stevie couldn't get to Arabella. All he could do was send those notes. But the *press* wouldn't know that. You and I both know a story about a star's personal life mirroring their on-screen life is catnip to editors—and to the public."

But I'd seen Stevie climb the gatepost and get onto the

grounds of Tate House. He hadn't been out of view long. Was he gone long enough to catch Arabella on the stairs and give her a shove?

The sound of a door opening and closing echoed through the house. Torrie started as her gaze flew to mine. "Who is that?"

"I'm sure it's the constable or one of the officers." But it was Detective Quimby who walked into the sitting room with Constable Albertson on his heels.

Torrie and I stood as Quimby crossed the room. He nodded to me and said, "Thank you for your help." Then he introduced himself to Torrie.

Despite the worries she'd voiced earlier, Torrie composed herself and didn't look nervous to me as she greeted Quimby. But Torrie had been an actress before she'd become Arabella's assistant.

Quimby said, "I'm sorry about Ms. Emsley. I have a few questions I need to ask you, if you feel up to it."

"Yes, of course." She motioned to the chair where I had been sitting, and said, "Kate, you wouldn't mind getting the DCI a cup of tea, would you?"

Her tone and manner were distinctly Arabella-like, and I was taken aback. How did I suddenly find myself in Torrie's position with her taking over Arabella's role? "Don't trouble yourself," Quimby said quickly. "I actually need to speak to Ms. Sharp first. Constable Albertson will ask you a few preliminary questions, Ms. Mayes."

Relief flashed across Torrie's face.

"If you'll come with me, Ms. Sharp," Quimby said, and I followed him to the kitchen.

At the table where Sylvester had played cards, he pulled out a chair for me so that I was seated with my back to the window then sat opposite me. I had a quick glimpse of people moving back and forth across the terrace as well as a man tracing a brush with delicate twists and swipes over the frame of one of the lounge chairs.

Quimby took out his phone and flicked through several screens. He looked exactly the same as when I'd first met him, a nondescript man with brown hair in a brown suit in his mid- to late-thirties, I guessed. I'd thought he looked rather bland when I first met him, until I noticed his sharp green eyes, which were startling in his plain face.

He trained those eyes on me, and I felt like I was under intense scrutiny, even though his question was innocuous. "I understand you're the go-between, running interference between this group and your film?"

"Yes. That sums it up."

"Not your normal job." It was a statement. The first time he'd interviewed me, I'd explained to him what being a location scout entailed.

"No, but when someone like Ms. Emsley asks for something, you give it to her."

"Why did she want you?"

"I have no idea. Maybe Torrie can tell you."

"You had perhaps met Ms. Emsley at some point in the past? Connected online?"

"No, nothing like that." I felt a twinge of unease. "I didn't know her at all." I stressed the last two words.

He tapped a quick note into his phone. "How would you describe the dynamic between the people here at Tate House?"

Glad that it seemed he was moving away from questions that focused on me, I said, "Well, Arabella was the center of it all, of course. They were all here because of her. Torrie was her assistant, and the Hibbert cousins were her security."

"Yes, the security detail," Quimby said, barely suppressing his sigh. "We'll come back to that. Tell me more about the personalities."

Torrie's worried questions popped into my mind along with the image of Stevie Lund vaulting over the gate. With a sinking sensation in my stomach, I asked, "It wasn't an accident, was it?"

CHAPTER 13

"WHY DO YOU SAY THAT?" Quimby asked, his tone careful.

"Well, I know the stairs are slippery, but your people seem to be taking a long time in the garden. It makes me wonder if something else happened besides Arabella losing her balance and falling." I looked over my shoulder at the crime scene technician by the lounger. "I don't imagine you normally search for fingerprints after an accident?"

"Every case is different," Quimby said in that same cautious way.

So he *was* suspicious. The sinking feeling in my stomach intensified. Dealing with an accidental death related to the documentary was bad enough, but a suspicious death....I rubbed my forehead. "This is not good. Elise will not like this. She'll..." I trailed off, not able to put into words what I suspected her reaction would be. I dreaded talking to her more than I had before.

On top of that, I'd been here. In fact, I found the body. I swallowed, realizing that I had bigger worries than Elise's temper. "My fingerprints will be out there, you know," I said quickly. "I was in the garden—several times, in fact." I didn't want to be in Quimby's crosshairs again.

He looked up from his phone, a slightly surprised look on his face.

I spread my hands. "I know you're thorough and look into everything and everyone." I waved a hand at the window behind me. "All that activity says that something is...suspicious. You once told me you suspect everyone, or something along those lines. I want to make it clear that I'm not hiding anything. I had no connection to anyone here before a few days ago, and even though Arabella was quite...er, trying...at times, I would never do anything that would cause her to end up on the stairs like that."

"I can't exclude anyone from my investigation, which at this point is focused on the threats Ms. Emsley received," he said, but he glanced out the window with a distracted air then returned his attention to me. "Let's stay focused on the threats for the moment."

His questions focused on the notes, so I stayed on the subject, summarizing how I'd found out about them, giving him a quick recap of the last few days, describing the run-in with the man in the garden, Gil's attempt to get on the set, and the threatening notes Arabella had described. He let me talk without asking many questions, mostly tapping away on his phone as I spoke. I described Arabella's narrow miss during filming and said, "After that—well—I'd already called Constable Albertson, but it seemed to be something serious."

"Quite." Quimby flicked through his notes then asked, "And Ms. Emsley thought the man in the garden wasn't Stevie Lund?"

"Right. She was very sure about that. Sylvester took a photo of the footprint. I suppose he might still have it. It looked like some sort of work boot. Arabella said Lund would never wear shoes like that and that he'd never climb the wall because it might ruin his suit."

"He is known to be quite particular about his wardrobe."

I raised my eyebrows. "So you already know about him, this Stevie Lund?"

"Mr. Lund has been on our radar for a long time," he said with a mix of exasperation and determination. "Ms. Emsley seemed relieved once she decided it couldn't have been Lund?"

"Yes. Once she saw the footprint, I got the feeling that she... well, that she enjoyed the attention. She obviously liked the idea that a fan would climb the wall and try to get to the house. But she was wrong about that part—that Stevie Lund wouldn't climb the wall. He went over the gate today—well, the gatepost first, actually. But he still climbed up and over. So he might have scaled the wall earlier."

Quimby's green eyes narrowed. "Lund was here? Today?"

"Yes, I saw him before I found Arabella. At first I thought it might be Gil, but it wasn't. It was definitely Lund."

Quimby thumbed back in his notes. "You assumed it was Gil Brayden, the paparazzi?"

"That's right. I was walking home from Parkview on the footpath and heard shouting—that's why I came up, to see what was going on. If something was wrong I needed to run interference. Gil was determined to get on the set, and I assumed he'd transferred his focus from Parkview to Tate House." I described Lund's angry yelling and how he'd vaulted over the gate.

"How long was Lund out of sight?"

"I don't know. Several minutes, at least. Maybe ten minutes or so."

We both looked toward the hallway at the sound of heavy footsteps. Constable Albertson came in holding Torrie's empty tea cup. He sent an apologetic grimace to Quimby. "Sorry, sir. She asked for more tea, and I thought it best to humor her."

"Right you are," Quimby said and swiveled back to me. "Carry on with your timeline. You saw Lund."

"Yes. You know, this house has a monitoring system. You should be able to get the times from it. You can probably track him on it and see exactly where he went."

Constable Albertson ran water as Quimby said, "I'm informed the cameras record only the main gate, drive, and the front entrance, but we'll check into it. If you'd continue…"

"Well, after I saw Lund I stood there a bit, debating what to do —whether I should call someone or wait. But then I heard a noise down the path to the village and thought that Lund had left the grounds that way, so I ducked into the trees," I said over the noise of Albertson opening and closing cabinet doors. "I didn't want to meet him, you know?"

"Understandable," Quimby said. "Good grief, Albertson. What is the problem?"

"Sorry, sir. Can't find the tea."

"It's on the counter—" I said.

At the same moment, Albertson retrieved a box of berry tea from an upper cabinet and shook it. "Found it. Sorry, sir. I'll be out of here in two ticks."

"Good," Quimby said, then checked his notes on his phone. "You'd taken cover in the trees. What then?"

"Nothing. I expected Lund to come along the path to get back to the gate so he could get his car, but no one came by. After a few minutes, I headed toward the village. Someone had knocked several of the stones from the wall onto the path, but I didn't see anyone except some cyclists in the distance. I'd called Chester and Sylvester, too, to let them know about Lund, so I went back to the gate to tell Chester that it looked like Lund had left the grounds. But when I got back there, Lund came running up from inside the grounds. He climbed over the gate again and drove away." I debated whether to tell him about the weird look on

Lund's face. I decided against it. It was only a look...but Arabella was dead at the bottom of the stairs.

"And...?" Quimby asked, interrupting my thoughts.

"That's it. That's all I saw."

Quimby put his phone down. "I think there's something else. You're considering if you should tell me or not. What is it?"

"Oh...well, yes, there is, but I don't know if it's important. It was only an impression."

"You never know what can be useful in an investigation."

"It was his face," I said slowly. "It's hard to explain, but he looked excited, keyed up."

"Not worried or scared?"

"No, not at all. More like exhilarated."

Quimby nodded then said, "Going back to the photographer, Gil Brayden. You showed his photo to Ms. Emsley. You thought he was the garden intruder, correct? What was her reaction?"

"She laughed it off. She said he was a nuisance, but Torrie said Arabella should be worried about him."

"Did she elaborate?"

"No, and I didn't ask. We were about to start filming so I didn't get a chance."

"Now, let's go over what happened when you found Ms. Emsley. Why did you come onto the property?" Quimby said as Albertson left with the tea.

"I wanted to check on her and make sure she was okay."

"You suspected something was wrong?"

I shifted in my chair. "No, I wanted to talk to her and make sure she wasn't upset or anything. Chester thought she was fine, but I figured Torrie might have called her after I spoke to Sylvester."

"But you'd already tried to phone Ms. Emsley, and she hadn't answered."

"That's true. I thought she might have ignored my call, but answered a call from Torrie."

"Makes sense. Chester Hibbert let you in?"

"Yes, he didn't seem to want to, but he did."

"He tried to convince you to leave?"

"No, I had the feeling he was more embarrassed about missing Lund. I'd asked if he'd seen Lund on the monitors, and Chester told me he had been in the loo, but he did open the gate for me. He said Arabella was in the garden so I went around the side of the house and found her on the steps."

Quimby pushed back his chair. "If you could show me exactly how far you went down the steps." I followed him outside, and as I crossed the terrace, I saw Chester and Sylvester standing on the grassy bit of lawn off to the side of the terrace. Chester had his hands in his pockets while Sylvester paced. They must be waiting for Quimby to speak to them.

We reached the stairs, and Quimby paused at the top step. I braced myself, expecting to see Arabella's body, but a tent had been set up over the lower portion of the steps, blocking it from view. Several people moved back and forth under the awning. The stone staircase dipped down the hillside, slashing through the banks of blossoms and greenery, but I couldn't appreciate the beautiful scene.

"You came directly to the garden?"

"Yes. I saw her right away and thought she was in a strange yoga position, but then I realized something wasn't right."

Quimby nodded. "And did you go down the stairs?"

"Yes, all the way to her. Once I got closer, I could tell from the angle of her head..." I stopped and looked away from the tent.

"I understand," Quimby said. "And when did Chester Hibbert arrive at the steps?"

"Right after me. Only a minute or two later, I think."

"So no one else was alone with the body?"

I looked at him, worry again surging inside me, but he was surveying the garden, sweeping his gaze across the bright patches of flowers that spilled down the hillside.

"I suppose not. I was only by myself down there a little while. Chester was right behind me. He was at the top of the stairs, running down. When I looked up he'd just hit the step with the slippery spot."

"*The* step with a slippery spot?" Quimby asked, his suddenly alert gaze shifting to my face. "Earlier, you said the stairs were slippery, not one specific place."

"Oh, I didn't mean the whole staircase, just a couple of steps here at the top. I slipped when I came down, but managed to catch my balance. The same thing happened to Chester. I think it was a puddle of water...that one there. See the low spot?"

Quimby moved a few steps below the one I'd indicated and squatted down so that his gaze was even with the step. Water filled a slight depression in the stone, reflecting the sky along with a few of the tiny purple flowers that grew over the edge of the step. He looked up at me, squinting in the sunlight. "Does this garden have an irrigation system?"

"I don't know. Claire—the agent—didn't mention one."

He nodded, but his attention was back on the steps. He'd shifted slightly and examined the area at the side of the steps near the landscape light. He pushed back the ground cover and revealed a furrow in the dark earth that ran from the light to the step.

Quimby dropped the ground cover and shouted, "Everyone off the steps," as he came up the steps and pushed me up onto the terrace, but I'd seen the thin copper wire that ran from the light through the furrow and ended in the puddle of water.

CHAPTER 14

"A WIRE IN WATER?" ALEX asked. "Are you serious?"

I shoved the phone between my ear and my shoulder as I leaned down to unhook the leash from Slink's collar. She knew what was coming and spun in a few anticipatory circles. "Completely serious."

"That's incredibly dangerous."

"I know." I took the tennis ball out of my pocket and heaved it as far as I could across the village green. Slink was off in an instant, her slender legs pumping in her graceful stride as she sped across the grass. She snatched the tennis ball and jetted back to me, running a neat figure eight around me before dropping the ball at my feet, her sides heaving. I tossed the ball again, and she was off.

"I can't believe no one noticed it," Alex said. "You said the police went up and down those steps."

"The wire was well hidden. If I hadn't told Quimby about slipping on the step, and if he hadn't pushed back the ground cover... well, I don't think anyone would have noticed it. Once they were sure the power was off and were able to get back on the steps, they found three other steps with the same set up." My stomach was still in knots, thinking about how awful it was that Arabella was dead, but my nerves edged up another notch when I thought about how much worse it could have been.

Quimby had made sure everyone cleared off the steps and then had gone in search of the power main. I'd told him about the power to the garden being connected through the potting shed and once everything had been shut off, the crime scene people returned to the staircase and examined every step. I shivered, remembering the shouts of "Sir, over here. Got another," that had floated up to the terrace where Quimby had told me to wait.

"Then that means it was intentional," Alex said, in a voice that wasn't his usual calm tone. "Thank God you didn't get shocked."

"I know. Good thing I was wearing my boat shoes today. Rubber soles, you know. I suppose that's why no one else was shocked. Arabella was the only one to go down the steps barefoot."

"So she stepped in the water and the current flowed through the wire to her foot?" Alex asked, his voice troubled.

"Yes, that's what they think happened. The landscape lighting is on a timer and is supposed to go off at midnight, but someone had changed the settings so that they stayed on all the time, even during the day. Arabella was wearing a gold toe ring, and that would have been a good conductor…at least, that's what I overheard one of the crime techs say."

Slink trotted back, shifting into a slower gear now. I tossed the ball a shorter distance. "Quimby had me wait on the terrace, and I think some of the techs didn't see me over in the corner. Once they realized Arabella might have been shocked, they checked her over and found some sort of mark on her toe around the ring. It must not have been obvious because they were giving one guy a hard time for missing it earlier, but he said that sometimes there isn't any external sign of low level electrocution—that's what he called it," I said.

Slink returned with the tennis ball and settled down to gnaw on it. I dropped down onto one of the benches that lined the green, suddenly feeling exhausted. The burst of adrenaline that had carried me through the afternoon had faded, leaving me shaky.

Once Constable Albertson told me Quimby had cleared me to leave Tate House, I'd called Elise immediately. Fortunately, she hadn't picked up. I had a temporary escape from the storm that I knew would come once she got the news, but I'd left her a message then gone directly to Alex's cottage where Slink had bounded to the door with her ears perked and long tail whipping back and forth in expectation of her nightly run.

Alex murmured, "Electrocuted," in an amazed tone. "That's so…"

"Odd?" I finished for him.

"Yes, that's what I was thinking. Who gets electrocuted nowadays?"

"More people than I realized, apparently," I said. "Constable Albertson told me that a man in Upper Benning died last year when he installed a dishwasher. He connected the wires, started it, then reached behind the counter to make an adjustment without turning off the power and died when his ring touched an exposed wire. Constable Albertson gives safety talks at the local schools. Warnings about electricity are part of his speech. He said it's often not the electric shock that kills people, but what happens after, which is what I gather they think probably happened with Arabella. The shock may have startled her and caused her to fall. Her neck was…just wrong…when I found her. Constable Albertson says the medical examiner will sort out whether she died instantly and broke her neck in the fall, or if she was still alive after the shock, and the impact of the fall killed her."

I switched the phone to the other ear as Slink rose and loped to my side. She must have picked up on the strain in my voice because she rubbed against my knees then rested her long nose on my thigh. I traced my hand over her narrow head then rubbed her ear. She closed her eyes and leaned into my hand. "Either way, it's scary."

"It was deliberate, you mean," Alex said, his voice grim. "Murder."

"Yes. I don't see how it could be anything but that. I suppose one wire might work loose and end up on the step somehow, but more than that? And into a waiting puddle?"

"No, and if the lights were switched on continuously, it sounds as if someone carefully set it up, which makes it even more frightening," Alex said. "Someone had everything in place. If Quimby hadn't examined the step and seen the wire it might have been written off as an accident."

"I don't know. Quimby and his team were taking their time out there. They must have suspected something. I mean, she'd had the threatening notes, so I suppose that would have caused them to look more carefully. And even though the burn on her toe wasn't spotted right away, surely it would have been noticed later. There would have to be an autopsy, right?"

"I suppose so, but there's a chance that it would have been missed, and—no, give me a minute," he said, his voice fading as he spoke to someone else. He came back on the line. "I have to finish up here. There's no way I can get out of here any sooner than tomorrow."

"It's fine. I'm okay," I said, but I would be glad when he was back in Nether Woodsmoor. "I'd love it if you came back, actually. I really miss you," I said in a burst of honesty. *Did I say that out loud?* I must have been more stressed than I realized. "What I meant was—"

"Okay, now I *know* I need to get back there. Spontaneous

admissions of affection are not your usual style, but don't stop. I like it."

"Alex," I said, a laugh bubbling up, which felt good after all the somberness and tension.

"I'll be on the road as soon as I can."

I was about to ask about his appointment that he'd been so cagey about, but before I could say anything, his playful tone faded as he added, "Seriously, be careful, okay?"

"I will, but you don't have to worry. No one set up that wire for me."

"Yes, but you pointed out the puddle to Quimby and then he found the wire. Someone can't be happy about that."

"I've been firmly ignoring that thought for the last few hours. And telling myself that whatever is going on, it's nothing to do with me. At least Elise can't accuse me of causing all this trouble."

"I wouldn't go that far," Alex said. "She'll be looking for someone to blame."

"But if Arabella was murdered, then it must have been someone from her orbit, one of her friends...I mean entourage," I amended. I doubted Arabella would consider either the Hibberts or Torrie a friend. She certainly hadn't treated them that way. "This has nothing to do with me."

CHAPTER 15

"*I*S IT TRUE?" LOUISE'S CONCERNED gaze skimmed over me as she bent to give Slink a rub.

"I'm afraid so." I hooked my tote bag over the back of the only free barstool and squeezed into the seat, twisting around so that I could talk to Louise, who had paused on her circuit through the pub. I'd dropped into the White Duck on my way home to pick up a takeaway dinner. Dogs were welcome in the pub, and Slink had followed me through the crowd to the bar, graciously inclining her head so the regulars could give her a pat. Louise had come over as soon as she spotted me. I wasn't surprised that she knew what had happened at Tate House. News moved through Nether Woodsmoor with an amazing osmosis-like speed.

She pushed the bangs of her black-cherry hair out of her eyes with the back of her hand. "Such a shame. How are you holding up? You look a little peaked." Despite her trendy hair color and only being in her thirties, she had a motherly manner and liked to look after people.

"I am a little frazzled," I admitted. "I'll be fine after I eat, I'm sure."

"I'll check on your food. Shannon is not pulling her weight tonight." Her padded figure bustled away, and I gathered Louise's new hire wasn't working out as well as she'd hoped.

Slink settled down between a woman on the next barstool and me. Slink compacted her long legs into the space and curled into a tight circle. The woman, who had a frizz of light brown curls around her freckled face, glanced down at Slink.

"We won't be long," I said. "I'm just waiting for takeaway." After years in the States where pets weren't allowed in restaurants, it still felt odd to me to bring Slink in the pub.

"No worries." She sent me a quick smile then took a large swallow of her gin and tonic as she tapped the edge of her phone, so that it spun in a half circle. She kept repeating the movement, so that her phone continued to revolve. I glanced around the pub, but didn't see anyone from the documentary, which was a relief. I wanted to get my food and go home, but…was that Gil Brayden? I twisted around a bit farther in an effort to get a better look, but I couldn't see the man's face. He did have dark hair and a light-colored scarf draped across the back of his neck, though.

Louise bustled up with a cup of tea that I hadn't ordered. "That'll fix you right up. Only a few more minutes on the food." I sipped the tea, which was sweet with sugar. There was no saying "no" to Louise when it came to food and drink. She dispensed it like a doctor gave prescriptions, and I did feel better after a few sips.

Louise returned with my sandwich packed in a box. "Here you are, luv." She set it in front of me.

"Thanks, Louise." I handed over a ten pound note.

"Was it…bad? You found her, right?"

"Yes. It was—shocking, but I didn't really know her, you know? So I'm not broken up with grief," I said, thinking of Torrie and how she hadn't been able to stop crying.

I noticed that the woman beside me had stopped spinning her

phone on the bar. She was staring at my takeaway box with a fierce concentration, her head tilted as if she was trying to listen to my conversation with Louise.

She noticed my glance. She picked up her phone and seemed to become absorbed in it.

"Arabella's assistant was pretty broken up," I said to Louise, lowering my voice a notch, but the pub was pretty noisy. "I had to take care of her, so I didn't really have time to get too upset."

"Caring for other people is a marvelous way to keep from concentrating too much on your own problems."

"You should know," I said with a grin as she dug in her apron pocket for my change. "You're an expert in watching over most of the village."

"We're not talking about me," she said, waving away my comment. Her expression turned serious. "Did the police give you a hard time?" After a friend of Louise's went missing at Christmas, the police had focused their attention on her. The situation had shaken her badly, and now she tended to view the police in a less generous way than she had before the incident.

"No, nothing like that happened," I said. "They're still figuring out exactly what happened." I was intentionally vague. I didn't want to get into a discussion with Louise about the details of the wire. Even though Quimby hadn't told me specifically to keep that bit of news to myself I was sure he wouldn't want me discussing it in the pub.

"Well, it was murder, wasn't it? That's what people are saying. And we both know that the police could decide you look like a convenient suspect—unless it was Constable Albertson who was there."

Louise gave our local constable an exemption from her new wariness toward law enforcement. "He was there," I said, "but it was Quimby who was in charge."

"Quimby? My, they *do* think it's serious, then."

The woman beside me asked Louise for directions to the loo then slipped off her barstool and disappeared down the short hallway to the restrooms.

I couldn't share that Quimby had originally arrived to investigate the threatening notes either, so I said, "No need to worry about me. I'm only on the edge of this investigation." Louise had finally counted out the change, and I reached to take it from her. As she handed it over she frowned, her gaze focused over my shoulder.

"Everything okay?" I asked.

"Hmm?" She looked back at me. "Just keeping an eye on things." She tilted her head toward a table behind me. "He's been asking around about Tate House. I don't like the look of him—something sly about him."

I looked over my shoulder and saw a man with dark hair. A group of people at a table in front of him were standing, sorting out jackets and pushing in chairs. They moved to the door and then I could see the expensively cut suit and the heavy brows over small eyes. It was Stevie Lund.

He looked up and caught me staring at him. I turned away. "That is—I mean, was—Arabella's ex-boyfriend. From everything I've heard, he *is* a load of trouble." I hadn't expected to see him at the pub. I'd have thought he'd be busy being interviewed by the police. I wondered if they hadn't talked to him yet or if he'd been able to answer all their questions.

Louise nodded. "I can always tell a rotter when I see one. I have too much experience in that department not to." She sighed. "He's staying at the inn. I should warn Doug."

I couldn't imagine Doug with his bulldog-like build having a problem dealing with Stevie. "I'm sure Doug can handle it."

"I'm sure he could, if it came to an outright confrontation, but that one," she tilted her head toward Lund's table, "he's the type who will skip out without paying. Too slick for his own good. I better give Tara a call and let her know they should run a deposit on his credit card to make sure it's good."

"I don't think that will be a problem. He's well-off, apparently."

Louise sniffed. "Then you'd think he wouldn't have tried to leave without paying yesterday. Slipped his mind, indeed." She swiped up several empty plates and disappeared through the door to the kitchen.

I finished my tea then picked up my box. I hopped off the barstool and bumped into someone who was passing right behind me. "Sorry—" I broke off. Lund stood directly behind me, one arm raised as he held a pint aloft.

A glob of foam trailed down the sleeve of his dark suit jacket. "Sorry," I repeated. "I didn't see you there. Let me get a napkin or something." I half turned back toward the bar, but he shifted a step closer, blocking my way.

"No need." He inched farther into my personal space as his pale blue eyes skimmed over my face. I felt as if I was under a computer scan, that he was studying each detail of my features. "It'll dry. You, however, should be more careful." He gave extra weight to the last sentence. I knew it was completely irrational to be afraid, but I was. Even surrounded by the noise and conversation bubbling around the pub, my heartbeat sped up as his cold blue gaze continued to buzz over me. "Careful about where you go and what you see." His eyes under his deep brows narrowed. "And about what you tell people. If you're smart you won't mention what you saw today."

Slink had stood when I slipped off my chair, and now she inched up under my hand. I felt a low growl rumble through her body. It was too loud in the pub for anyone else to hear, but Lund glanced down at Slink then back at me. "If you can't control your dog, you should keep it on a lead." He leaned even closer. "Don't forget what I said. I only give people one warning." His face transformed from deadly serious to a fake smile. "Cheers!" He lifted the pint and pushed past me, causing me to have to step back and bump into my empty barstool.

CHAPTER 16

"GOOD GIRL, SLINK," I SAID as I stepped into the darkness outside the pub. "You don't need a lead, do you? You were doing exactly what you should, letting him know he shouldn't be a jerk."

Slink pranced beside me, keeping up with the quick pace I set, her ears up. Her nails clicking along and the jingle of her collar were the only sounds as we briskly climbed the incline to Cottage Lane then swept along the low dry-stone wall that enclosed the cottage gardens. The golden stone of the cottages had faded to a pearly gray in the dim light.

I continued to compliment Slink as we walked, and despite the fast pace, my breathing and heartbeat were returning to normal. Lund obviously didn't want me to tell the police I'd seen him at Tate House. "Well, too late for that," I said to Slink. She had raised her gaze to me as I spoke, but then she pricked her ears and turned back the direction we'd come, her body tense and alert.

I spun around. The quiet street stretched out behind me. Lights glowed from some of the cottage windows. Down below in the village, a car purred along, its headlights slicing through the night. A shadow shifted. I looked down at Slink. She stayed alert, but silent. I waited a few moments more, but nothing moved. "Must have been a tree branch blowing in the wind. Come on, Slink." I wanted to get into my cottage and lock the door.

She reluctantly turned away and followed me to Alex's cottage, where I stopped off to pick up Slink's bed and food. Normally, she stayed in familiar surroundings at Alex's place, but tonight I wanted some companionship in my cottage. I tucked Slink's enormous cushion under one elbow, grabbed her food and bowls in one hand, and my own dinner in the other. With my tote bag bouncing against my back, I resembled a pack mule.

As we left Alex's cottage, I approached the street cautiously. Had Lund followed me so he could reiterate his warning? But Slink wasn't wary. She seemed much more interested in the aroma of my sandwich than anything on the lane. It was only a few steps to Honeysuckle Cottage. It took some maneuvering to get Slink and everything I was carrying inside the gate and up the stairs at my cottage.

As I unlocked the door, the clatter of plastic wheels sounded to my right as my neighbor Annette Phillips trundled her wheelie bin to the curb. I made a mental note to remember to put out my bin tonight. I opened the door, and Slink trotted inside, her collar jangling, which drew Annette's attention.

"Oh, hello there! I thought you were already home." Annette paused with her bin at her side. Her jeans were dirt-stained at the knees.

"No, just getting in." I dropped the dog bed, the food, and my tote bag inside the door and took one step inside, signaling—I hoped—that I wasn't up for an in-depth neighborly chat. I held onto my sandwich. Slink had impeccable manners, but I wasn't about to tempt her by leaving it unattended.

Annette had moved into the recently reconstructed cottage next door. She worked in a nursery school in Upper Benning. She was never short on words—all those hours with toddlers all day, I supposed, gave her a hunger for adult conversation.

"I don't see how you keep up those long hours. Did you hear about the poor woman up at Tate House?"

"Yes, I did." Conversing with Annette wasn't actually that tiring. I only had to contribute a few words. She carried the weight of the conversation almost single-handedly.

"Terrible situation. It will be a long while before that place sells now," she said cheerfully, clearly delighted to discuss Arabella's death in an abstract way, considering only the impact it had on the village. I couldn't think of it so casually, but I suppose I might have felt differently if I'd only heard about it instead of experiencing it firsthand.

Annette stepped back. "I won't keep you. I'm sure you have another early start tomorrow. How you do it, I don't know. Well, good night."

I locked the door firmly behind me, realizing that I didn't know if I had an early morning or not the next day. Another full day of filming was on the schedule, but most of it involved either on-location interviews with Arabella, or shooting more footage of her strolling through Parkview—this time in modern clothes instead of a period costume. None of that would happen now.

I hadn't had time to consider what would happen with the documentary, but now I thought about the footage we had. Would we have enough to complete the documentary or would we have to come up with something else?

I completed my circuit of the house, closing curtains and shutters while Slink sniffed around the back garden. Once she trotted into the kitchen, I locked the door behind her, poured out a serving of kibble, and filled Slink's water bowl. She swept her long nose over her dog food then looked at me reproachfully.

"Sorry, that's what is on your menu."

Slink gave me one more big-eyed look, then went into the sitting room and collapsed onto her back on her huge cushion that I'd placed near the couch. I brought my sandwich into the front room, kicked off my boat shoes, and curled up on one corner of the couch to eat while I checked my messages. Several calls and texts had come in while I was in the pub, but it had been too noisy to hear the ringer. I scrolled through the texts. Most of them were from Melissa, demanding to know if I was okay and what had happened. Holding my sandwich in one hand and texting with the other, I tapped out a message that I was fine and that I'd meet her for coffee in the morning with all the details.

I listened to my voicemails. Elise's voice came sharply through the phone. "Why didn't you call me the moment this happened? The death of Arabella Emsley will affect everything—absolutely every aspect of our schedule. I expect a call back the minute you get this."

I sighed and deleted the message. The next one was from Ren. "So sorry to hear about Arabella. How are you? Please let me know if there is anything I can do. And if you could convey our sympathies to everyone there, that would be appreciated. The schedule has been shifted. Elise agrees that we should move Saturday's day off to tomorrow."

I bet she hated changing the schedule, but it was the smart thing to do. Everything would be in disarray tomorrow. What would we shoot if the person who was supposed to be in almost every scene wasn't there?

Ren's soothing voice continued, "Take tomorrow to rest and recover. That had to be a stressful incident. Let me know if there is anything either I or the production team can do to help."

The next message was from Elise. "Really, Kate, I can't imagine where you are or why you haven't checked in with me. I *must* hear from you immediately. We have to come up with a contingency plan to fill the last segment of the final episode. This is an all-hands-on-deck moment, Kate. I want to hear ideas from everyone by tomorrow. Seven-thirty a.m. at the conference room in Upper Benning. Be prepared."

The final message was from Ren. "Sorry to disturb you again. You may have received word about a meeting tomorrow morning. It's been canceled. *I* will contact you," he added, "when a new time is set. Again, call if you need anything."

The tug of war continues, I muttered to myself, glad I'd missed that battle. Slink opened one eye, saw that the food was gone and shifted her long legs into a more comfortable position. I tipped my head back against the couch. I checked the time. Nine o'clock was really too early to go to bed, but I was exhausted. I pushed myself off the couch, then I threw away my takeaway box, and towed the rolling bin out to the street. I locked the front door, picked up my boat shoes, and went into the kitchen to double check the locks on the back door.

I'd left my tote bag on the kitchen table beside my laptop, but my bag had toppled onto its side. I picked up a couple of papers that had cascaded to the floor, the copies of the hand-drawn maps that I'd sketched for the crew so they could get from the resort in Upper Benning, where most of them were staying, to Parkview. GPS and Google maps were great, except when they sent you to a completely unrelated location. Old-fashioned paper maps were good for double-checking routes, and some people on the crew actually preferred paper maps. I'd handed out copies to everyone who needed one, so I tossed the pages in the trash under the sink and climbed the stairs to the brass bed under the A-line roof with wooden beams.

I thought I might have trouble falling asleep. With everything that had happened, I expected it to be one of those nights when I fell into bed only to suddenly have my mind whirring through the events of the day to the point that I had trouble drifting off. But I must have dropped off as soon as I curled up on my side. When I opened my eyes the next morning, I'd hardly moved and the sheets were barely rumpled.

Full sunlight glowed around the edges of the shutters. A pair of dark eyes on the same level as my face gazed at me intently. I gave Slink a rub as I sat up. For a second, I felt a horrible sense of panic, thinking I'd slept through my alarm, but then I remembered about Arabella and that today was an off day.

"Overslept, did I?" I said to Slink as I reached automatically for my phone to check the weather. But I didn't have to do that today. "Off day," I muttered as I scrubbed my hand across my face. "Coffee. I need coffee."

As I slid out of bed, Slink's ears perked up and her mouth parted in a doggie grin. She stepped back, her long body shimmering in a good morning greeting. I rubbed her ears then shrugged into a robe because even though it was summer, the mornings were chilly. Slink flew down the stairs ahead of me. I let her out into the back garden, and a burst of cool air surged into the kitchen. I topped off Slink's water bowl, put the coffee on, then climbed the stairs again and took a quick shower. By the time I threw on khaki shorts and a white V-neck T-shirt, the aroma of dark roast had filled the cottage.

I poured myself a big mug and, after checking the refrigerator, decided to have a real breakfast. Even though I was meeting Melissa this morning, and it was nearly nine, she wasn't a morning person. *Morning* to her meant anytime after ten o'clock.

I wasn't much of a cook, but I could make a mean omelet. I cracked some eggs, whisked them, then added them to the skillet on the two-burner stove. I let them cook while I chopped the little bit of ham I had in the back of the refrigerator and shredded some cheese. By the time I'd sprinkled the cheese and ham across the eggs, Slink was sitting prettily while watching my every movement.

I sipped my coffee while I gave the omelet a final flip, then slipped it onto a plate. As I settled at the table, trying to ignore Slink's devoted gaze, my bare foot touched something that was a different texture than the hardwood floor. I twisted sideways and saw a piece of paper squished up against the central wooden pedestal of the heavy table. I picked it up as I chewed a bite of the omelet. It was a wrinkled oblong envelope.

It must have fallen out of my tote bag when it toppled over last night. The envelope had slid to the far side of the table where I couldn't see it. Between bites of the fluffy eggs, I smoothed out the wrinkles and turned it over. The front was blank, but it was thick enough that I could tell something was inside it, at least a sheet or two of paper.

A knock sounded on the front door, and Slink and I exchanged puzzled glances. I shoved the envelope into the pocket of my shorts and glanced around for my phone. Had the brainstorming meeting been rescheduled? Had I missed the message? Was it Elise, steaming with anger, on the other side of the door?

The knocking continued. As I hurried toward it Slink crisscrossed my path, nearly tripping me. I caught the deep timbre of a male voice on the other side of the door. Thinking it was Alex, I threw the door open, then stopped short. "DCI Quimby."

"Sorry to disturb you. I have a few more questions. May I come in?"

"Yes, of course." I waved Slink back, and Quimby extended his hand for Slink to examine, then he followed me back to the kitchen. His suit today was somewhere in between a light gray and a taupe with a tie to match. How did he find such bland ties that matched his bland suits so exactly? He gave new meaning to the word plainclothes policeman.

I offered him coffee, and he said, "Sure," then noticed my half-eaten omelet. "Sorry to interrupt your breakfast. Go ahead." He looked around the room, his gaze traveling over every inch of it. Was it an occupational hazard, assessing everything, or was he looking for something specific?

I handed him a mug, then sat down at the table and took a small bite while Quimby seated himself opposite of me and sorted out his phone and coffee. I pushed my plate away. The eggs were cold, and something about sitting across from the police made my appetite fade. I'd never thought of Quimby as overly friendly, but there was a new degree of coolness in his manner that made me wary. I realized I was thinking like Louise and gave myself a mental shake. Quimby was probably tired. Dark circles under his eyes indicated that he hadn't had a full night's sleep like I had.

He took a long sip of his coffee. "That's good." He took another drink, then said, "You stated yesterday that you hadn't met Ms. Emsley before she came to Nether Woodsmoor."

"That's right."

He stared at me, and I fought off the urge to squirm.

"Are you sure that's correct?"

"Yes," I said. "She's the sort of person you don't forget."

Quimby's expression didn't reflect my light tone. "Are you absolutely sure you didn't have some sort of interaction with her? Perhaps in California? Maybe a chance meeting either on a 'shoot,' I believe it's called, or socially?"

I leaned back in my chair. "I suppose it's possible she could have been associated with some project I also worked on, but I had never talked to her until she came here. In fact, I barely talked to her once she was here."

"Then why did she request to work with you?"

I shrugged. "I don't know. I told you all this yesterday."

"Could it perhaps have something to do with your friend Melissa Millbank?"

"Melissa?"

"Ms. Millbank was friends with both Ms. Emsley and Ms. Mayes."

All the formal names took me a second to work out. "Oh, you mean that Melissa knew Arabella and Torrie back in the day? Yes, that's true, they were all in some regional theater or something like that. They had a falling out. I don't know exactly what happened, but that has nothing to do with anything now."

"So you didn't put yourself forward to work with Ms. Emsley...perhaps at the suggestion of your friend Ms. Millbank?"

"No, not at all." I didn't like these questions and felt a growing sense of unease. "Just what are you implying?"

"I'm not implying anything, just checking facts."

"Well, the facts are that Melissa hasn't had anything to do with Arabella, and she didn't want to be around her either."

"Bad blood between them, still?"

"No," I said impatiently and felt Slink stir. She'd come to sit beside me. I rubbed my hand down her long neck and told myself to calm down. "Honestly, I don't think Melissa cared a bit about Arabella. Melissa's wrapped up in her own world right now." Almost all her conversations revolved around Paul, but I didn't want to tell Quimby that. I wasn't sure where he was going with his questions and the less info I gave him, the better. "Anyway, Elise assigned me to work with Arabella because Arabella insisted on it."

He gave a small nod as he sipped his coffee. "Do you mind if I have a look around?" He glanced toward the sitting room and the stairs then brought his gaze back to my tote bag beside my laptop.

"Why?"

His gaze sharpened. "You'd rather I didn't?" he asked, his tone surprised.

"Well, to be honest, no. Why should I let you?" I asked. The uneasy feeling had ratcheted up to full-on anxiety.

"Because it would be the quickest way to clear up a tip we received."

"You received a tip...about me?"

"Yes, that you were writing the threatening notes."

It took me a second to form an answer because what he said didn't make sense. "Me?" I finally said. "That's absurd. Why would *I* send notes to Arabella? I didn't even know her...oh, I see," I said, realizing that he'd put together my friendship with Melissa and her past connection with Arabella and made a triangle between the three of us. "You think I'm sending notes to Arabella *for* Melissa?"

"Perhaps Ms. Millbank enlisted you to help her harass Ms. Emsley, and things got out of hand."

"That's...I don't know...I take back the word *absurd*. It isn't strong enough. Arabella received those notes before she ever came to Nether Woodsmoor." Suddenly, I thought of the envelope that I'd shoved in my pocket, and my breathing quickened. I didn't normally put paper in blank envelopes in my bag. I resisted the urge to shove my hand in my pocket and make sure the envelope was still there.

"No reason you couldn't have sent those notes as well."

"I didn't know where she was before she came here. I didn't *care* where she was. Neither did Melissa." I leaned forward. "I can't believe you seriously could think for a moment that I had anything to do with her death. What about the man in the garden? What about Stevie Lund? They're much better suspects than me."

"I agree," Quimby said quietly. "Except in the case of Lund. The security cameras at Tate House show that Lund walked up the drive, had a verbal confrontation with Chester Hibbert at the front door, then left. Lund never went into the garden. I do have other leads to pursue, though. That's why I asked to have a quick look around. I have to follow up on the tip, and while I consider it extremely doubtful that you are involved in this, it is a murder investigation now. I'd hoped that because of our past association you would trust me, and we could clear this up now without waiting for warrants and such. I'd rather get on to more serious inquiries."

I tilted my head. "I had nothing to do with Arabella's death, and I have nothing to hide, but surely you understand that I'm not going to let you prowl around my cottage. Would you give a police officer an okay to do that at your house?"

A slight smile flickered across his face. "Probably not." He stood. "I'll be in touch."

I followed him to the door and locked it behind him. I waited, watching out the sitting room window until his car pulled away then I went in the kitchen and took out the envelope. I had a very bad feeling about it.

The flap wasn't sealed. I put it down on the table and ripped a paper towel from the roll by the sink. I used it to cover my fingers as I pushed the flap back and pulled out a single sheet of paper. Still using the paper towel, I opened the page, which was folded in thirds. It was stiff and didn't move easily, so I only lifted the edges until I could see the interior. A mishmash of letters cut from the pages of a glossy magazine wavered in a sloping line across the center of the page, spelling out the message, "Arabella Greta Emsley." Under it was another string of numbers, today's date, I realized. The last line was the shortest, "R.I.P."

I should call Quimby and hand this over to him right away. I knew that, but my thoughts jumped ahead to questions that would come up. *Why hadn't I turned it over to him earlier this morning during his visit? How was it possible I'd found it moments after he mentioned the tip the police had received that said I had sent the threatening notes? If I didn't make the note, how did it get in my bag? If it fell out last night, how had I missed it?* And then we'd be off on the same circuit about Melissa and why I was the liaison for Arabella.

A hammering at the door made me jump.

CHAPTER 17

SLINK LET OUT A VOLLEY of barks and raced to the front door and back. I stared at the note, my body going hot then cold. Was Quimby back with a search warrant already? No, it couldn't be, I told myself, but my hands trembled as I used the paper towel to press the folds of the paper down and cover the message. I dragged my laptop over and set it on top of the paper towel-covered note, and followed Slink to the door.

"Kate?" called a feminine voice.

I unlocked the door and pulled it open an inch.

Melissa stood on the porch holding a to-go cup of coffee steaming in each hand. "You really should get a doorbell—what's wrong?"

I swung the door open and checked the street as she came inside. "So much." Quimby wasn't in sight. I closed the door. "I thought you were Quimby, back with a search warrant."

She held out one of the cups to me then bent over to say hello to Slink as she said in an accusing tone, "Have you not had your coffee yet?"

It was a mocha and smelled wonderful. I took a long sip. "Actually, I have. I'm not groggy at all. Quimby was just here, asking about you and Arabella and Torrie." She followed me to the kitchen as I summarized Quimby's visit then removed the laptop and used the paper towel to unfold the note. "Then I found this. It must have fallen out of my tote bag. No, don't touch it. I've already handled the envelope. Don't add your fingerprints to the note—we'll be in even bigger trouble then."

Melissa's eyes, heavily rimmed with her signature black liner, skimmed over the note. "What rubbish to think you'd do something like this. Of course, I'm sure our tame detective could picture *me* sending those notes—I am rather an odd fish."

I glanced over her ensemble for today. She was clearly dressing down for the day off in a black-and-white polka-dot shirt that was vented in the back and had an asymmetrical hem. She'd paired the shirt with billowy white slacks that looked like something out of the *Arabian Knights* along with thick-heeled white wedges that tied around her ankles. I would have looked clownish and ridiculous in the outfit, but on Melissa it looked perfect—slightly quirky and fun. "You have a flair for fashion. That doesn't mean you're odd—or that you'd send a note like this."

"In some people's books it does. And I think that Quimby is one of those conventional people who might think that way. I mean, look at how he dresses. No imagination!" She leaned over the note again. "I wonder if he'll ask me about knowing Arabella and Torrie years ago?"

I pulled open a drawer and took out a large plastic bag. "I imagine he will." Slink watched me with interest, then realized food wasn't about to appear and loped off to sleep on her cushion.

"He's completely daft to think you'd do something like that." She motioned to the note with her coffee.

"Yet, I did have a threatening note in my tote bag." I slid the note into the plastic bag without touching the paper then sealed the top.

"Is it like the others?"

"You heard about them?" I asked, thinking that Torrie had been right about word getting around quickly about the notes.

"Rumors, but I figured since it was Arabella that the rumors were true. I mean, she was the sort you'd *want* to send nasty notes to, you know? So...is it like the others?"

"I don't know. I didn't see them. Arabella said they were words cut out of magazines, so I assume they looked like this."

Melissa frowned at the note. "Not much creativity in the phrasing. You'd think if you were sending threats to a person you could come up with something better than R.I.P."

I blew out a breath. "Unfortunately, I don't think Quimby will be concerned with how trite the message is."

She looked up sharply. "You're not planning to give this to him, are you? That would be idiotic."

"Yes, I know. But it *is* evidence. He should have it. It could be tested for fingerprints."

"If someone went to the trouble to put this in your bag, I doubt they would have been careless enough to leave a fingerprint on it. I wonder how long it's been in there?"

"I don't know. It must have been in with the copies of the map that fell out when my tote bag tipped over yesterday. I didn't notice the envelope until this morning, though."

"So anyone could have dropped it in during the last few days?"

"I suppose so—no wait. I thought I'd lost my phone yesterday. I was searching for it at the end of the day right before I left Parkview. It had slipped out of the little pocket inside the tote bag that I usually put it in, but I took almost everything out of my tote bag to look for it." I focused on the floor and tried to remember exactly what I'd pulled out of the bag. After a second I said, "No, the envelope wasn't in there. I remember removing the extra copies of the map. I would have noticed an envelope, even if it was in with the papers. It's not the same size as the papers, and it's thicker."

I pressed the plastic bag. The layer of glue made the paper stiffer and distorted it a little so that it didn't lay flat. "And I did take the maps out. I know I slapped them down when I cleared everything out, so if the envelope was in there it probably would have fallen out and separated from the pages like it did last night when the bag tipped over."

"So someone must have put it in your bag between when you left Parkview and when you came home."

I dropped into the chair at the kitchen table and took a long sip of the mocha. "It could have been anyone at Tate House. I put my bag down at the top of the garden steps when I went down to check on Arabella. Then later, it was on the kitchen counter inside the house. I figured Constable Albertson probably brought it in. Everyone came through there at some point."

After the wire had been discovered, I'd waited on the terrace along with the Hibbert cousins until the police were sure the stairs were safe. A lot of confusion occurred right after the wire was found, though, and either one of the cousins could have slipped into the kitchen to put the envelope in my bag, or Torrie could have done it while I was outside because she never came out at all.

Melissa pulled out a chair and sat. "You came here after you left Tate House, right?"

"Ah—no. I took Slink for a run then stopped at the pub. Stevie Lund was there—you know who he is?"

"Arabella's angry ex, or that's what they're calling him in the paper that I saw at the market."

"That's about right," I said, thinking of how he'd shouted and shaken the gate. Could he really be in the clear when it came to

Arabella's death? "And I think I saw Gil Brayden in the pub, too, but it was only a glimpse. I looked around for him when I left, but either he'd slipped out, or it wasn't him at all."

"Who's Gil Brayden?"

"That's right. You don't know about him." I brought her up to date on the man in the garden and how the next day, Gil had tried to get onto the Parkview grounds.

"So you're pretty sure this Brayden bloke was at Tate House sneaking around the gardens?"

"Both Arabella and Torrie thought it was him. He's paparazzi. They're not known for good manners."

"Or playing by the rules." Melissa took a sip of her coffee, her frowning gaze fixed on the plastic bag that I'd placed on the table. "Threatening notes sent to a star would make a good story. Maybe Arabella was wrong and the notes weren't from Lund. Maybe this Gil manufactured a story so he could cover it. He could have been sending Arabella the notes, but when he heard she'd died, he dropped one in your bag and gave the police a tip to divert suspicion from him."

"That's possible, I suppose. But he's a photographer, not a reporter. Or Lund could have put the note in my bag. Arabella thought he was the one sending the notes. Lund even bumped into me as I left the pub, so he could have put it in my bag then... but anyone could have done it, actually. I had my bag hooked on the back of the barstool. *Anyone* in the pub could have dropped something in my bag."

"But of all the people in the pub, only the photographer bloke and Stevie Lund have any link to Arabella."

"That we know of." A gloomy feeling settled over me. "The pub was packed. Who knows what—or who—I missed. And then there's everyone at Tate House—Torrie and the Hibbert cousins." I swirled my mocha around. "Something was...I don't know...off, at Tate House. I felt it every time I was there. Weird undercurrents that I couldn't quite put my finger on."

"I'll bet there were undercurrents. Someone was murdered there." She wrapped her free hand around her waist as if she felt chilled. "I'm sorry you're messed up in this, but I'm so glad that Arabella didn't want me around."

I put my coffee down. "What happened between you two? I never did get the full story." Unlike Quimby, I didn't think for a minute that Melissa could be involved in some scheme to harass Arabella, but I wanted to know the full story.

Melissa became very interested in the grain of the wood on the tabletop. "It's one of those things I'm not proud of." Her voice was uncharacteristically quiet. "I stole her boyfriend. She'd landed the lead in the play—the role I'd hoped to get—and she was so smug about the whole thing, it made me furious...so, I flirted with her boyfriend until he broke up with her and went out with me. Not my best moment," she said with a grimace.

"As an adult, Arabella was hard to deal with. I'm sure she wasn't any easier when she was a teenager."

"Still, I shouldn't have done it." She sighed. "But that's what happened, and Arabella is not one to forgive and forget. Once you crossed her, you were on her black list forever."

"Until you mentioned it the other day, I didn't know you acted."

"Oh, I tried. I was *terrible*," she said, drawing out the last word. "I realize that now, but at the time I had my heart set on being a star. It was a summer workshop. We put on two plays: one in July and one in August. I see now that the whole point of it was to expose us to all aspects of theater. For the first play, half of us worked behind the scenes, lights, costume, that sort of thing. Then we switched for the second play. The people who were actors the first time around were behind the scenes and vice versa."

Melissa smiled. "After playing the lead, Arabella was assigned to lights. She hated every moment of it. It wasn't a bad gig. Torrie was with her, so she should have been happy about that, but she wasn't. Pouted her way through the whole thing. But, like I said, she wasn't one to let things go. I'm sure that's why she vetted the list of cast and crew before she arrived here. Although, it looks like she had more to be worried about than cutting out the people who'd wronged her."

Melissa checked the time and finished her coffee. "Paul will be here any minute. Because we have the day off, we're going to a swanky restaurant near Upper Benning for lunch. Would you like to come? Get away from all this for a bit?"

"And be a third-wheel? No thanks. Besides, Quimby would probably assume I had skipped town. I think I'd better keep a low profile for now. Maybe try to work out where Brayden was yesterday and where Lund went after he left Tate House," I said, mentally running through who would be a good source of information about the men.

Lund was staying at the inn. Was Brayden staying there, too? Doug and Tara, the owners, were a nice couple. Since I'd helped them out in the past when a guest went missing, they might help me now.

I could hear Alex's voice in my head telling me those things were Quimby's job and that I should leave it alone, but Quimby had gotten a tip that pointed him in my direction. I didn't like sitting around waiting for things to happen to me. I'd much rather be out front, making things happen.

Melissa looked doubtful. "Are you sure you don't want to go?"

"Positive."

"Okay, well, then," she gave me a stern look, "You'll not hand that off to Quimby, will you? I don't fancy having to cut short my day in the country to come spring you from jail."

"I doubt Quimby could arrest me with only a piece of paper as evidence, but I don't like the idea of hanging on to it either."

"Then pop it in the post—minus that envelope with your fingerprints on it—and send it to him anonymously. Or keep it a day or two, and then turn it over to him later. Who knows? They might find the person who really sent the notes, and you'll be in the clear by then. You could always tell him you found it buried in the depths of your bag—and it would be true, too. Just leave out the part about *when* you found it."

"I doubt Quimby would forget to ask me about that."

Melissa's phone buzzed with a text. "That's Paul. He's outside."

"Have a nice afternoon," I said firmly, following her to the door. Paul waved and shouted hello from the car's open window. As Melissa trotted down the steps, I said, "Have you heard anything about a meeting today?"

Melissa opened the gate at the end of the walk. "Emergency meeting late this afternoon. Looks like tomorrow will be a wash as well. Check your email for all the details."

"Thanks. I will." I returned to the cottage. I thought Melissa's idea of posting the note was better than keeping it, so I slipped on my winter gloves, then took an envelope from the back of the box I'd bought for mailing my occasional letters to California. I knew I wouldn't have touched the envelopes at the back of the box. I slid the single sheet of paper into the envelope and retrieved Quimby's business card from the mantle. He'd given it to me before I left Tate House yesterday, and I'd propped it up there so I wouldn't lose it. I carefully printed the address in letters so neat it would have made my first grade teacher proud.

I removed the protective strip that covered the self-sealing flap and pressed it into place. I couldn't bring myself to destroy the envelope, so I left it in the plastic bag and stuffed it into the back of a junk drawer in the kitchen under a stack of receipts and coupons that I'd saved but never used.

Feeling better now that I had a course of action, I took off the gloves, then sat down at the kitchen table to read my email before

I left to post the letter. I didn't want to give Elise any reason to be more upset with me than she already was, and I wouldn't put it past her to give me some other assignment—one of the kind she always described as "little," but could take hours or days to complete.

I lifted the lid of the laptop, picked up the mouse, and turned it over to switch it on, but the bright beam at the bottom of the mouse was already on. I set it down with a frown. I was sure I'd switched it off the last time I'd used it—I always did. The screen-saver faded as I swirled the mouse and the background image came up, one of my favorite shots, a photo of Alex and me grinning at the camera, which we'd held at arm's length. The green undulating hills of Derbyshire spread out behind us under a cloud-dotted sky. Normally, I smiled when the image came up, but not today. Hadn't I left the browser open?

I had been in the middle of scanning job postings for location scouting jobs yesterday before I left for work. The documentary was winding up and, even though I didn't want to think about my time in Nether Woodsmoor coming to an end, I had to start looking around. Many of the location scouting jobs I'd landed had come through word of mouth, but it didn't hurt to keep an eye on the job boards. There had been a promising one in New York. It was for a medical drama and needed locations for a hospital. New York was on the other side of the Atlantic, but it was closer to England than California.

I clicked through a couple of open documents, but the browser window wasn't hiding behind any of them, and it wasn't minimized either. With an apprehensive feeling, I opened the browser, thinking about identity theft and how foolish it was that I hadn't taken time to set a password for the computer. I had a passcode on my phone, but not on the laptop. I didn't carry it with me all the time and it didn't seem like I needed one on it.

I gave myself a mental shake. If someone had been on my

computer, then that would mean someone had been in the cottage and everything had been fine when I got home last night, nothing disturbed or out of place...except the computer mouse was on.

The browser window opened, and I clicked to the history section as I glanced at the door to the back garden. I'd learned last year that the locks on the doors fell into the antique category and were quite easy to pick, if someone knew what they were doing. Beatrice owned the cottage along with several others, and I'd meant to ask her for newer locks, but it hadn't seemed urgent.

The page loaded, and I sucked in a breath as I read down the list of page titles of the recently visited sites: *How electricity works. Basic house wiring. Voltage of power lines. Man electrocuted in home. Worker dies after electric shock.*

My fingers trembled as I cleared the search history. I clicked the commands to shut down the computer and restart. But was that enough? I didn't know enough about computers to know if I'd completely erased the data. As the computer powered up again, I looked around the cottage, my heart hammering.

Someone *had* been inside and planted those search terms in the browser's history to make me look guilty of Arabella's death. And someone had told the police I was involved in sending threats to Arabella. What else had they done?

CHAPTER 18

*A*N HOUR LATER, I CLOSED the door to the storage nook under the stairs then sat down wearily on the bottom step. I'd been through the whole cottage, checking everywhere I could think of—drawers, cabinets, under the sofa cushions and the mattress—but nothing else looked different or out of place. I felt a little steadier and not quite so frightened now that I'd searched the cottage. I hadn't found any more envelopes or pages with cut-out words pasted to them, but I still had the note I'd found in my bag, and I wanted to get rid of that.

Slink shook herself awake and trotted over to me, then rested her nose on my knees. "Good thing you stayed with me last night," I said.

For a moment after I'd found the strange search history on my computer, I'd been afraid that someone had gotten inside the cottage last night, but it couldn't have happened, not with Slink around. She wouldn't sleep through someone breaking in and messing with my computer. And now that I'd calmed down and thought about it, I realized that the search history had been dated. The searches on electricity and electrocution had been at the top of the list under yesterday's date. Since Slink had been in the cottage with me last night it must have happened before I returned home. At least I knew it hadn't happened while I was sleeping unaware upstairs.

I gave Slink's ears a final rub and stood. "Time to post a letter." Slink looked hopeful, but I shook my head. "Not this time, girl. I think it's much better if you stay here."

In my search of the cottage, I'd found what had been a full sheet of first class stamps shoved into the back of a drawer in the kitchen with a few remaining on the page. The previous tenant must have left them. I donned my winter gloves again and attached more postage than the envelope needed. I wanted to make sure it got to Quimby.

I checked the locks on the door, used a tissue to tuck the envelope into my pocket, then transferred my phone and other essentials to a slender crossbody bag. On non-shooting days, I didn't need to carry all my extra items and downsized from my tote bag to the smaller bag.

I picked up my laptop, considering if I should bring it with me. I didn't want to leave it in the cottage in case Melissa was wrong, and Quimby did get his warrant. Just the thought of Quimby returning made my heartbeat skitter. I took a deep breath and told myself to calm down. I'd make sure that if Quimby returned, he wouldn't find my computer...at Honeysuckle Cottage.

I tucked it under my arm, gave Slink a pat on the head, and made a quick trip to Alex's cottage. I let myself in and went to the storage area under the stairs that was positioned in the same place as the one in my cottage. The similarity ended at the location. While my storage area held an empty suitcase and a few boxes that had been left from prior tenants, Alex's storage closet was completely packed.

A kayak paddle swished toward me when I opened the door.

I caught it and pushed it back into place beside the snowboard. Stacks of boxes and books lined the shelves on the back wall along with a sadly deflated soccer ball, a radio with a broken antenna, and a manual typewriter with a limp ribbon. I shoved aside some boxes on the floor, opened one of the dusty board games, and set my laptop under the colorful playing board. After replacing the lid of the box, I brushed off my hands, thinking that it should be safe from Quimby at least temporarily. I felt slightly better. Now I just had to get rid of the note.

As I came back down Cottage Lane, I heard the noisy clatter of Annette retrieving her wheelie bin from the street. My steps slowed as I remembered something she'd said yesterday. Hadn't she thought I was home early?

"Annette," I called, but she'd seen me and was waiting for me. She was always up for a chat. She looked much more polished than she had yesterday in her gardening clothes. She wore a yellow cotton top, tan slacks, and flats. A name tag was clipped to her shirt.

"Good morning," she said. "Looks like we'll escape the rain for another day."

"Yes, I suppose so." The weather was the last thing on my mind. "I can tell you're on your way to work, so I won't keep you." I didn't want to be pulled into a long conversation with her. I wanted to get rid of the letter in my pocket. Even though it was slim, I was very aware of it as it crackled with each step.

"Oh, it's fine. I'm on the afternoon shift today. I have a few minutes."

"Oh...er, good. Well, I have to be off soon." It was always good to have a deadline when chatting with Annette. "Yesterday, you said something about me being home early...?"

She tipped her head to the side, "Did I? Oh, yes. I was in the back garden, weeding. With all this rain it's been difficult to keep up with the garden, you know?" She parked the bin and settled in, leaning her hip against the gate.

"Yes, I imagine so." Thank goodness Beatrice employed a gardener to stop by the cottage and maintain the flowerbeds. My thumb was more black than green, and I was sure the plants would be in sad shape if they were left up to me.

"I heard your back door close, and I thought what a difficult job you have, such long hours."

"I think working with toddlers would be more difficult."

"They can be a...challenge at times, but then they put their fat little arms around your neck, and it makes it all worthwhile, you know?"

"I'm sure it does," I said vaguely since my experience in that area was limited. "So that would have been about what time? That you heard the door, I mean."

Her gaze sharpened. "Around eight or so, I think. It was still light out, but getting darker. I had so much to do that I worked until the light was completely gone. I would have come over and said hello, but I was almost done with the flowerbed by the wall, and I wanted to finish it off."

"Oh, that's fine. I just wanted to make sure my...friend was able to get in."

I knew it had been closer to nine when I arrived at the cottage. It had taken several hours before the police let me leave Tate House. Then I'd taken Slink for her run and stopped by the pub. I swallowed, a feeling of unease sweeping over me. What if I'd walked in on the intruder?

Her attentiveness faded. "Yes, no problem. I didn't see who it was. I was hunkered down next to the wall that separates our gardens. It blocked my view, but I knew it was probably your boyfriend." I didn't correct her, not wanting to launch into a long explanation, but something else had caught her attention behind me. She leaned a little to the side and called out, "Hello! How are you? I see you were able to get your bike fixed."

I turned and saw the woman who had been seated next to me at the bar last night. She was on a cruiser-type bike, one of the older designs that let you ride sitting up. Nether Woodsmoor was a cycling destination because of the beautiful countryside. While I saw some of the traditional bikes on the streets and paths, more often than not, I saw riders on sleek modern bikes, whipping by, hunched over their handlebars.

Her crinkly hair was pulled back in a ponytail. She wore light blue capris with a T-shirt. At first glance, I thought it had some sort of abstract design on it. But as she came closer, I realized the marks were dried streaks and splotches of paint. She put out one sandal-clad foot and hopped off the bike, tilting it sideways as she stopped. "Yes, thank you so much for letting me borrow your bike pump. I was able to get down to the repair shop where they patched it for me. You saved me quite a walk."

Annette waved her hand. "No worries. I couldn't leave you stranded, not with the sun at its peak. You would have had a long, hot walk down to the village. Visiting Nether Woodsmoor, are you, for the biking?"

"No, I'm not much of a cyclist, really. It's just a break for me, to get out a bit."

"But you're not from here." Annette said it with assurance. Nether Woodsmoor was small enough that, while I didn't know everyone's names, I did recognize almost all of the villagers. Annette had grown up in the village—she'd given me an overview of her history when she moved in—so she would know a visitor when she saw one. "Where are you staying? At the inn?"

I hid a smile as the woman inched her bike backward. She didn't like the nosy questions, but Annette was oblivious to any discomfort she was causing.

"No, I'm in a bungalow on the other side of the village," the woman said vaguely.

"One of those Internet house rental things, then." Annette's forehead wrinkled then cleared. "Henrietta Philbank's bungalow? Red door with the frosted glass panel on the side?"

The woman looked half-surprised, half-frightened. "Yes, how did you know?"

"Women's Institute. Henrietta teaches at a nice day school in Yardley. She always takes a holiday in the summer and goes to see her mum in Devon. She's done that house share thing the last few summers. Wouldn't like to do it myself as you'd never know who would be staying in your place."

Annette seemed to realize that she'd said something that could be taken the wrong way and quickly added, "Of course, if they were like *you*, it would be fine. You're the sort who would take care and not leave a mess. Oh goodness, I didn't realize it was so late. I must be off, which is a pity. I'd love to have you in for a cup of tea. I could tell you about the cycling paths." She gripped the handle of the wheelie bin and maneuvered it through her gate. "There's one that goes around Parkview, which is quite nice, although a bit crowded. Another one goes over to the old Hillary place. Not as popular, but even nicer views, I've always thought. I like to walk it myself, but the path is wide, and you could ride it." As she towed the bin toward the side of the house, she called, "Do come by again if you get the chance."

Once she'd disappeared around the side of her house, I looked back at the woman's slightly bemused face. She said, "She's rather, um, overpowering."

"She means well," I said, my tone apologetic, "but doesn't realize how she comes across."

"It was really you I wanted to speak to. I saw you at the pub last night..." She rotated her tight grip on the handlebars backward and forward a few centimeters.

"I remember. We sat next to each other."

"Right. I'm sorry, but I couldn't help but overhear your conversation. I realize I should have said something the moment I realized who you were, but I was so stunned. The shock of everything, I suppose…anyway," she released her grip on the handlebar and held it out toward me, "I'm Violet Emsley."

CHAPTER 19

I WAS ALREADY SHAKING HER hand as I processed the name. "Violet? You're Arabella's sister."

At first glance, I didn't see any similarities between the two women, but then I realized that they both had the same shade of brown hair, but Arabella's had been sleek and shiny while Violet's coarse frizz stuck out wildly. They both had dark brown eyes and a similar brow line, but Arabella's eyebrows had been plucked and shaped into delicate arches that emphasized her eyes. Violet looked like she had never worried about shaping her eyebrows, or much else related to fashion, grooming, or makeup. Her face was free of makeup, and her hair was escaping from an elastic.

"Do you have a moment to talk? I'd like to hear about Arabella. The police are being quite beastly about it. I hoped you'd tell me how she was these last few days."

I felt like the note was burning a hole in the pocket of my shorts, but how could I put off a woman whose sister had just died? I hesitated, my mind racing. She'd been on the path yesterday with a broken-down bike. Could she have tampered with the wiring at Tate House? Apparently, anyone determined enough could climb over the wall, and if she was cycling around

Nether Woodsmoor, she wasn't exactly delicate. And Violet had visited the house earlier when Torrie turned her away. Maybe yesterday Violet had made her way onto the grounds without going through the gate and...what?...Set up an elaborate electrical trap for her sister? If her distraught expression was genuine, that wasn't what happened.

She motioned to the keys I held. "I can see you're on your way out. I can come back later. Or I could meet you somewhere later. Perhaps the pub?"

The only date I had was with a postbox, but she didn't need to know that. Although she looked genuinely grief-stricken, I didn't want to be stupid and invite a stranger into my home. "I'm on my way into the village now. Why don't we go that direction? We could take the path that goes down to the river. There are some benches there where we could talk. That wouldn't put you out of your way, if you're going back to the bungalow where you're staying."

She swung her leg over the bike to dismount. "Yes, let's do that."

As Violet and I walked down the lane, Annette reappeared on the way to her car, which was parked on the lane, and gave us a sharp once-over.

"Looks like you'll have some questions to answer later," Violet said.

"Don't worry, I'm getting quite good at evading her. If she does catch me, I'll tell her we discussed bike paths." I tried to ignore the faint crackle that came from the envelope in my pocket with each step.

Violet gestured to the basket on the front of the bike that held a wooden box and several glass jars with screw-top lids filled with brightly colored water. "I'm not getting anywhere today so I might as well head back."

Arabella had said something about her sister being a painter.

"What sort of paintings do you do?" I asked as she pushed her bike beside me down Cottage Lane.

"Watercolor." Her mouth turned down at the corners. "Arabella called them nursery school art, but many serious artists work in watercolor."

"I'm sure they do," I said since I wasn't well informed on watercolorists.

She wrinkled her nose. "Sorry. I tend to get a bit defensive about it, but she was so...so snobbish, which was quite ironic, considering that she made her living playing pretend." We had made our way down the sloping streets and were now in Nether Woodsmoor. As we paused on the curb to wait for the traffic, she said, "That sounds awful."

Her voice was contrite as I motioned for us to take a street that would bring us out at the path that ran along the river. "It was an old argument," Violet continued. "Arabella didn't understand that other forms of artistic expression are just as legitimate as hers. And the thought that I could be happy with my "pale little doodles" as she called them—well, she didn't understand that. Unless everyone knew your name, and you were paid millions of dollars for a few months of your time, you were a failure in her eyes."

We had reached the pedestrian zone beside the river, a wide swath of flat water that flowed by with a low murmur. Restaurants and shops lined the walking area. Since it was a sunny day, it was filled with tourists and locals alike. Some strolled while others spread blankets for an early picnic lunch. I spotted a free bench and headed for it, walking by a red postbox. I ran my hand over the outside of my shorts pocket where the square of the folded envelope pressed against the fabric. I would have liked to drop it in the postbox, but couldn't figure out how I'd explain using a tissue to hold the thing. "That must have been difficult," I said, trying to put the note out of my mind and focus on Violet. "I don't know what it would be like to have a sister—or brother for that matter. I'm an only child."

Violet parked her bike at the end of the bench and sat down beside me. "Arabella and I shouldn't have fought so much. I probably shouldn't speak of her this way, with her...gone...but it's how she was." Her voice turned fierce. "She *was* selfish, even as a little girl. She never would share. And she didn't change once she got older. A few thousand pounds was nothing to her. She spent more than that on a *handbag*, but she'd never give it to me even though I'd put it to good use. There are plenty of people who would love to learn to paint—children and adults."

"Your art school," I said.

She turned toward me. "She mentioned it? Had she decided to fund it?"

Arabella hadn't sounded the least bit interested in it when I heard her mention it—in fact, her tone had been disparaging, but I couldn't say that, not with Violet looking at me so eagerly.

"I have no idea. I wasn't involved with her much. I only spoke to her a few times."

"Oh. Well, perhaps after the will is..." She waved her hand and shrugged a shoulder. "...probated or whatever it's called. Maybe then I'll be able to open the school. I mean, if she hasn't changed her will. And she wasn't the sort of person to dwell on things like that. I doubt she gave it another thought after she signed it."

"So she did have a will?"

"Oh, yes. She called me out of the blue one day and said I would get half her estate and not to do anything foolish with it if she were to kick off before me. Like leaving the other half of her estate to fund an acting grant wasn't foolish. Her business manager made her draw up the will after she got together with Stevie Lund. He said that Stevie was the sort of person who would cause no end of trouble if something were to happen to Arabella." Her tone became quieter. "I think, too, that he wanted her to do it as a preventative measure to keep Stevie from getting any...ideas about, you know, hurting her—or worse."

"You think Lund would have killed her for her money?" I asked. "Is that what you're saying?"

Her gaze slipped away from mine. "That sounds so... horrible when you put it like that, but Stevie is quite vicious, and look at his family—criminals, all of them. Not white-collar criminals, either. Mobsters, that's what they are, no matter what the papers say. They run drugs. Arabella and Stevie always had a stormy relationship. If they were on the outs, and he thought he could get Arabella's money, then I think he'd do it. Or, actually he'd probably have someone else do it."

Arabella had said the same thing, I remembered, and suddenly I felt as if I was standing in a cold draft. I crossed my arms. But how well informed was Violet about Arabella? From what I'd seen, Arabella hadn't wanted anything to do with Violet and had kept her at a distance. "Stevie Lund is here in Nether Woodsmoor. Did you know that?" I asked.

"Stevie Lund?"

"He was at the pub last night."

Her eyes widened. "Are you sure?"

I nodded. "In fact, he bumped into me when I left, didn't you see him?"

"No. I went to the loo, and when I came back, you'd already left. I'd been working up to asking you about Arabella, but then when I heard the word *murder*...I went all funny inside. The police had told me, of course, but when I heard you mention it, it hit me hard—that it was real. Too many drinks probably had something to do with it, too, I suppose. After I washed my face, I felt better. When I got back and saw you were gone I didn't look around to see who was in the pub. I left as quick as I could, hoping to catch up with you. Your dog made you easy to spot. I saw you turn to go up the lane to your house, and I followed. But then I realized that if I ran up to you on a dark street and began asking questions about Arabella you'd think I was absolutely mad, so I hung back and watched which house you went into."

"I thought there was someone at the end of Cottage Lane last night. It wasn't my imagination."

"No, that was me. I decided I'd wait until today to talk to you. I'd already been by your cottage once today on my way to paint this morning, but couldn't get up the nerve to knock on your door. And then I couldn't concentrate at all, so I pitched my painting things in the bike's basket and came back to the village, passing your cottage again."

"I'm afraid I can't tell you much about Arabella. Like I said, I only spoke to her a few times, and she didn't mention the art school to me."

"The art school doesn't matter. That's not really why I wanted to talk to you."

I refrained from pointing out that the art school had been the first thing that had come up. It was important to her, no matter what she said.

"The police have been so cagey," Violet said. "They won't tell me anything. I don't know why they're making such a fuss about *me* being in Nether Woodsmoor, if Stevie is here, too. He's obviously the best suspect."

"What have the police said?" I asked.

"Only that she fell down the stairs."

So they were keeping the bit of news about the wiring to themselves. I wondered how long it would be before it came out. I decided I'd better not say anything about it to Violet. I cast around for something that I could tell her. "It looked like Arabella was on her way to do yoga."

"She would be. She was always working out. And if it was nice, she'd be outside. It was the one time she'd allow herself to get some sun." She gazed at the river, watching a group of ducks float under the bridge. "Was she…did it look like she had been in pain, or anything like that?"

"No, I don't think so. It must have been quick."

Still looking at the river, she drew in a deep breath, then let it out slowly. "I wish I could have seen her. Even though we had our moments, I still—" She looked down at her hands clasped together in her lap.

"Were you hoping to see her yesterday?"

She nodded as she sniffed and got her emotions under control. "I actually went by Tate House twice. Your neighbor only saw me at noon, but I went back later, after I'd had a bite at the tea shop. I figured it was worth a try." She unlocked her hands and picked at a patch of dried blue paint on her shirt. "I suppose that's why the police went so funny. Why did I go back when I'd already been turned away? Wasn't I welcome?" She made a face. "Of course I couldn't deny it. Blooming security cameras every-where these days. Nothing's private anymore."

"Tate House does have quite a bit of monitoring equipment."

"And the security lads, too." A corner of her mouth turned up. "Arabella did know how to play up the drama. She was always good at that. *One* security person would certainly not be enough for a star like her."

"So it was late when you went back? It was after you'd had tea?"

"Yes, it was around five or so, I think. I figured, one more go. I'd made a special trip here. I had to give it another try before I left."

"When were you leaving?"

"I'd planned to leave this morning, which is another tick against me according to the police. I had no idea she was going to die, did I? I came up to see my sister for a few days. I couldn't stick around forever." Her gaze sharpened on something behind me. "And speaking of that, I should go," she said briskly. "I have to clear up and pack so I can get out of here today." She stood and rolled the bike to her hip, again taking a quick glance over my shoulder.

I looked back, but only saw milling families, cyclists, and a group of teens making their way toward the river. "So the police haven't asked you to stay on?"

"In Nether Woodsmoor?" she asked as if the village were in the Arctic Circle and no one could be expected to stay and survive. "They shouldn't have any problem with it. London is only a train ride away. They know where to find me. And besides, I need to get on with the arrangements for the funeral." She swung up on the bike and said goodbye. She pushed firmly on the pedals and picked up speed. She followed the curving bank of the river and disappeared behind a group of trees that edged the water.

Did Violet realize Arabella's will—if it contained the bequests she thought it did—gave her a motive? The way she spoke so freely about it seemed to indicate that the thought hadn't crossed her mind. I twisted around, running my arm along the back of the bench as I looked over the pedestrian area behind me. The group of teenagers parted, half of them darting toward the bridge. That's when I saw Constable Albertson.

I tensed, and my hand went to cover my thigh so that it rested over the envelope in my pocket, but then I realized that Albertson wasn't interested in me at all. His attention was focused on Torrie, who was several yards in front of him.

CHAPTER 20

J STAYED SEATED ON THE bench and watched Albertson watch Torrie. He was in street clothes, a brown knit shirt and jeans. Torrie was several yards ahead of him, making her way speedily toward the red postbox that Violet and I had passed. One of the Hibberts was at her side, and she held a flat box clutched to her chest. She must be sending off the last of Arabella's mail. Maybe she was a better assistant than I gave her credit for. Just because she seemed to dislike Arabella, didn't mean she wouldn't do her job.

The man with her turned his head. I didn't see a glint of an earring, so I assumed it was Sylvester. Torrie dropped the box in the slot of the postbox, while Sylvester waited behind her, hands clasped loosely while his head turned, his gaze sweeping the area. His posture reminded me of the pose Secret Service agents took around the president. When Sylvester looked in Albertson's direction, the constable melted into one of the shops that fronted the pedestrian area.

After Torrie turned away from the postbox, Sylvester nodded in my direction. They weren't looking at me, were they? I glanced around, hoping that some other person had drawn their attention, but except for a pair of joggers who trotted swiftly by, there was only me. Torrie said a few words to Sylvester then he headed toward the river while Torrie strode toward me. Behind her, Constable Albertson moseyed from one shop to the next, but kept his attention on Torrie as she made a beeline for me.

Great. Just what I didn't want. The police were obviously keeping a discreet eye on Torrie. The last thing I needed right now was for her to draw their attention to me—especially while the envelope felt as if it was burning a hole in my pocket.

"Kate," she said, sounding an awful lot like Elise's peremptory tones, "Where have you been? I called you several times this morning, but only got your voicemail."

I took my phone out of my pocket and checked the display. "I'm sorry, Torrie. I must have forgotten to switch on the ringer this morning." I was completely out of my routine and off my game. I usually checked the weather and turned on the ringer on my phone first thing each day.

"At least I've caught you now," Torrie said, but she still sounded displeased. "I'm *attempting* to get everything in order—all Arabella's things—so we can clear out of Tate House, but I can't find her charm bracelet. Was she wearing it yesterday when you found her?"

"Um…I don't know…no, I don't think so." I stole a glance over her shoulder. Albertson had wandered down one of the side streets that branched off from the pedestrian walkway, but he reappeared, his gaze checking on Torrie's location briefly before he turned away to study a clothing display in a shop window. "I remember she had a toe ring and an ankle bracelet, but I think that was the only jewelry I saw. Could it be in her room?" If it was in her messy room, it could take a while to find it.

Torrie pulled a face. "No, it wouldn't be there—thank goodness. She never put anything away. Never. Her room was always a tip."

147

"I'm sorry I can't help, but I don't think she had it on. Wouldn't she have taken it off since she was about to do yoga?" The jangle of the charms wouldn't exactly fit with the exercise that was supposed to be calming and relaxing.

"No. She always wore it, or if she couldn't wear it, like if she was filming, she put it in a little pouch that was lined with foam. It didn't make any noise inside the pouch, and no one knew about it."

"Oh, yes. I think I saw it on the day we filmed in the gardens. When she picked up her reticule, it almost fell out."

"If she took it off at all, she would have put it down somewhere on the stairs while she worked out. But Chester says it wasn't there." Her voice held a note of suspicion. "The police tell me it's not listed as either a piece of evidence or part of her personal property."

She must not trust Chester since she wanted to check his story against what I had to say. "I'm sorry. I wish I could help you, but I don't remember seeing it."

She tilted her pointed chin down as she studied the ground, her thoughts concentrated on the past. "She had it on when we arrived back from Parkview that day, so it has to be in the garden somewhere. I *must* find it." She said the last sentence under her breath, but not low enough that I couldn't hear her. The intensity of her voice surprised me.

It was only a piece of jewelry, and not an extremely valuable one, at that. She noticed my expression and flushed. "It was one of her favorite pieces...her good luck charm. I know her sister will want it...for sentimental reasons. I have to go." She turned away, and Sylvester immediately left the edge of the river. They met and walked back through the village. After a few moments, Constable Albertson fell into step behind them.

I followed the path along the river for a few moments, keeping an eye out for anyone interested in me, but no one seemed to be dogging my footsteps. I crossed the bridge and wandered around on the far side of the river for a bit then crossed back, pausing in the middle of the bridge.

I wasn't looking at the smooth flow of water, but the buildings around the area. Violet's mention of cameras everywhere made me realize that despite making sure I didn't leave my prints on the envelope, there was another way Quimby could trace it back to me. I spotted one camera mounted high on a light pole, aimed at the pedestrian area.

I supposed there could be others that I wasn't able to see. I considered hopping in Alex's little car for a drive to Upper Benning or some other more populated area to mail the note, but I really didn't want to hang on to it for another moment.

I crossed the bridge and went into one of the shops where I bought a baseball cap and a T-shirt with an outline of Parkview Hall on it. I managed to get the items into my crossbody bag then I went down a few yards, popped into a tea shop with baskets of flowers hanging under a bright awning. After sipping a cup of tea, I went to the loo, pulled the souvenir shirt over the one I was wearing, and twisted my hair up under the cap. I emerged from the tea shop and was relieved to see a large group of tourists following a woman with an umbrella held high in the air. They were heading for the river, so they'd pass right by the postbox. I was quite a bit younger than most of the group, who wore name tags and carried identical bags that read, "Beautiful Britain."

I fell into the group that was following the woman with the umbrella like ducklings waddling after their mother. "The five-arched stone bridge dates from the thirteenth century," she announced, "and was very important in establishing the village as a market town…"

I managed to get the envelope out of my pocket with the tissue protecting it from my fingers. I dropped the envelope in the slot and peeled off from the group as the woman pointed out the church and began a detailed description of its history. I wound my way through the village and took a circuitous route back to Cottage Lane. I wanted to pick up Alex's car and drive over to the inn so I could ask about Gil Brayden, but I wanted to ditch my new shirt and hat and let Slink out, too.

Once I was in the shade of the path that ran behind the cottages, I took off the cap and removed the extra T-shirt. I was relieved to get rid of the note, but I still felt on edge and started when my phone rang.

I checked the screen, afraid it would be Torrie—or worse, Elise—but it was Alex. I barely let him say hello before I said, "I have so much to tell you. I don't even know where to start."

"Then let me tell you my news. It's short: I'm done. On my way back tomorrow."

"I'm so glad," I said. "Was your appointment canceled?"

"Appoint—? Oh, right. No, it wasn't." His voice was wary, and the tension that I'd felt in the garden when I asked him about the appointment was back.

"Okay," I said uncertainly, but I didn't understand at all. If the appointment was still on why was he coming back?

He muttered something in a frustrated tone that I didn't catch, then after a short pause he blew out a sigh. "Oh, forget it. I didn't want to tell you over the phone, but I'm tired of trying to keep it a secret." My heart seemed to dip to my stomach. I couldn't form any words, but before I could gather my thoughts, he went on, "Are you near a computer?"

It was the last thing I expected him to say, and it took me a moment to answer. "Ah—no," I said, thinking of my laptop hidden in his cottage.

"Well, you're on your phone. That'll work. Put me on speaker and go to this web address."

"All right." I slowed my pace until I was barely moving as I brought up the browser and tapped in the address he gave me.

The page loaded as Alex's voice came through the speaker. "Can you see it?"

I stopped walking altogether and leaned against the dry-stone wall in the shade of a tree so that I could see the screen better. The words *Elegant Locations* headed the page. Two tabs under the words read, "Find your location" and "List your location." A grid of images filled the rest of the page, all of them stately homes. I recognized Parkview and a few other local manors. As I thumbed down the page, the images scrolled, showing many more locations. "Alex, what is this?"

"Our website." Pride tinged his voice. "It's not finished yet. I'd planned to camp out at a hotel this weekend and get it done."

I reached the bottom of the page and read the fine print. "K & A Consulting?" I asked. "That's...me and you?"

"Of course," Alex said. "I mean, if you're interested in going into business with me..."

My thoughts were spinning. I'd seen plenty of location scouting websites, but usually they were broad, covering any and all locations around the world, or they specialized by region but covered all different types of locations in that area. "Specialize in stately home location scouting...Alex that's brilliant."

"I thought if we have an online catalog of all the manor houses we could be a clearing house for that niche. You know, go narrow, but really cover that section of the market in-depth. If someone needs a drafty castle on the Highlands we'd have those, but we'd have specs on interior rooms, too. Say someone wants a Georgian ballroom or an Art Deco dining room, they can search for those details and view images of the locations along with information on size and availability. The initial setup will be a lot of work. I think we need more specifics on each location and more images. Right now, I only have exterior shots, but once we start filling out the catalog, we could have details on rooms, grounds, outbuildings—the works. And we could include dates things are available. The flip side is that people could list their properties as well. We could have a sliding scale for listing properties and then we could still do scouting and location management as well."

"A sort of middleman for country manors and stately homes," I said, thinking of how much time it could save producers and production companies. Searching for locations ate up a lot of the budget because travel and in-person site visits were expensive. Of course, they'd still want to visit their finalists in person, but this could save tons of legwork.

"Facilitator is a better term, I think," Alex said.

"Yes, definitely. Oh, Alex, this is great. It means…so many things…" I stopped as it hit me. "It means I can stay—here, in England. And we wouldn't be scrambling to find work on the same location, or near each other."

"That's the main reason behind the whole thing," Alex said, his tone going quieter. "Are you in?"

"I'm *so* in," I said, excitement rising in me at the thought of working with Alex all the time and being able to stay without the constant worry about where the next job would be. "Will it pay enough…for both of us, I mean?"

"Once it gets off the ground, I think it will. It'll be a little sketchy in the beginning, but you or I can take on some extra scouting work until we get it going, if we need to."

"I wish you were here so I could give you a hug." I pushed off the wall. I was too excited to be still and headed down the path to my cottage. "So this is what you've been so secretive about."

"Yes, well…I wanted to surprise you with it. I wanted to be able to show you the finished product, but I could tell keeping it a secret was creating a distance between us. I didn't like that."

"I didn't either. I'm so glad you told me." All that worry and stress, I thought, mentally chiding myself. So much angst, for no reason.

"Yeah. I probably should have let you in on it from the beginning."

"Well, you certainly won't be able to keep me out of it now." I opened the gate and went in the back garden. "You'll probably be sick of me before this is over."

"Never that," Alex said, his voice soft, then he cleared his throat. "Now, you had something you wanted to tell me?"

"Oh, that's right." My spirits dipped as I thought about the note and the convoluted mess that I was in. "Hold on a second. I just got back and need to let Slink out." She must have heard me approach because as soon as I unlocked the back door, she shot out of it like an arrow released from a bow.

She circled the tiny garden, flying over the small area in a circle that made me dizzy. She clearly wasn't interested in going back inside and paused hopefully by the gate. "Later," I promised and dropped into one of the chairs under the oak tree near the back garden wall. I'd recently upgraded from flimsy plastic chairs to low-slung wooden models in a smooth grain that let you stretch out your feet while you tipped your head back and studied the pattern of green leaves against the blue of the sky. Slink relented and came over to sprawl, panting, at my feet.

"Now what's happened?" Alex asked, concern shading his words.

I almost told him about the note and the computer searches, but I checked myself. I was feeling skittish and wasn't sure I wanted to share anything on a cell phone. I'd learned recently that it was fairly easy to listen to mobile phone conversations, and after watching Albertson follow Torrie around, I didn't want to take any chances. Especially after I'd gone to all the trouble to get the note to Quimby without him—hopefully—being able to trace it back to me. So instead I told Alex about my conversations with Violet and Torrie.

"She wanted to talk about a charm bracelet?" Alex asked when I finished.

"Yes. I thought it was weird, too. Especially since Violet didn't mention it at all. If it were a family heirloom or something like that, you'd think she would have asked about it, too. But she seemed most interested in whether or not Arabella had mentioned funding the art school."

A cyclist zipped by, helmeted head tucked low then another figure, this one familiar, moved down the path. I watched until he went by me then hopped up and took a quick look over the garden wall.

"Kate, are you still there?"

"Yes. I just saw the oddest thing. It was one of the Hibberts—Sylvester, I think—coming up the path from the village on his way to Tate House, carrying a crowbar."

CHAPTER 21

*W*HY WOULD ONE OF THE Hibberts need a crowbar? Why would anyone at Tate House need one? I pondered those questions on the drive to the Old Woodsmoor Inn but hadn't come up with an answer by the time I parked in front of the two-story white stucco and wood-beamed building with leaded glass windows. It was set back from the road with open countryside stretching out behind it. I'd again left Slink in my cottage, sort of an impromptu security system. She'd hoped for a run, but I'd promised her one later after the meeting, which was still on for late this afternoon. I'd checked my email on my phone and found Ren's message about the meeting.

Alex had to cut our conversation short, which was probably a good thing since I was leaning toward giving him a recap of the whole incident with the note and the computer searches, despite my reluctance to talk about it on a cell phone. He would be back tomorrow, which would be soon enough, I told myself. And we were going into business together, I thought, hugging the idea to myself. We had so much to talk about.

I climbed out of Alex's MG Midget and swung the door closed. As I crossed the gravel to the inn, my steps slowed. A white Ford Fiesta with a dent near the front wheel well was parked near the inn. I scanned the rest of the cars in the parking area, but didn't see a bright yellow Italian sports car.

The inn's restaurant was popular and guests came from around the world to stay in the quaint atmosphere, so I wasn't surprised to hear voices coming from the dining room. Even though his back was turned, I recognized Doug's squat, bulldog build behind the reception counter. As I crossed the wide plank floor, he closed a filing cabinet drawer and turned, his weathered face splitting into a smile when he saw me. "Kate Sharp." He thumped his palm against the counter. "It's been an age."

"Good to see you, too, Doug. How's Tara?" Where Doug was blustery and expansive, Tara was quick and efficient, zipping around the kitchen preparing food and overseeing the maids who came in daily to clean the rooms.

"Fine. Fine."

"Looks like business is good." I glanced out the window to the full parking area.

"Yes, but we haven't seen you around."

"I know. Work." I shrugged one shoulder. "Not much time for a leisurely dinner." My workday often ran past dinner. I usually picked up a quick meal from the pub or the Chinese restaurant.

"Or dinner at all, from what I hear from Louise. She says you work all hours of the day and night. Aren't there laws about that?"

"Not any my boss cares about. Actually, I'm here about something work-related."

He scratched his temple and glanced at the computer. "If you're looking to film here, I don't see how we could do it. We're booked solid through the summer."

I'd once scouted another of Doug and Tara's properties, a B & B, that they owned. "No, it's nothing like that. You heard about the death at Tate House?"

"Sad news, that. I heard you found her," he said with a sympathetic look. "I didn't want to bring it up, unless you did."

"I wish I could ignore it, but I can't. I can't give you any details, but I was hoping you could give me a little insight into some of your guests, like Stevie Lund. Louise told me he was staying here."

Doug ran his hand down over his mouth as he gave a nod. "I think I understand. Your business is involved, and you—or the people you work for—need some information."

"You could put it that way." It wasn't exactly the reason I was there, but I wasn't going to quibble with Doug's interpretation of my request.

"Guest privacy and confidentiality are important to us," he said, and I felt my shoulders sag. "I could never reveal anything confidential...but," he leaned his elbows on the counter as he added, "if you wanted to discuss something that would be obvious to anyone who happened to be in the area, like the location of a certain flash car....that I could talk about."

"Oh, that's good because there is one showy car I'd love to discuss. A canary yellow one."

Doug nodded. "It's been parked here off and on since the day before yesterday."

That was interesting. Stevie had been in Nether Woodsmoor since Wednesday, the day before the finial fell from Parkview's roof and all this craziness started. I didn't need to ask about yesterday. I had seen Stevie Lund myself at Tate House. "I don't see it out there now. I wonder if it will be back later or if it's gone for good...?"

"I'm sure it will be back, unless the owner doesn't care to collect some very expensive luggage and clothing. Tara says the suits are like the car—Italian." He grinned. "Clothing isn't covered under hotelier confidentiality rules."

"I see. Well, in that case, there's another vehicle that I think is very interesting. It's out there now." I described the white car that I'd seen Gil Brayden get into after he was escorted off Parkview Hall's grounds.

Doug tilted his head. "That one's been here longer. Sunday night, I think was the first night it was parked here overnight."

I raised my eyebrows. "Sunday?" Then that meant Gil Brayden had been in Nether Woodsmoor as long as Arabella and her group had been. Of course, if he was stalking Arabella, trying to get photos of her in unguarded moments to sell to the gossip papers then it made sense that he'd arrive shortly after Arabella. But how had he known she was here? Had all the secrecy and decoy cars failed to throw Brayden off the scent?

I had one of Tara's flaky chicken and ham pies for lunch, hoping that I would see either Stevie Lund or Gil Brayden, but neither one made an appearance. I headed back to Cottage Lane where I let Slink out then gathered up my notebook and camera for the meeting in Upper Benning. I didn't think I'd need to take any pictures, but it was better to be prepared in case Elise sent me off on an impromptu assignment.

I didn't bother shifting everything back to the tote bag, just put my work essentials in it and slipped the crossbody bag across my chest. I grabbed the keys to Alex's car, locked up the cottage, and found Quimby blocking my front gate.

"Oh, I didn't see you there." I hoped he put down my sudden quick breathing to jumpiness rather than the jolt of fear I felt on seeing him. I glanced up the lane looking for more police officials, but he was alone. Surely, if he had a search warrant, he'd have more people with him. Unless he'd come to pick up something small, like my tote bag or laptop. He wouldn't need anyone with him for that, I thought and felt as if my insides had turned to ice.

"I thought you'd be interested to know that the Emsley case will be transferred to Scotland Yard."

"Oh, really?" The frigid feeling inside me intensified.

"It's not surprising, of course. The case covers multiple jurisdictions and involves a celebrity," he went on, but his voice was drowned out by the words Scotland Yard, which seemed to be echoing in my head.

I tried to fight off the wave of worry that engulfed me and focused on what Quimby was saying. "...not sure what Scotland Yard will make of you. You're a peculiar case."

"I'm not following."

"Normally when someone pops up in multiple murder investigations, it's a cause for concern." He paused, and I swallowed because my throat was suddenly dry. "But with you I think it's something else. Perhaps an intensely curious nature combined with incredibly bad luck. Whatever it is, you've proved yourself valuable in the past. Several times, in fact. Yes, I heard about Bath. The point is, I understand that it's happenstance, but Scotland Yard might not take that view. Looks peculiar—a civilian involved as frequently as you have been in crime cases. In light of that fact, I thought you might prefer to...share, let's say...any information you might have regarding the case with me before it goes up the chain."

For a second, I wavered. I could tell him everything about the note and hand off my laptop. But would I be out of it then? Would he say *thank you very much for this information* and walk away? No, it would mean more questions. And it would tie me even closer to Arabella. Right now, the police viewed me as someone who'd met Arabella a week ago and happened to find her body. I didn't want to be someone who, in their eyes, could have sent threats to her and researched how to kill her.

I swallowed again. "I'm afraid I can't help you. I don't have anything to share." I reached for the gate latch. "I have a work meeting and really must go."

He stepped back. "I don't believe you, you know—that you're

going on about your normal life and have no interest in Ms. Emsley's death, but if that's the way you want to play it..."

He watched me walk up the lane to Alex's car, which was parked in front of his cottage. I managed to get it started and shift into gear, despite my unsteady legs. I spun the wheel and executed a U-turn under his gaze then watched him in the rearview mirror as I drove away. He remained planted in front of my cottage, his steady gaze following the car until I turned the corner.

~

"Kate, your thoughts?"

"Well, I'm not sure...," I said, playing for time. My thoughts had not been on the meeting. As Elise's voice droned on, covering various last minute options we could put into play to cover the gap in the episode, I'd been thinking about Stevie Lund. Even though the cameras at Tate House had shown he only went to the front door and back to the gate, could he still be responsible for the wires that had shocked Arabella? But then I had to wonder if a murderer would drive a bright yellow sports car to the scene of the crime and leave it in sight of the road. Would anyone be that stupid? Could it possibly be a feint? Could Stevie Lund be that clever?

From my few interactions with him, I thought he wasn't the type of person who liked to confuse or secretly laugh at people. He seemed the sort who liked confrontation. He'd relish seeing fear in an adversary's eyes.

And Brayden...I'd searched out what I could find of his photos while waiting for the meeting to begin. He only had a few recent photos of Arabella posted in the gossip news. And it wasn't like Arabella hadn't been available to be photographed during the first part of the week. Her daily walks to the village would have been a prime opportunity to photograph her. Where had Brayden been then? He had to have known she was in town —the whole village knew.

"You *must* have an opinion on whether or not a segment on Jane Austen-inspired video games would be a good idea or not," Elise said from the head of the conference table. Arabella's death had barely made a ripple in the meeting. It had been discussed— shocking and terrible—but Elise clearly viewed it as something that had happened on the periphery of our work. She believed that, except for the bad luck of me being the one to find Arabella's body, none of our crew had been involved or were suspects— and I wasn't about to let her know that it looked like someone was trying to push me into that role. Unlike other times when a death had happened around our filming and it had taken center stage, this time the only discussion about Arabella concerned how her death affected our schedule.

I cleared my throat and tried to drag my thoughts back to the snippets of the discussion I'd caught. "It's intriguing that Austen's influence has extended to things as modern as video games." I nodded at Felix Carrick, our cinematographer, who had a wicked glint in his eye. "But I don't think the topic would appeal strongly to our typical viewers, women from thirty to forty-nine," I added.

Felix said, "That's true, most likely." He waved his hand, indi- cating the floor was open for the next idea.

Working with Elise did have its drawbacks, but in the area of idea generation and brainstorming, she had become quite demo- cratic lately. Or perhaps she was more desperate for new ideas, my cynical side whispered. Whatever the case, she did ask for and listen to input from the entire crew. Felix leaned back in his chair, looking content. A bit of a troublemaker, he enjoyed riling Elise. I bet he threw out the video game idea just to see what reaction he could get from her. I hadn't seen much of him lately. Any day off he had, he was off meeting his new girlfriend. The relationship had softened his personality somewhat, but hadn't completely erased his subversive streak.

The silence stretched, and then Elise shot a disapproving glance at Ren. "You've been almost as quiet as Kate." He had only spoken a few words so far during the meeting.

"I'm perfectly happy to listen to everyone's ideas and will chime in when I have something to say," he said mildly.

Elise turned back to me, eyebrows raised. "We haven't heard an original idea from you."

I pushed all thoughts of Arabella and Tate House out of my mind. "I like Melissa's idea of looking into the modern resurgence in the popularity of Regency paper dolls." Melissa and Paul had arrived a few minutes late, hand-in-hand which drew an evil-eyed look from Elise, but neither of them seemed to notice, and both had been tossing out suggestions during the meeting.

Elise said, "Yes, but that centers on fashion, and we've done several segments on that. We need something *new*. Something we haven't touched on yet."

After a few beats of silence, I said, "We haven't done anything on money." We'd explored the literary side of Austen's work from the plots themselves to the actual writing of her books. We'd also delved into the modern film adaptations, Austen's family life, her time in the city of Bath, courtship, marriage, fashion, etiquette, and military history—several of Austen's brothers were military men as were some of her characters—but we hadn't touched on the theme of money.

Elise said, "Go on." Coming from her, that was lavish encouragement.

"Not necessarily the bills and coins used in her day, although that could be mentioned, but we could focus on the value of money. What was enough to live on in the Regency? Why were the Dashwood women poor with only—what was it?—something like five hundred pounds a year? And why did everyone always seem to know how much money everyone else had to live on? And why was it always mentioned as a certain amount per year?"

I leaned my elbows on the table as I warmed to the idea. "Money is a theme in all Austen's books—not enough of it, like in *Pride and Prejudice* and *Sense and Sensibility*—or the opposite, which is one of the themes of *Emma*. What happens when you have an excess of it and a meddling personality to boot? We could even touch on the changing attitudes toward wealth and money in her fiction. Darcy inherits his wealth, but by the time Austen wrote *Persuasion*, Captain Wentworth has earned his fortune and is a self-made man."

Paul, sitting beside Melissa, pulled his pencil from behind his ear and tapped the table. "We could bring back that author, the one we interviewed for the second episode about food in the Regency, who kept veering off to talk about other things. Didn't she have several books? One of them had something about commerce or money, I think." He dropped the pencil and picked up his computer tablet. "Yes, here it is. It's called *A Regency Primer: Daily Life* by Deborah Clayton. Table of contents...household, food and drink, transportation, education, work...and yes, money—a whole chapter on it. Looks like exactly what we want." After another flurry of typing, he'd brought up her contact information. "She works out of York. If she's free during the next few days..."

Elise drummed her fingers on the table. "I remember her. She was personable and entertaining. We do have Monday as a contingency day at Parkview. If she were able to come here on short notice, it might work out. Where could we film it?" Elise looked to me.

I ran through my mental list of options. "We haven't used the Tapestry Gallery. Good light in there, the colors are rich and textured, and there are a couple of big globes we could arrange in the background. That would look nice."

We all turned our attention to Ren. "Excellent idea. Let's see if we can make it happen."

Elise handed out assignments, and the meeting broke up. I didn't linger. After I'd jotted down my assigned tasks, which were to coordinate with Beatrice about possibly using the Tapestry Gallery and to check with Torrie about the exact date that Tate House would be vacant, I said a general goodbye and left. There was still plenty of daylight left, and I wanted to get back to Nether Woodsmoor. Slink would be ready for her run, and I wanted to make sure all was well at the cottage. I hadn't liked leaving Quimby standing outside my gate, but at least Slink was inside. I hoped Quimby wouldn't execute a search warrant with her inside.

I navigated back to Nether Woodsmoor through the quiet countryside lanes. As I approached the village, I decided to talk to Torrie first and get that off my list. When I spoke to her earlier today, I should have nailed down an exact time she and the Hibberts would leave Nether Woodsmoor, but I'd been shaken up from finding the cut-and-paste note. Coordinating move-out details had completely slipped my mind. I'd need to do a walk-through of Tate House after Torrie left—if the police would let me. Since they'd let Torrie and the security guards remain, I didn't see why I shouldn't be able to check the premises before I handed the keys over to Claire.

I turned the car toward the road that climbed through the trees to Tate House. I rounded the curve at the top and saw the gate was open. I cruised through and rolled to a stop beside one of the hulking SUVs with the dark tinted windows. It was parked at an angle, nose toward the house, and one of the Hibberts was opening the back passenger door.

As I levered myself out of the MG, I saw the silver hoop in his ear and said, 'Hi, Chester."

The engine of the SUV was running. The low mumble must

have drowned out my car's approach because he jumped and looked around quickly.

I remembered the gun that had made a brief appearance when Stevie Lund climbed the wall, and I halted, with the open car door between him and me.

CHAPTER 22

*I*T WAS A SMALL CAR with small doors, totally inadequate as a shield. But Chester didn't pull out a gun, only nodded a greeting, then opened the passenger door and chucked in a duffle bag. He shrugged his shoulder and his backpack dropped from his shoulder to his hand. He tossed it in as well then slammed the door.

He wasn't wearing his usual outfit of a dark suit and white shirt. Instead, he had on a navy T-shirt, jeans, and running shoes. "Off duty?" I closed my car door.

"Yeah," he said sarcastically. "You could say that." His gaze skipped around the grounds then over his shoulder. It wasn't the confident surveying sweep I'd seen Sylvester use when he scanned the pedestrian walkway. Chester's glance was nervous and darting.

He climbed into the SUV and closed the door. I hurried across to him and knocked on the window. When he rolled it down halfway, I said, "You're leaving, aren't you?" The casual clothes, the bags, and the furtive glance around…had Torrie let him go?

He nodded. "And you'd be smart to make yourself scarce, too." He fastened the seatbelt with a click. "They're looking for someone to pin it on, and you're an easy target. I'm one too—that's why I'm out of here."

"Wait. Are you talking about the police?"

He jerked his chin in the direction of Tate House. "No, Torrie and Sylvester."

He shifted into reverse. I gripped the edge of the car window. "Slow down. What are they trying to pin on me? Arabella's murder?" I had an uneasy feeling I knew what he was going to say, but I wanted to make sure of what he was hinting at.

He removed one hand from the wheel and ran it over his shaved head. "They're scared. Their plan is smashed to pieces, and they're afraid they'll be blamed for the murder, so they're making sure someone else looks good for it—not them. Get it?"

"No, I'm afraid I don't. Look, I know you're not a chatty kind of person, but I need more details to understand. If they didn't murder Arabella, then what are they worried about? And how do you know all this?"

He sighed and looked longingly into the rearview mirror then put the SUV back in park. "I heard them talking. They thought I was out of the house this morning. I'd gone out to tell Ms. Emsley's sister that I couldn't let her in."

"Violet?" I asked. "I thought she'd left Nether Woodsmoor."

"No, she was here a few hours ago. Wouldn't go away either, until someone came out to talk to her."

"What did she want?" Violet had seemed so anxious to leave the village earlier. Why was she hanging around Tate House?

"She wanted to look around the house and garden, but I couldn't let her in. Police orders, I told her, which wasn't exactly accurate, but Torrie didn't want to let her in. Once Ms. Emsley's sister left, I came back into the kitchen quietly, not that I meant to sneak in or anything. I just happened not to make much noise. But they probably wouldn't have heard me even if I was noisy because they were in the sitting room arguing."

I nodded, remembering how the voices of Arabella and Torrie had carried into the kitchen. "What were they arguing about?" Getting Chester to talk was harder than trying to get Elise to give me a day off.

"The notes," he said in a tone that indicated it should explain everything. He reached for the gearshift.

"The threatening notes...you mean Torrie and Sylvester sent them?"

He shrugged. "It was Ms. Emsley and Torrie in it together, sending the notes before we showed up. Sylvester caught on to what they were doing, and then he wanted in on it. He's wily and likes to be part of anything like that."

"Did Sylvester and Torrie know each other before you went to work for Arabella?" I asked. Torrie hadn't been able to tell the cousins apart the day they arrived—or she'd pretended not to know them.

"Nah, but they hit it off right away."

"Torrie did say something about publicity and the threatening notes...that Arabella wanted to play up the story in hopes it would help her get a part in that psychological thriller, *The Darkness*, that's casting right now." Had Arabella engineered the whole thing—the threatening notes and the press coverage as well? If that was true, then Stevie Lund was a convenient scapegoat to blame the notes on, and it would explain why Gil Brayden arrived in Nether Woodsmoor the same day as Arabella.

I spoke slowly as I worked through my thoughts. "If they were doing that, planting false threats, and then Arabella was killed, they'd be worried about how it would look once the police found out."

If Torrie had another threatening note prepared to "send" to Arabella, and she wanted to get rid of it, my tote bag would be a great place to drop it. Either I would carry it off the grounds of

Tate House unknowingly, or if it were found, it would implicate me and draw the police's attention to me.

Chester nodded. "That's what happened. Sending a couple of threats is bad, but it's in a whole different league than murder."

"Yes, I can see how Arabella's death would rattle them. What did you hear them say?"

"When I came inside Torrie was yelling, saying she wouldn't stand for it, and then Sylvester said he'd take care of it. She calmed down a little, and I couldn't hear exactly what they said. I wasn't paying that much attention then. Torrie has been on edge since yesterday. I figured she was having another one of her temper tantrums and ignored it, like I had been. Then I heard my name. Sylvester said whatever they did, they'd make sure it looked like I did it. Torrie said that wasn't any good. 'Too close to us,' were her exact words. Then she said you'd be a better choice."

"When was this?" I asked, realizing now I was the one glancing around the grounds of Tate House nervously.

"A few hours ago. I went and slammed the door. They got quiet then, and I didn't hear anything else. I laid low then went to pack when they weren't paying attention. They think I'm going out to pick up dinner."

"But you're not. Where are you going?"

"Away. The train station in Upper Benning for a start. I'll park the SUV there and leave the keys under the floor mat. They have an extra set and can pick it up later. You seem like a nice lady. You always treated me right, didn't look down your nose at me like some people. That's why I told you this, but now I have to go." He gave a little nod, like he'd completed a job and was satisfied with the results, then put the SUV in reverse.

"But what about the investigation into Arabella's death? You can't just leave."

"The police haven't told me not to, and they know where to find me."

"It won't look good—you leaving. The DCI will think…"

He patted a sealed letter on the console. "I wrote out everything for the police, why I'm leaving and where I'll be, but I'm not sticking around here. I didn't kill Ms. Emsley—I barely knew her. Why would I want to murder her? But I know how these things go. If they can pin those threats on me somehow, then the police will think I might have had something to do with getting rid of Ms. Emsley. Being the only one here with Ms. Emsley that afternoon is a strike against me. I'm not waiting around so they can pin the threats on me, too."

"If you leave, the police won't see it that way," I said.

"I've got a kid, and if my ex ever gets wind of this, she'd be back in court so fast. She's looking for an excuse to cut me out of my son's life."

"How could she not know? Arabella's death has been in the news."

"My ex-wife doesn't know I was working for Arabella Emsley. She doesn't even know I'm in the UK I don't think the death of a British actress will be at the top of the news in Vancouver."

"Won't Sylvester tell her?"

"Nah—he never liked her," he said with a small smile. "Besides, he'd never sell me out…well, not to her. He does have some standards—they are low, but he wouldn't do that to me." He gave me another little nod and released the brake. I let go of the window as he said, "Good luck."

The tinted window glided up, a square of blackness hiding his face, and then he swept away through the gates.

CHAPTER 23

*A*FTER CHESTER DROVE AWAY, I stood in the driveway, debating if I should ring the doorbell and talk to Torrie, which had been my original reason for stopping at Tate House. It didn't seem like the smartest move after what Chester had told me. He could have made up the whole story, but I believed him. He'd looked genuinely pained when he mentioned the possibility of being cut off from his son. And someone *had* planted a threatening note in my bag. Torrie could certainly have done that at some point without me noticing.

A phone call to Torrie would work fine, I decided. I climbed into the car and headed back to Cottage Lane. I parked the MG in front of Alex's house. As I walked back to my cottage, I called Torrie. She didn't answer, so I left her a message telling her I needed to coordinate with her about when they were leaving Tate House. I ended the message and hung up, thinking that even if she didn't call me back I did have the codes to enter the house. If she didn't want to meet with me—which sounded like a good idea now—I could have her leave the keys and remotes inside and pick them up later.

I was glad to see no sign of Quimby either outside my gate or inside my cottage. I did a quick walk-through. It didn't look as if anything had changed. I didn't find any stray papers, and my only computer was still locked away in Alex's messy closet. Slink had greeted me enthusiastically and then went into raptures when I picked up the leash.

I locked up again, then Slink and I headed for the village green. The network of paths that crisscrossed the village offered a variety of walks, but it was getting late, and I didn't want to be anywhere lonely. A sprinkling of people were on the green, including a man doing what looked like Tai Chi and a woman sitting on a bench talking nonstop into her cell phone. I went to the other end of the green where we wouldn't disturb anyone. I unhooked Slink's collar then tossed a long stick for her.

As she skimmed along the grass, I thought about the computer searches. If Torrie dropped the note into my tote bag, had she also managed to get into my cottage and type in the search terms that were so incriminating? Or had it been Sylvester? Chester had said his cousin was wily. Would Sylvester's skill set include something shady like lock picking?

But if they had already settled on me as a good target for the notes why were they arguing about throwing suspicion on Chester? Did they have more notes to get rid of? If they did, wouldn't it be easier to destroy them...burn them or tear them into tiny pieces and flush them down the toilet?

I sat there for a long time, letting Slink enjoy the freedom of galloping across the wide space as the sun sunk lower in the sky. Eventually she trotted back and dropped at my feet, exhausted. I bent down and rubbed her ears. "I hear you, girl. I'm tired, too." It had been a long day. Too many unanswered questions were floating around in my mind, not to mention the stress of worrying about Quimby showing up with a warrant. Soon, Scotland Yard would be involved. I didn't want to think about that topic.

Quimby should receive the note I'd put in the mail by tomorrow. I was sure he'd have it analyzed, and I hoped I hadn't inadvertently left anything that could identify me...like a stray hair or smudge of a partial fingerprint. I shook my head, trying to dislodge my worries. At least I wasn't still carrying the note around or hiding it in the cottage. "We need food," I said, and Slink pricked up her ears.

I wasn't up for dropping in at the pub tonight. It was Friday, so it would be even more crowded. Louise would have her hands full and no time to chat anyway. I stopped and placed a takeaway order at the Palace, the Indian restaurant a few blocks from the green. While I was waiting for my order, my phone rang. I knew Alex would be busy today clearing up last minute details in Chawton, and I hadn't expected him to call, but I still felt a bit of a letdown when I saw it was Torrie.

I used my brightest voice as I said, "Torrie, hello," hoping it disguised any wariness that I felt after talking to Chester.

"Kate. Are you at your cottage? Can you come here now?"

"Ah—no, I'm afraid I can't." I smiled a thank-you to Mrs. Sardana as she handed me my dinner. "You got my message?" I asked Torrie.

"Yes. We're not leaving for a few more days."

I pushed the door of the restaurant open with my shoulder and let Slink head home. It had taken a while to get my food. It was dark now, and the evening air was cooling rapidly. The breeze felt chilly on my bare arms. "Okay, that's fine. Just leave the keys and remotes in the house. I'll have Claire meet me there to let me in for the walk-through."

"Someone else has a key to Tate House?" she asked sharply.

"Yes, of course. The property manager has a key. Ms. Emsley only rented it for a few days."

"Right. Yes. I hadn't thought of it—with everything that's happened I'm extra cautious."

"I understand." I was, too, that's why I wasn't going to meet her at Tate House alone.

"I suppose this property manager is on the police's list as well? She certainly should be if she isn't."

"I have no idea. I'm sure they're checking everything."

"Well, it's about time they asked someone else questions besides me. Just because I was her assistant doesn't mean I knew her every movement or stayed with her every second of the day. And now Chester has disappeared. At least, if the police go chasing after him that will mean I'll get a break from them."

"Chester's gone?"

"Yes! Left to go pick up food and didn't come back."

"Do you think he was...involved...?" I asked. I didn't think Chester had anything to do with Arabella's death, but I wanted to see what she had to say about it.

"I *don't know*. That's what I keep telling the police. I only met him a few days ago. I have no idea what type of person he is. I know he was cleared by the agency Arabella used to find the Hibberts, but that's all. Now that he's bolted, though...it does make you wonder..."

I heard a long intake of breath. I supposed she was drawing on a cigarette and hoped she wasn't smoking inside Tate House.

"I can't wait to get out of this horrible village and away from the police," she said. "They don't listen. I've told them over and over again that I know nothing about the garden or that messy little shed, but they keep asking about it. They found some sort of wires in there. The police went on and on about how the wires were the exact length needed to replace the wiring that was tampered with. But really, how do they know that's what they were for? They could just be bits of wire left over from some project that didn't get in the rubbish. That's what all this is—rubbish. They're quite fixated on those scraps of wire. It makes me wonder about their ability."

If what Torrie said about the wires was true, the murderer had planned not only a stealthy way to kill Arabella, but also had prepared to remove all the evidence of the electrocution. I shivered at the thought of such meticulous planning.

Torrie drew in another breath. "It's frightening to think how dim the police are—it really is—when you think of the power they have. That's why I'm leaving as soon as I can."

"So the police don't want you to stay until the inquest?"

I hadn't thought of the inquest until now. I would have to be there, and Chester, too.

"I'm not going to ask them if I can leave, am I? I learned that lesson a long time ago. If the answer could be *no*, don't ask. I'm willing to come back, if they need me. But why they would need *me*, I don't know. I was in Upper Benning—*and* Sylvester was with me."

She said she had to go. I said goodbye automatically, thinking about her confident statement that she wasn't at Tate House when Arabella died. But that didn't matter at all. A trap had been set for Arabella—or someone. Would anyone else have gone down the stairs barefoot? I didn't think so. Torrie wouldn't even go on the back terrace because of the plants and bees, and I couldn't picture either one of the Hibbert cousins going for a barefoot stroll in the garden. No, someone had set up the wires for Arabella and waited, someone very patient.

WHEN WE GOT BACK to the cottage I fed Slink and changed into a pair of comfy pajamas then went back downstairs and transferred my food to a plate. I settled at the table, but didn't bother to get either my phone or a book. I'd been so wrapped up in getting rid of the note that I hadn't thought of much else, but now the questions were popping into my mind.

I tore off a piece of naan. Why was Arabella killed? I'd barely stopped to think about the answer to that, but it was the elephant in the room, so to speak. Chester, Sylvester, and Torrie seemed to be the best suspects—they were staying at Tate House and had easy access to the stairs and could have set up the wiring. But why would they? Arabella was difficult to work for, but she was their employer. Now they were all out of a job.

If Torrie thought she was in Arabella's will, that might have been her motive, but after talking to Violet, it didn't sound as if Arabella had left anything to Torrie. Could Stevie Lund really have orchestrated—or had someone orchestrate—Arabella's death? Just because the cameras at Tate House showed he didn't go into the garden didn't mean that someone else hadn't set it up for him.

And what about Violet? She had been to Tate House several times. If Gil Brayden could get over the wall, she probably could too. She was young and fit. Did she know anything about electricity? Did Gil? But then I thought of the computer searches someone had planted on my laptop and realized that anyone who knew how to do an Internet search could find out how to go about setting up the wires. And who had knocked the stones off the wall into the path?

I moved the food around my plate. I wasn't eating much. Slink was stretched out with her head on her paws a respectful distance away, but her steady gaze communicated, *if you don't want that, I'll finish it off.*

"Sorry, girl. If Alex comes home and you won't eat your dog food, *I'll* be in the dog house."

I pushed the plate away, took my Moleskine notebook, and began to jot down everything that had happened along with all my questions. It took a long time to get it all written out, and when I was done, I still had more questions than answers. I was tapping my pen against the pages when Slink lifted her head, her ears pricked. She turned her long nose toward the door to the back garden.

I heard a faint metallic clicking sound, the latch of the back gate closing. Slink stood and turned to the door, her nose at the frame. I glanced at the time, nearly ten, and felt a twinge of worry. I lifted the curtain at the window over the sink. There were no lights along the walking path behind the cottages. Bright squares of light from the windows in the back door and kitchen were the only illumination. I switched on the feeble light over the back door, and it lit up about half the garden, which was empty.

Slink was weaving back and forth beside me, dancing from foot to foot, but she wasn't growling, just on alert. I waited a few moments more, but nothing moved. I opened the door. She ran lightly down the steps, nose to the ground, and crisscrossed the garden to the deeper darkness under the oak tree at the back of the garden. I had on flip-flops, and the cool air swept over my bare feet. She whined and ran back to me then darted away beyond the light to the tree. She made the circuit again, whining louder.

"What is it, girl?" I made my way across the garden leaving the splash of light and plunging into the darker area, but it wasn't complete blackness. With the faint light glowing from the cottage, I could see the dim outline of Gil Brayden seated in one of my new wooden chairs under the oak tree.

CHAPTER 24

"GIL, WHAT ARE YOU DOING?" I meant for my voice to be sharp, but it came out in a hoarse whisper. He didn't move. Slink went forward, paused, then nudged Gil's hand, which dangled over the chair arm. No response.

I stepped closer. Gil's legs were stretched out in front of him, loose and relaxed like the limbs of a rag doll. His head tilted forward and to the side so that his chin was almost resting on his shoulder. I could make out the longish curtain of dark hair that fell over one of his eyes. He looked pale, but that could be because the darkness had bleached the color out of everything in the garden.

"Gil." I shook his shoulder. His upper body tilted and slid a few inches. Only the arm of the chair kept him from toppling to the ground.

Not another one, I thought as my skin prickled. "Please just be passed out," I muttered as I leaned down to look at his face, but I needed more light. Where was my cell phone? It had a flashlight on it. I patted my pockets, then remembered I was in pajamas. I had left the phone in the cottage. I reached out and felt for a pulse in the wrist of his hand that dangled even farther over the arm of the chair now.

His skin was clammy, and I recoiled, then swallowed and made myself grip his wrist again, searching for a pulse. Maybe he wasn't…? Was that a flutter? I pressed harder and held my breath. Slink had stopped pacing and whining and now sat at attention beside me.

After a few moments, I released his wrist and pressed my hand over my heart, which was now pounding away. I had to call the police, but—what a mess. A dead man in my back garden. My thoughts tumbled around in my mind. What would they think? And so soon after I'd been the first on the scene when Arabella died…this couldn't be a coincidence.

I turned and made for the cottage, my legs feeling like they might give out at any moment. I blinked and squinted in the strong light of the kitchen. My crossbody bag was on the table where I'd dropped it beside the tote bag. I unzipped the purse and dug around inside, but didn't find my phone. Thoroughly rattled thinking about Gil's clammy body in the chair outside, I couldn't remember where I'd left my phone. I checked the tote bag then threw it down. My phone must be upstairs in the pocket of my shorts. I raced up the stairs with Slink at my heels and found my phone in the pocket of my discarded shorts.

I tapped out the code to unlock my phone as I trotted back downstairs and out the door, once again plunging into the pool of blackness under the tree. I skidded to a halt.

The chair was empty. I turned on the flashlight and aimed the phone at the ground around the chair and the base of the tree. The glowing screen showed nothing but the smooth grain of the chair's wood and springy tufts of grass. I turned in a circle, scanning the garden. No sign of Gil…or anyone.

Slink trotted to the gate. I opened it, stepped onto the hard-packed path, and pointed the light up and down the path. It was deserted. I went to the wall that ran along Annette's garden and swept the light over it, seeing only glossy leaves and furled flower buds in sparsely planted beds. She'd installed a little shed at the back corner of the garden, but the new padlock, still securely in place, glinted as I aimed the light at it. I stepped away from the wall and saw a light coming down the path toward me from the direction of the village.

A powerful flashlight, it cut through the night, sweeping from side to side along the path. The reflective vest and the distinctive outline of the hat were unmistakable. I hurried forward.

"Constable Albertson," I called. The beam of light flashed full in my face, blinding me. I held up a hand, and the light moved down to illuminate the path.

"Can I help you?"

I blinked away the spots and focused on the man's face. I didn't recognize the voice. "Oh, I thought you were Constable Albertson."

"Constable Carnay here. Constable Albertson's off tonight. Who are you?"

"I'm Kate Sharp. I live in the cottage back there. There was… um…" I stopped, at a loss. How could I say there had been a man —I'd *thought* he was dead—in my back garden, and now he was gone? This constable had found me in my pajamas poking around the path late at night. He probably already thought I was a tad crazy.

He asked, "Is there a problem? We had a report—" He turned sharply at the jingle of Slink's collar as she trotted up.

"Slink! There you are. Thank goodness," I ad-libbed. To the constable, I said, "The gate must not have latched, and she got out. I was…looking for her." Slink had her liquid eyes fixed on me during my little speech. She tucked her hind legs under and sat on her haunches, the very picture of a well-trained dog. "So sorry. Come on, Slink, let's go home."

Slink sprang up and trotted ahead of me docilely through the open gate. Constable Carney focused the light on the gate then swept it around my garden. My breathing was fast as my gaze followed the beam, but everything was just as I'd seen it a few minutes before, only much clearer in the brighter light.

"We had a report of a disturbance. Did you hear anything?" he asked as I stepped in and closed the gate.

"Ah—no."

He looked back the way he'd come and used the beam of the flashlight to pick out the gates on this side of the path as he counted under his breath until he got to my gate. "Yes, at this cottage. Any problems?" He lifted the light and moved it over the garden, slower this time.

"No. Just a lost dog—temporarily lost, that is. All good now."

"Anyone inside your cottage?"

"Only me. Good night, Constable."

I hurried away from the gate, my flip-flops making slapping sounds against the soles of my feet as I crossed to the door. Slink was already sitting in the light of the doorway. She reversed out of my way, and I closed the door, locked it, then leaned against it.

"A report," I whispered. A report that drew the police to my back garden at the exact moment that Gil, his dead—or unconscious?—body was also there. I ran a shaky hand over my forehead. Cottage Lane was a quiet street and there was no disturbance tonight to draw the police, but someone had made sure the police were here. Someone wanted Gil found in my backyard.

I pushed away from the door and hurriedly checked rooms and closets—I had left the back door open and thought Gil might have slipped inside—but the cottage was empty. Upstairs, I went to the window in the bedroom. I left the light off and cracked the shutters.

The constable moved up and down the entire length of the

path, his light tracing carefully over every garden. He looped around and checked the front of each cottage, too. Once he'd left, I pushed the shutters closed and sat in the dark a moment.

I was confused about lots of things, but I was pretty sure of one thing—wherever Gil was now, he certainly wasn't anywhere around Cottage Lane. I changed into a lightweight taupe sweater, a pair of jeans, and my boat shoes. A visit to the inn was in order.

CHAPTER 25

*T*HE RECEPTION AREA OF THE inn was empty when I arrived, but a few dinner guests were lingering over their coffee and dessert in the dining room. Doug wasn't in the reception area, but Tara, in a white chef's smock, was chatting with a group at a table. I caught her eye. She came across the room to me.

"Sorry to interrupt," I said.

"It's fine. We're winding down. Nothing to do now but wash the dishes."

"Still, I don't want to put you behind. Is Doug around?"

"No, he's at the farmhouse. The telly is out, and the guests must have a working telly. What can I help you with?"

"Can you ring Gil Brayden's room for me?"

"Sure." She tilted her head to the side, giving me an inquisitive look. "Although, he doesn't seem your type," she said with a hint of a smile.

"Far from it," I said with an answering grin. "Not my type at all."

She nodded her head. "Thought so. Course, not many can compete with your Alex."

"He's not my Alex." I felt a flush creep up my face.

"Oh, I think he is."

I cleared my throat. "This is…something else."

She went behind the counter and picked up the handset. "Ah, I see. Work related." She punched a few buttons and handed over the phone. "Has Mr. Brayden been giving you problems? I can have Doug speak to him."

"No, it's not that," I paused and listened to the phone ring. "He did try to get on the set earlier, but this is about something else." I handed the phone back to her. "He's not answering."

I looked out one of the windows to the parking area. "I think that's his car there, the white one." I'd seen the car on the way inside and expected him to answer the phone in his room. "I suppose he might have walked into Nether Woodsmoor…"

Tara said, "I can let him know you want to speak to him when he gets in."

"It's more than that. I'm worried about him," I said, thinking it would be better not to go into the whole incident in my back garden. "I wanted to make sure he was okay. I think he might have been…hurt."

She checked the row of keys behind the counter. "His key is gone." She frowned. "But guests often forget to turn in their key when they leave." She tapped her fingers on the counter as she stared at the keys a moment more, then she looked up at the clock on the wall. "You must be quite concerned—it's nearly eleven."

"I am."

"Right then. We better check."

She unlocked a drawer, withdrew a set of keys, and headed for the stairs. She didn't tell me to wait, so I climbed the stairs and followed her along the low-ceiling passage. She paused to unlock a closet and pick up two fluffy towels. "Our excuse," she said, then continued on to Room Four where she tapped on the door. "Mr. Brayden?"

Tara tapped again. "Mr. Brayden?" she said in a louder voice. "I have your fresh towels." After a moment, she transferred the towels to the crook of her arm and pulled out the keys. She opened the door an inch, then pushed it wide and flicked on the light. "He's not here."

I joined her at the doorway. "And I thought Alex was messy."

She let out a gusty sigh. "The maids weren't exaggerating."

It reminded me of Arabella's room, except Gil had a lot less clothing to leave lying on the floor and furniture. He still had managed to cover every flat surface and most of the floor with clothes, empty soft drink cans, Styrofoam takeaway containers, crumpled gum wrappers, carrier bags, and used towels.

Tara stepped carefully across the floor, gathering used towels as she went.

I followed her inside and picked up one of the gum wrappers. It smelled of banana and had the diagonal print across the paper that I'd seen before. The spurt of anger that I'd felt when I realized someone wanted Gil found in my yard had fizzled and transformed to worry. As I looked around the room, the anxious feeling that had been dogging me since I found the note intensified.

"Did you see him today?" I asked Tara. She pushed open the door to the adjoining bath. I could see an uncapped tube of toothpaste by the sink and a disposable razor resting in a dried blob of shaving cream. She paused with a bundle of towels in her arms. "You know, I saw him tonight, now that I think about it. About eight, I think. I had to go out back and call in one of the waiters who was late coming in from his break. I noticed Mr. Brayden because he was on the path that goes through the fields. Do you know the one I mean?"

I went to the desk where a tangle of charging cords sat by a closed laptop and a couple of camera bags. "The one that circles around the village and crosses Grove Road?"

"Yes, that's it. It was rather odd to see him walking out so late in the day. Most guests, if they're going out, walk into the village along the main road."

I knew that path circled around Nether Woodsmoor and eventually merged with the footpath that ran behind Cottage Lane. "No one was with him?" The larger camera bag was open, and I looked inside. It was a duffle-type bag with separate padded sections. "Nice," I murmured. Gil might look scruffy and unkept, but he had a top-of-the-line camera along with several expensive lenses.

"No. In fact, he's kept mostly to himself while he's been here, which I think is a bit odd. He works for the newspapers. I expected him to pester both Doug and me with questions, but he never asked us about the village or any of the other guests." She picked up a padded book that listed the inn's amenities, which had fallen to the floor, and put it on the nightstand. "The only person I saw him talking to was Mr. Lund."

I looked up from the camera bag. "Really?"

"He bought Mr. Lund several drinks the other night—can't remember when it was, exactly—but they had a long conversation about investments."

"Investments?" I asked, surprised. It wasn't the topic I would have expected those two men to discuss.

"Well, I suppose that was it. I heard snippets—liquidity, assets, and security. Mr. Brayden probably wanted some investment tips since that's Mr. Lund's specialty."

"Investments are his specialty?"

"He's an advisor…financial things—stocks, bonds."

"I had no idea." I'd never thought about what Stevie Lund did for a living. I'd assumed he worked for his father in the "family business." I made a mental note to search for Stevie Lund's name online and see what came up.

I let the flap of the camera bag fall back into place, then peeked into the smaller bag next to it and froze. A very nice Canon took up most of the space, but a gold charm bracelet with tiny diamonds sparkled against the black nylon interior.

CHAPTER 26

"WE HAVE TO CALL THE police." I angled the bag so that the charms of the bracelet dangled separately. A gold key was the largest charm and was the easiest to distinguish, but the little Cartier purse and the diamond-encrusted sandal were there, too.

"What?" Tara turned back from the door to the hall. "Why?"

"This bracelet belonged to Arabella. I recognize some of the charms. She wore it all the time."

"Then what is it doing in here? In Mr. Brayden's bag?"

"I don't know," I murmured as I took out my phone. Tara frowned at me. "We have to report it," I whispered as the operator answered.

Once I'd explained what we'd found, the emergency operator repeated, "Jewelry that belonged to a victim?" in a doubtful tone.

"Yes. It could be important," I said, thinking of Torrie's questions about the bracelet.

"Your location?"

"The Old Woodsmoor Inn." Tara's frown deepened into a look of disapproval. "DCI Quimby will want to know about it," I added, still speaking into the phone.

"I'll relay the message," he said with a note of finality.

"Wait—you're not going to send someone to pick it up now?"

"That will be up to the DCI. I'll relay the message," he repeated.

I hung up. "I don't know when they'll be here. Sounds as if it may be tomorrow. You'd better take that down with you. Do you have somewhere you can lock it up?"

"We have a safe for guests' valuables."

"That's where this needs to go. No—here, use one of those towels to pick up the strap," I said.

"You think...it had something to do with that woman's death?" Now instead of irritated, Tara looked worried.

"It's connected to it...somehow."

I WAITED at the inn for a while in case a constable or sergeant showed up to take charge of the bracelet and wanted to ask me questions, but after about twenty minutes, I could see that Tara was ready to begin shutting down for the night. I also realized it would look very strange if the constable who had been on the path behind the cottages showed up and found me fully dressed and poking around the inn's rooms with Tara.

She locked the whole camera bag in the safe and promised to call me if someone came for it. On my way through the parking area, I stopped and looked in the white Ford Fiesta. It was locked up tight, and the inside was spotlessly clean. Could it really belong to Gil? Then I saw a pair of heavy-duty work boots on the back seat beside a light-colored scarf.

I unlocked the MG and drove home, with what seemed like a million more questions running around in my mind. The drive only took a few minutes. The streets of the village were deserted and quiet, except for a few pockets of activity around the pub and a couple of other establishments that stayed open late. As I turned onto Cottage Lane, I was glad to see the parking slot in front of Alex's cottage was still open. The later it got in the day, the harder it was to find parking on the street.

I shifted into reverse and carefully eased the MG into the space then shut off the engine and sat in the car for a moment, listening to the clicks and pings of the engine. It was nearly midnight, and light glowed from only a few windows along the lane—one of them, mine. I felt tired, drained, and confused.

Had Gil killed Arabella and kept the bracelet? I couldn't think of a good reason he'd take the bracelet and then leave it in his belongings. Maybe he found it? But if that was the case, why was it hidden in one of his camera bags? He *must* have recognized it. Arabella wore it all the time. He would have seen it in the photos he took of her. Why had he kept it instead of calling the police? Was he afraid of what the police would assume if he turned in the bracelet, like I had been with the note? Had someone planted the bracelet like the note had been planted in my bag?

I couldn't figure out any of those questions, so I climbed out of the car and turned for my cottage, but then remembered that Alex would be back tomorrow. The production had rented a large van for the trip to Chawton, but it would be returned tomorrow, and he might need the keys to his car. I wasn't sure if he had his set with him or not. He could have left them in the cottage. He let me borrow the car whenever I needed to, but I didn't feel right keeping the keys with me, especially since he was arriving back tomorrow.

I slipped through his gate, unlocked the door, and automatically flipped on the hall light as I tossed the keys in the little bowl on the table near the door. The layout of Alex's cottage was similar to mine. The front door opened into a long hallway that stretched between the door and the kitchen at the back of the cottage, and I was already swinging around to leave by the time my brain processed what I'd seen—a man standing motionless at the far end of the hall in the kitchen doorway.

CHAPTER 27

*I*T WAS GIL. HE LOOKED so different that it took me a moment to recognize him, but despite the washed-out, ashy complexion, it *was* Gil. The cocky charm he'd displayed when he tried to slip into Parkview had vanished. Now he radiated tension. *He looks as if he's been ill or in a horrible accident.* The thought flashed through my mind while we both stood frozen in place.

He took two steps forward and collapsed in a pile on the floor. I gripped the door with one hand, poised to run out of it if he stirred, but he didn't move. "Gil?"

He groaned, shifted, and made an effort to stand, but only managed to lift himself slightly, then he clutched the kitchen doorframe and leaned his head against it. His face was even whiter than a moment ago, except for a large red welt on his temple. Part of me wanted to run out the door and call the police —Arabella's missing jewelry was in his camera bag, after all—but he looked so awful that I couldn't leave.

I left the front door open and inched toward him. "Are you okay?"

He swallowed thickly and began to shake his head, but

checked his movement. "No," he said after a moment. "This room —the whole world, in fact, has a tendency to spin at the most inconvenient times. Or just go completely black."

"You better put your head down between your knees." He wasn't faking. He looked like he was about to pass out.

I could see into the kitchen where a bundle of dissolving ice cubes were melting in the folds of a kitchen towel. The upper portion of the back door had a window in it, and a pane was broken out of it. It would be easy to reach inside and unlock the deadbolt and the night latch.

He folded over at the waist and said in a muffled voice, "But then you might be able to bean me on the head, too. Unfortunately, since I can't seem to stand, I'll just have to trust you'll be nicer than Torrie."

"Torrie caused that bump on your head?" I stepped around Gil and went into the kitchen to search Alex's tiny freezer for more ice cubes. The refrigerator was more modern than the one in my cottage. It had squared off corners instead of rounded ones and a slightly bigger freezer. I pulled out the last tray of ice cubes and cracked it over the sink.

Gil winced at the noise. "No, her thug of a boyfriend."

"Sylvester?" I found a dry towel and poured some of the ice in it, then put the tray back in the freezer.

"Yeah, that's what she called him. It was supposed to be just her. He must have been waiting for her signal."

I went and closed the front door then returned to his side. I squatted down in front of him. "Feeling a bit better now?"

"One step up from death, I think." He inched his head upright. "Okay, yeah, I'll sit here for a few minutes more."

"That's a good plan," I said. "Here's a cold compress."

He took it with a wary look in his hooded eyes. "Thanks." He put it tentatively against his temple.

I had slipped my crossbody bag over my shoulder when I got

out of the car. I unzipped it and took out my phone. "I'll call an ambulance—"

He jerked upright, his hand with the towel dropping away from his face. "No." He closed his eyes and breathed in and out a few times. "No. You can't," he said more slowly.

"Okay, we'll wait on that," I said, scared by how his color fluctuated. He was back to the sickly pale shade. "Why shouldn't I call for help?" I asked in an even tone.

"Because they'll ask questions, and I'm in a big enough mess right now. I need a few minutes to recover, that's all. It's why I came in here. Sorry about the window in the back door."

"Oh, it's not my house. I was just dropping off some car keys for a friend, but I'll tell him." I kept my tone conversational. His breathing was calming down, and his face was taking on a more natural skin tone.

I sat down on the floor, my back against the leg of the little table by the front door, afraid that if I made any sudden move, he'd react by trying to jump to his feet, and the sudden change would cause him to pass out. Maybe if we talked for a bit, he'd calm down and let me get him some medical attention. I wasn't scared of Gil—he couldn't even stand—but I bet he could answer some of my questions.

"So I take it you went to meet Torrie and Sylvester tonight, and they weren't too pleased with you."

He pressed the towel to his head again, squeezing his eyes shut as the fabric made contact with the lump on his temple. "Torrie," he said through an unsteady breath. "Only Torrie was supposed to be there."

"About the bracelet."

His eyes flew open. "How did you know—"

"You made a brief appearance in my back garden tonight. I can see now that you must have been out cold, but at the time I thought you were dead. I couldn't find a pulse. I must not have done it right, or your pulse was so faint that I couldn't find it. I'd make a very poor nurse. Anyway, I went off to find my phone. When I came back, you were gone."

"Yeah, it nearly killed me to climb that tree."

"You *climbed* the oak tree?"

"I felt better then," he said, his tone defensive. "I woke up and didn't know where I was. The last thing I remembered was turning my head just enough to catch a glimpse of Sylvester as he swung something—a board or pipe or something—at my head. I was still pretty confused. I had no idea where I was, but I wasn't about to run inside that cottage. For all I knew, Torrie and her heavy-handed friend were in there, but I wasn't going to wait around to give Sylvester another go at me. I heard someone coming from the cottage—that must have been you, I guess—but I didn't know that. I didn't have enough time to get out of the garden, so I just went up the branches."

"In the state you're in?" I asked. Some of the branches on that tree were pretty low. Still, it was hard to imagine Gil scrambling up them nimbly in the dark.

"I told you, I felt better then than I do now. I mean, at first, I did. Once I got up there, the sick feeling hit me. I thought I was going to pass out again, but I kept still, and it got better. The constable came, so I settled in until he left. I stayed up there a while then got myself down, which was much harder, by the way. I needed somewhere to recover. This was the only house without lights on, so I gambled, hoping whoever lived here was away."

"I get the feeling you gamble a lot."

"Yeah, you could say that." One corner of his mouth turned up briefly.

"That's what happened with the bracelet, wasn't it?" I asked.

He went to shake his head, but stopped abruptly and swallowed.

I leaned forward. "I don't think you killed Arabella. But it might be what the police think when they pick up the bracelet from the inn. Yes, they know about it." I told him what had happened at the inn, then said, "I've been thinking about that bracelet, and I can't believe that if you'd killed Arabella, you would keep something that was hers. Knowing that you like to play all the angles, I think you took it for a specific reason. Somehow, you thought you could work it to your advantage."

He looked at me around the edge of the towel for a moment then said, "I think I better tell you what happened in case I go out again. At least, that way one other person will know what happened. The more people who know, the better. Makes it less worth killing me, that way." He rubbed the uninjured side of his forehead with his free hand then said, "I was gobsmacked to see Arabella like that—dead, I mean. She'd set up the meeting, and I knew she'd be alone. She'd gotten everyone out of the house except one of the security guys."

I nodded, thinking of the tea bags that Constable Albertson had found in the kitchen. Arabella wasn't out of her special blend of tea. It was an excuse to get Torrie and Sylvester out of Tate House, and she'd told Chester she wanted to be alone in the garden.

"When I found her..." He shook his head and sighed. "I thought something might go wrong with her plan, but I never expected anything like that."

"Her plan—that was to do with the threatening notes, right?"

He shifted, sitting up a bit straighter. "Who's telling this story?"

"Sorry. Go on."

"The threats were part of it. She wanted me to help her make sure the word got out about the threats. Torrie didn't like Arabella involving me. I think that's why Arabella wanted to meet me alone."

That would explain Torrie's angry reaction when I showed

her the photo of Gil on the day he tried to get into Parkview. She hadn't trusted Gil and didn't like him being involved. No wonder Arabella had sent them away on a useless errand. "What were you meeting Arabella for?"

"To talk about the next phase of her plan to get publicity about the threats. I'm not sure what she had in mind...she was going to tell me about it in the garden."

"How did you get onto the grounds of Tate House?"

"Over the wall," he said with a small grin. "Just like that first time when you spotted me."

"And you left the same way?"

"Yep. Both times. Although, I did knock off the stones when I left that last time. I wanted out of there, so I didn't stay to put them back. Yeah, climbing over the wall was the safest way in and out, with the cameras on the gate and the house. It was much easier getting in there than getting inside the grounds of Parkview."

"So the finial falling off the roof at Parkview, that was part of the plan?" I asked, thinking that if Arabella was coordinating the notes, why would she stop there? She'd probably arranged some of the dramatic near misses as well.

"Of course. She had Torrie and one of the security guards scope it out the day before. The next day he climbed that scaffolding and tossed the piece of stone down. You mucked up that one, not letting me on the grounds. She hadn't counted on you blocking me. So, yeah, the faulty brakes, the threats, the narrow miss—all great copy, she thought. That's why she wanted you, too. She knew you'd been involved in that other case down in Bath and thought she could get some mileage out of that, too. You know, once the first wave of publicity had died away over the threats and 'accidents,' she could leak your name and say that you were involved, trying to help her figure out who'd sent the threats."

I was literally speechless for a moment. "Of all the—that's crazy and so...so...manipulative."

He began to nod, then caught himself. "Yep. She had—ah—tunnel vision on some things. Didn't really see where things could go, you know? She thought it would help her get a part, and that was her only concern. I was happy to help her out. The money would have been good," he said with a flash of a grin. For a second he looked like the cocky paparazzi guy who'd tried to talk his way onto Parkview's grounds, but then his expression turned sober. "She certainly didn't think through the money thing."

CHAPTER 28

"THE MONEY?" I ASKED BECAUSE Gil had retreated into his own thoughts.

He blinked and focused on me. "She thought Stevie was her biggest worry there, but I don't know…I wonder if…"

He seemed to drift a bit and then slumped down against the wall. "Hey, are you doing okay?" I asked. "I think it would be a good idea to get your head looked at. I could take you to a walk-in clinic."

"No," he said firmly and focused on me. "Nothing like that. So…the money. Arabella took it from her ex. You know about the break-up?" I nodded, and he went on, "Arabella wanted revenge for the way he broke up with her. Once he realized she had the money, Stevie was furious. Arabella needed a place to hide out while she moved the cash. She thought Stevie wouldn't come here, but he found her."

I was lost. "When did this happen? When did she take the money, I mean?"

Gil said, "Let's see, it would have been last week…ah, Thursday. I'm pretty sure she said it was a Thursday. Yes, it was. The woman across the hall remembered the date because she'd had her cleaning lady in that day."

"So Arabella stole some money from Stevie? That's what you're saying?"

"Exactly. I'd been keeping a close eye on Arabella...her associates and such. I sometimes supplement my photography income gathering drips and drabs of information on celebrities."

"And sell it to the celebrity gossip press," I said, understanding him perfectly. "You find the 'close friends' who are always quoted anonymously in the articles."

"Right. Sometimes it really is a friend," he said, quickly.

I raised my eyebrows. "Was it this time?"

"Ah—a bit. She knows Arabella and Stevie...more of an acquaintance than a friend, if you want to be *exact*. She lives across the hall from what was Stevie and Arabella's flat when they were together. She saw Arabella taking the money."

"So you were already working with Arabella, helping her make sure the news about the threatening notes got out when you found out she'd taken money from Stevie?"

"Yes. It changed the scope of our arrangement, you might say."

He bargained for a bigger payment, I bet. "How much money did Arabella take?" I asked.

He lifted his free hand and shrugged his shoulders. "No idea. She took what she could get her hands on. A couple million, at least. She didn't know exactly how much. With all the different exchange rates it was kind of hard to calculate everything."

"Whoa, wait." I sat forward. "Millions?"

"Yeah, it was mostly in euros, but there were dollars and pounds as well."

"Why—oh, Stevie's family," I said thinking of what Tara had overheard. "Stevie's not in investments, is he?"

"Nope. He moves the money for his dad's 'enterprise.' His job is to get the cash out of the country. Arabella said he usually didn't keep cash in the flat, but they had a mix-up, and he had to bring some back. She knew it was there. She still had her key, so she went in when he was gone, loaded it up into carrier bags, and walked out with it. The neighbor could see the outlines of rectangular bundles pressed up against the side of the bags. The doorman knew Arabella, you see. No questions. No fuss. She made a couple of trips, too," Gil said. "You have to admire the simplicity and audacity of it. She walked in and took it out in full view of everyone, bold as you please."

"You mean she literally carried out bags of cash, and no one said anything?"

"That's exactly what happened. No one would have ever known, except that on the last trip with the carrier bags, she had a run-in with a man walking his dog. There was a scuffle, and in the confusion, the neighbor saw some bundles of money. She kept quiet about it because she didn't want the police getting too close to her, something to do with her au pair's visa not being quite up to snuff, but with a little monetary incentive she was willing to tell me about it."

"I see," I said. "And Stevie couldn't exactly call the police and report the stolen cash." The word Gil had used earlier, gobs-macked, described exactly how I felt. "Money. Cash," I murmured, rearranging everything that had happened in view of this new bit of information, which finally answered the question about why Arabella had been killed. That sort of cash would certainly give everyone in Arabella's orbit a motive.

"Arabella called it the perfect crime," he said, his tone flat. "It wasn't perfect, though. Someone killed her for it. It wasn't me," he said. "I took the bracelet, but I didn't kill her."

We'd come full circle, back to the bracelet. I put aside thoughts about stacks of cash and focused on Gil and the bracelet. "I still don't understand why you took the bracelet."

He looked a little shamefaced. "After I saw that she was

dead...well, I knew that they hadn't moved all the money. Some of it was still around. That bracelet was the key. Arabella said that once. She didn't trust Torrie, not completely. I knew Arabella had the money stashed somewhere that Torrie couldn't get to. Since Arabella never let the charm bracelet out of her sight, I figured Torrie would need it to get to the money. If I had the bracelet, I could get *my* money. Arabella hadn't paid me. That was the only way I'd get anything," he said, his tone defensive.

I wasn't about to argue with him about the pros and cons of his plan—obviously, it hadn't worked out too well for him. He could see that as well as I could. "You really need to talk to DCI Quimby," I said. "Tell him the whole story."

"Right. I have zero proof they stole the money. Arabella was shuttling it out of here as fast as she could, and I'm sure Torrie is doing the same. Obviously, they figured out how to get to the cash since they didn't wait to get it from me before bashing me on the head. Once the police have that bracelet and realize I was involved in the threats..."

He looked like he was going to be sick, so I said quickly, "But then how did you get that injury and how did you end up in my back garden? They can't discount those things either."

"That is weird," he drew himself away from the wall and sat up straight. "Why did they dump me there?"

"To implicate me. It's a little campaign they have going on. You're just the latest attempt to make sure the police focus on me. They had to wait until it was dark and the path was deserted before they put you in my garden and called the police with a story about a disturbance."

"So I'm a pawn. What a lowering thought. You never see yourself as a bit player, only the star."

"Are you kidding? You're the only person who can explain this whole situation. You have to talk to DCI Quimby. Explain everything to him. I'll back you up. I'll tell him about finding you in my back garden and everything." I still had my phone in my hand, and I held it out to him.

"No. That's not a good idea." His face took on a stubborn cast as he pushed the phone away. "No chats with the police. *You* know everything. You can pass it on. I'm leaving for somewhere warm and sunny and Third World. This has worked out better than I thought. Now I'm not the only person who knows about Torrie and Sylvester, which lessens the effectiveness of killing me —very important to me—*and* it will let you give all the details to the authorities. I won't get my money, but I'll be alive. That's all that matters at this point."

"You'll be safer if you tell them everything."

"No. Not happening," he said shortly. "But I do think I might be able to stand up. He gripped the doorframe and slowly stood. "Okay, not so bad. I think I will sit down for a moment, though."

I'd hopped up and had been holding my arms out in case he suddenly went down, but he didn't sway. He walked carefully to the kitchen table and pulled out a chair. "Is there any more ice?"

"A few cubes." I stuck my phone in my pocket and took the towel from him. I went to the sink and shook out what was left of the tiny cubes then opened the freezer.

The chair scraped on the floor. I thought Gil had gotten dizzy and fallen out of the chair, but that wasn't what happened at all. By the time I'd turned around, he was pulling open the front door.

As I raced to the door, a car engine revved. I was in time to see Gil circle the wheel of the MG and gun it.

CHAPTER 29

I RAN DOWN THE STEPS and stopped at the gate. The only sign of Alex's car was two red taillights getting smaller and smaller by the second. I gripped the rough wood of the gate as I waited for the little car to reappear at the base of the hill. Cottage Lane was built on a rise that gave me a view of the village. The MG barely paused before turning onto the high street, but he didn't take the route to the inn. Instead, he crossed the bridge and headed for the main road, the road that would take him away from Nether Woodsmoor to Upper Benning.

I pulled my phone out of my pocket and scrolled through the contact list until I found the inn's phone number. The phone rang several times, then I got an automated message with their regular business hours and instructions to leave a message. "Tara, this is Kate. I just saw Gil. I don't think he's on his way back to your place, but I suppose he could loop around...sorry, I'm not making any sense. Just be careful, if he does show up. I think you better call the police if you see him."

I ended the call, wondering how long it would be before Tara got it...in the morning? They had an electronic entry code system so that guests could arrive after hours and let themselves in—that way, they didn't have to have someone on duty all night long. Theoretically, Gil could slip in during the night, pack up, and leave without anyone knowing. My fingers hovered over the phone keypad. I knew I needed to call the police. I had to report that Gil had stolen the car...but how could I explain everything that had happened. *Yes, officer, he was in my back garden earlier tonight, then he disappeared. No, I didn't tell the constable about it when he came earlier.* And that wasn't even including finding the bracelet at the inn or anything Gil told me.

I rubbed my forehead. I didn't think I could handle trying to summarize everything to an emergency operator. If they let me get through the whole convoluted story, they'd be more likely to send a mental health professional than a police officer. I knew in my gut that I needed to get in touch with Quimby...and tell him everything.

But I couldn't leave Alex's cottage wide open. I trotted back up the steps then slowed as I entered the bright hallway. The little bowl with the keys was empty and had been shoved back against the wall, but otherwise, everything else looked the same. I found a piece of cardboard in the storage closet and taped it over the hole in the back door. I put a kitchen chair under the door handle. That was the best I could do for a security measure.

As I stepped inside my cottage a few minutes later, Slink, who had been stretched out on her back, flipped onto her feet, shook head to toe, then ambled over to greet me. It was the first normal thing that had happened in hours, and I went through the routine of letting her out and refilling her water bowl before I called Quimby.

It rang several times. I glanced at the clock. It was after midnight. So much had happened that I'd completely lost track of time. "Quimby," he said in a sharp voice.

At least it didn't sound as if I'd woken him. I identified myself, and he cut in quickly. "I got the message about the bracelet. It will be picked up first thing tomorrow."

"Oh, good, but I was actually calling about something else. Alex's car has been stolen. Gil Brayden took it."

"Brayden? How do you know this?"

I described exactly how I'd found Gil in Alex's cottage. "He's hurt. A head injury." Quimby muttered something under his breath then asked for a detailed description of Alex's car. "I'll call this in. I'll be out there shortly. Are you still in his house?"

"No, I'm at my house."

"Fine. I need information on a few more things. For instance, I'd like to know why you and Mrs. Owen were searching Gil Brayden's room."

My heart sunk. I *would* have to tell him everything. "Yes, I have quite a bit to tell you."

"See you shortly," he said and ended the call.

I rubbed my forehead. "Coffee." I would probably be up for hours. Maybe the jolt of caffeine would help me think more clearly. A good cup of dark roast might soften up Quimby, too. I doubted it would actually have much impact, but it was worth a shot. Once I had the coffee brewing, I called Alex. It was late, but his car had been stolen. He should know about it.

"Sorry to call so late. I've got some bad news, I'm afraid," I said as soon as he answered.

"What?" he asked, his voice suddenly serious.

"The MG has been stolen."

I cringed in the silence. He loved that car.

"Is that all? You nearly gave me a heart attack, Kate. You said it was bad news. I was picturing you hurt or something..." He stopped and cleared his throat.

"No, I'm fine, but I know how much you like that car."

"We've been through this before—it's only a car. As long as you're okay...and you are okay?"

"Yes. Perfectly fine. I may not be after Quimby gets here, though. He's not going to be happy."

"Quimby?"

"Yes. It all has to do with Arabella's death. I better start with the notes," I said, thinking it would be a good rehearsal for my upcoming conversation with Quimby. I'd been reluctant to explain what had happened in detail over the phone, but since I was planning to tell Quimby everything soon, I decided it didn't matter now.

"So this paparazzi guy, Brayden, stole my car," Alex said after I'd caught him up. "And he also had jewelry that Arabella always wore?"

"Yes."

"You said Quimby is on his way over right now?"

"Yes," I said, still dreading what Quimby would have to say about me withholding evidence.

Alex's breath came out in a whoosh. "Okay. That's good. I'm leaving now."

"To come back? It's the middle of the night."

"I don't care what time it is. You're in the middle of something very dangerous."

"You don't have to do that."

"Yes, I do. I'm already packed. I can be on the road in a few minutes."

"Alex, I'm fine. I have Slink here with me."

"I'm coming back," he said.

My phone beeped with an incoming call. "I've got to go. That's Quimby. Call you back?"

"Yes. Definitely," Alex said.

I switched to the other call. "Ms. Sharp," Quimby said after identifying himself, "I just got a report that the MG was spotted on the side of the road a few miles outside of Nether Woodsmoor."

"Abandoned?"

"No, with Mr. Brayden still in it. A passing motorist reported the car went straight off the road into a field. No damage to the car, but when emergency got to him, he was unconscious. That head injury you mentioned, probably. I'm going to the hospital he was taken to as it's on my way to Nether Woodsmoor. I'll be along after I've seen Brayden, but it may be tomorrow, depending on how long it takes at the hospital."

A reprieve from Quimby's questions, then. "I'll be here in Nether Woodsmoor all day tomorrow...er, today," I amended. Technically, it was Saturday. "It's a day off for the documentary," I explained.

"Good. I'll speak to you soon," he said.

I called Alex's number, but it went to voicemail. Maybe he was already on the road and couldn't answer since talking on cell phones while driving wasn't allowed. I was sure he'd call or text the next time he stopped. I left him a message then drained the last of my coffee and put the mug in the sink.

It didn't sound as if Quimby would make it here before tomorrow, but I was too wired for sleep. I picked up my Moleskine notebook. I wanted to write down what Gil had told me in case he wasn't able to speak to Quimby. My thoughts skittered away from that scenario. I tucked my legs under me, curled up at the end of the couch, and started writing.

The paper was covered with scrawls, lines, and notes by the time I finished. It took me quite a while to get it all down on paper, and by that time, I'd burrowed farther down into the cushions and rested my head against the back of the couch. I stifled a yawn as I looked over the messy paper...something flickered in my mind...something about shapes...rectangles and squares and boxes. Lines, too, but I couldn't quite grasp it. I blinked and refocused on the paper, thinking I should go make more coffee, but it seemed like too much work even to get up off the couch.

GRADUALLY, I became aware of a growing light in the room. What was I doing sleeping on the couch? I rubbed my neck and struggled upright. Then I saw my notebook open on my lap, the pages covered with my handwriting and lots of little arrows and stars and exclamation points.

I swung my feet to the floor and scrubbed my hand across my face then went to brew some coffee. The sky was lightening, brightening the room, but it was still very early, four thirty. Slink dragged herself off her bed and followed me slowly into the kitchen, then went to stand by the back door, a slightly reproachful look on her face. I got the coffee going, then opened the door for her. "Sorry, girl. I know it's too early to be up."

The cool morning air engulfed me as she brushed by me and trotted down the steps. I returned and waited in front of the coffeemaker like a zombie.

I poured myself a huge, aromatic mug and sipped. It burned but it was so worth it. I checked my phone and saw I had a text from Alex saying he was on the road and had stopped for coffee. He'd call or text later. I retrieved my notebook and skimmed over what I'd written last night, trying to revive that fragment of thought that I couldn't quite grasp. It had seemed so important… something to do with shapes…and lines, too, I thought. Something geometric…? And then I had it.

I scrambled for my phone and flicked through the photos I'd taken of Tate House before Arabella arrived. I checked them, skimming through, looking at the furniture and decorative objects. I found the photos of the upstairs hall and went still as several things crystalized in my mind.

The jingle of Slink's collar as she came up the steps to the back door pulled me out of my reverie. She was ready to get back to her bed and headed straight for it when she came inside. I was closing the door when a male voice carried through the half-light from the direction of the path.

"Don't see why we have to go down so early."

I recognized that voice. It was Sylvester. I watched through the half-closed door as Torrie's short frame appeared. Her arms were crossed over a flat box she had pressed to her chest. Sylvester, taller, but moving more slowly, was a step behind her. She stopped and spun toward him. "Because we don't want that annoying constable to see us drop this off. He's been there the last two days. I don't like it."

"Don't see why it matters. We're out of here today—"

"Shush." Torrie made a chopping motion. "We're getting rid of this one now." She turned and went on. After a moment, Sylvester dragged on behind her, an irked expression on his face.

I didn't move until they'd disappeared down the path. They were leaving, and Quimby wasn't here. I doubted they were going somewhere nice and respectable where the police could track them down. Once they were gone, there would only be Gil's story about what had happened, and he wasn't exactly the most reliable witness, I thought with a sinking feeling. Quimby might give me the benefit of the doubt when it came to the threatening note, but I didn't think Scotland Yard would be so lenient. And now I was linked to Gil—sneaky, car-stealing Gil. Would they believe his story? Would they believe mine?

What I needed was something solid, proof that Gil's story was true. If I'd worked it out correctly...then I knew exactly where to find it. My breathing quickened. No one was at Tate House...and I had the code to unlock the gate and the door. It was too good an opportunity to pass up. I set my coffee on the counter and hurried back to the front room. I'd kicked off my shoes last night while I was on the couch. I put my shoes on, grabbed my phone, and switched it to silent. Slink, who was back on her cushion, watched me without moving her head, her gaze tracking me. I patted her head. "Don't worry, girl. I'll be quick."

CHAPTER 30

*J*TUCKED MY HAIR BEHIND my ears, added my keys to my crossbody bag then went out the back door and through the garden. I paused at the gate. The footpath was empty. I slipped through the gate, closed it soundlessly behind me, and jogged toward Tate House. It would take Torrie and Sylvester at least fifteen minutes to get to the village and back to Tate House. I knew this because I'd walked the path so often. I didn't linger and kept up my quick pace. The sky was shifting to a pale lemon-yellow as I hurried along, but the trees lining the side of the road were in deep shadow.

I'd almost reached the point where the drive branched off the path and curved up to Tate House when a whisper of movement made me freeze. I stood in the deep shadow at the side of the path as the swishing sound grew louder. I stepped back into the trees. It couldn't be Torrie or Sylvester. They were on the way to the village. They couldn't have doubled back without me seeing them. A figure on a bike swept out of the drive, coasted around the sweep of the curve in the path then resumed pedaling. I barely had time to process the thought that it was Violet on the bike as she zoomed away, her figure diminishing. Was everyone in Nether Woodsmoor an early riser this morning? Was Violet out for her morning exercise? I shook my head. Not this early. And Tate House was not remotely close to the bungalow where Violet said she was staying. Did she know about the money? Was that why she hadn't returned to London? In any case, it didn't look like she was coming back, so I stepped out of the trees.

As I climbed the steep incline to the gate at Tate House, I paged through the notebook until I found the code then punched it in. After a pause, it began to creep open. I slipped through the opening then punched in the code to close the gate. It halted then labored back the other direction. I went up the drive, checking over my shoulder to make sure the gate closed. I put in the front door code and tried the handle, tensed for the shriek of an alarm, but the door opened smoothly. I stepped into the silent house and took a few deep breaths. The quick pace up the drive had nothing to do with my winded breathing. It was my nerves that made me sound so out of shape.

It was still dark enough outside that most of the room was in shadow, but I didn't want to turn on a light. I took a step, and my foot bumped into a large bundle. Several suitcases sat beside the front door, packed and ready to go. Torrie and Sylvester weren't kidding about leaving. A piece of paper folded in thirds stuck up from the exterior pocket of an overnight bag. I pushed the folded paper open enough to see that it was a printed airline ticket reservation, Manchester to Heathrow, departing this afternoon with two passengers listed, Torrie and Sylvester.

My phone vibrated in my pocket, and I jumped. Telling myself to calm down, I took out my phone. I was completely alone and had plenty of time before Torrie and Sylvester came back. A text message from Alex read, *Almost back to Nether Woodsmoor. Talk to you later today.*

Best to be methodical and check the downstairs first, I thought, giving the ground floor a quick tour. I punched the buttons to call Alex as I walked through the rooms. He answered and said, "Hey, sorry to wake you. I thought you wouldn't get the text until later."

"You're really here?"

"Almost. I'm a few miles out. I missed most of the traffic. Roads are quiet. I'm getting more coffee. Did you talk with Quimby?"

"No, he had to take a detour to the hospital." I explained what had happened with Gil.

The ground floor rooms looked unchanged. The suitcases by the door were the only sign of Torrie and Sylvester. I made a quick tour of the kitchen where the light over the island was on, and I saw some signs of habitation. The trash bin was overflowing, and two mugs sat in the sink, dark rings of coffee at their base.

"What are you doing up so early? It's not even five."

"Searching Tate House for a pile of cash," I said.

"What?"

I went back through the large room to the frosted glass staircase. "It's why Arabella was killed, but there's not a shred of proof, and with Quimby coming today, and the case going to Scotland Yard...well, when Torrie and Sylvester went out, I came up here to have a look."

"Scotland Yard?" Alex asked.

"Yes, I didn't get to tell you about that last night. Quimby says Scotland Yard will take over. I guess the transfer hasn't been made yet or isn't official because Quimby went to talk to Gil, and he's coming to talk to me." I paused at the top of the stairs. "Of course they wouldn't leave it here, out in the open," I murmured. It had to be in one of the bedrooms.

"Leave what out in the open?" Alex asked. "Wait—Torrie and Sylvester went *out*? Where would they go at this time of the morning?"

"To the postbox—that's how they're moving the cash. I worked it out last night and this morning. They're mailing it— that must be what they're doing. They're sending it off through the Royal Mail so they can pick it up somewhere else. I saw one of the boxes had a customs form so they have to be sending it out of the country. Arabella said she was leaving on a long foreign holiday. I bet she was traveling to wherever she was sending the cash. Now Torrie and Sylvester have their bags packed and boarding passes for a flight to Heathrow. They can go anywhere from there."

I stopped at the door to Arabella's room to make sure my memory was right. The tangle of clothes and shoes still ranged around the furniture and floor, and the luggage was all there, except for one piece. The only other change that I could see was that the ironing board was no longer in the room.

"What cash?"

"The cash that Arabella stole from her ex, Stevie Lund. His family is rather shady—drugs." During my short trip upstairs on the day that Arabella died, I hadn't explored all the rooms, but I did now, working my way down the hall. The next door opened to a bare and utilitarian flight of stairs descending to a landing. It was the back staircase, the one that went down to the kitchen.

I looked in the bath at the end of the hall, but it was too small. "Remember his dad was in the news?" I said, "Drug lord, got off on a technicality? Gil said Stevie moves cash for his dad. I'm fuzzy on how that part worked exactly, but Gil Brayden inter- viewed a woman who lives on the same floor as Stevie. She says Arabella went to his flat alone and made several trips out of there, carrying heavy bags filled with cash. Then she had Torrie contact Paul and move up their arrival date." I had worked out the timeline last night when I jotted down everything. "The day after she took the cash, Arabella made plans to arrive here in Nether Woodsmoor early and insisted we move her someplace more secure. The threatening notes were an excuse to hire two guards and retreat to a secure house, but they weren't guarding her. They were guarding the *cash*," I said, working my way up the other side of the hall now.

The next room had probably been Chester's. The bed was made, but looked rumpled. The rest of the room was bare and devoid of any personal possessions.

"And you think Torrie and—what was his name...Sylvester?— killed her to get the cash?"

"Either Torrie did it alone, and then Sylvester got on board with her later...or they worked together to pull it off. My bet is that Torrie came up with the idea and once Sylvester worked out what was happening, he teamed up with her." I crossed the room and checked a little alcove by the windows...nothing but chairs and a table. "The wiring and timing controls for the outdoor lights are separate from the house. It runs through the potting shed in the garden. Torrie is supposedly highly allergic to pollen and deathly afraid of getting a bee sting. She wouldn't even go onto the terrace with me on the day they arrived, but later she told me that the police kept asking about the potting shed. She said she had never been in the garden or the 'messy' shed. How did she know it was messy, if she hadn't been in there? I suppose Sylvester could have told her, but then why would he be in there? Either Torrie had set it up by herself, or she and Sylvester had worked together." I went back into the hall.

"They decided they didn't want to cut the money three ways," Alex said, his voice grim.

"Must have."

"Kate, you need to get out of there. It's very dangerous...if you're even close...if what you think happened is the truth, these are ruthless people."

"It will only take a second more. The money *has* to be here. It's got to be in the trunk. I almost worked it out last night right before I drifted off to sleep, but it got all muddled up with boxes and the rectangles of money that Gil described, and I couldn't sort it out. But this morning it all came together. Arabella was very specific about one piece of luggage when she arrived, a trunk—that was the box that I kept thinking about. It was the only piece of luggage she cared about. I think she kept the key to it on the charm bracelet that she wore all the time. I saw the charm bracelet last night, and the key was bigger than the rest of the charms. It wasn't a charm at all—it was a real key. And that's why Torrie wanted the bracelet, to open the trunk."

I continued to open doors. The next door revealed a linen closet, then I found another bare and empty bedroom, but I stepped inside and looked around to make sure the trunk wasn't hidden on the far side of the canopied bed. "On the day Arabella died while I was downstairs making tea for Torrie, she came upstairs and dragged the trunk out of Arabella's room, leaving two long scuff marks on the hardwood. They were most noticeable right at Arabella's door. She must have used the carpet runner down the middle of the hall to move the trunk the rest of the way. She knew the police would search Arabella's room, and she had to get the trunk out of there. I came up to check on Torrie after I made her tea and saw the marks she left on the floor when she dragged the trunk out of Arabella's room, but didn't put it all together until this morning."

I looked into another room, which looked as if it had been recently occupied. Drawers hung open, and the sink in the bath was wet, but there was no trunk. I went back to the hall. "There was a trunk in the upstairs hallway on the day Arabella died," I said looking at the now empty space. "It had a crocheted tablecloth draped over it and a few framed pictures on top of it. Torrie must have hoped that if the police searched the house, they'd assume the trunk was part of the furnishings that went with the house and overlook it, which they must have. I think the police spent most of their time outside. If they were indoors, they probably focused on Arabella's room. I only noticed the trunk that day because I bumped my shin on it. It stuck out a little too far into the hallway, but that must have been the only place Torrie could find to put it in the short amount of time she had. That trunk isn't in any of the pre-arrival photos I took of Tate House. And the items on the trunk, the framed pictures and tablecloth, are all from other upstairs rooms."

The next room must have been where Torrie stayed. The faint scent of cigarette smoke lingered when I opened the door. The bedding was massed in a pile on the floor at the foot of the bed, the doors of the heavy empty wardrobe gaped open. The ironing board was set up beside the wardrobe.

I stopped in my tracks for a second then raced across the room. "I've found it, the Louis Vuitton trunk. They've ruined it, of course. It's why they needed a crowbar. When they couldn't find Arabella's charm bracelet with the key, they ripped the trunk open."

One corner of the trunk had been pried apart, the leather and brass detail crushed and wrenched out of the way. But the trunk's workmanship was excellent. The opposite corner of the trunk still held its shape, and the lock on it was fastened tight. They'd had to work hard to make even a small opening, and once they had that, they hadn't bothered to crack open the other side. I knelt down and looked between the edges of leather and wood that had been bent back to create an opening about eight inches across, expecting to see stacks of money.

I sat back on my heels, stunned. "It's empty. The money must have been in there. It all fits so perfectly. It's the only thing that explains everything." I jumped up and scanned the room again.

Alex was saying something, but I overrode him. "Wait—the boxes." I saw a stack of flat boxes, already addressed and stamped, sitting on the ironing board. I'd been so focused on finding the trunk I hadn't even noticed them. I snatched one up and groaned. It was empty, the flaps unsealed. "They're empty, all of them," I said. "Well, maybe Quimby can use the address to track the money." I paused, studying the address. "Oh—I thought—it said New Jersey..."

A roar came through the phone. "Kate!"

"Sorry. I found some mailing boxes—"

"I don't care if you found Fort Knox in there. You need to get out. *Now*."

"—like the ones I saw Arabella mailing. I caught a glimpse of the address earlier this week and thought it said *New Jersey*. I can now see it only lists Jersey as the address," I said excitedly. "Isn't that somewhere in the Channel Islands?"

Alex stopped shouting. "Yes, it is," he said, his tone thoughtful. "It's also something of a tax haven, I think." His voice hardened. "Kate. I love you and want you to get out of there now. Do you understand me? I want us to spend the rest of our lives together, but that's going to be extremely difficult if you get yourself killed."

My arm fell to my side, the box forgotten. "You love me?"

"Yes. God help me, I do. Every bit of your adorably irritating super-focused, take-charge, I-must-do-it-myself nature."

"And you want us to grow old together?"

"Yes, that's generally what people in love, do—get married and spend their lives together," Alex said. "I know I shouldn't have sprung that on you, especially right after the business thing—"

"Sounds wonderful," I said, realizing it was true. I'd held Alex off and resisted thinking about how I felt about him, but the idea of spending our lives together *was* what I wanted. Suddenly, it was all very simple. I wanted to be with him—always, even with his clutter of sticky notes and his roll-with-the-punches attitude.

"Good," Alex said. "Excellent, now will—wait. Did you just agree to marry me?"

"Yes, I think so," I said happily. "It's all so clear when you put it like that—I want to be with you, too. All those things that I thought were important—our different temperaments and habits and all that—they don't matter. Well, they matter a little bit, but we'll work that out. The being together part is what matters."

The line was completely silent for a moment. "Oh—well—good."

"You don't sound very excited."

"I didn't think it would be that easy," Alex said.

"I didn't either—to figure out what I wanted, I mean—but you caught me off guard. I can't explain it."

"You don't have to explain it to me. I feel the same way," he said, then his voice changed and had a note of exasperation in it. "Now will you get out of there? I can meet you at your cottage. I'm almost there."

"Only if you say it again." I happened to glance in the mirror above the dresser and saw I had a huge smile on my face.

"The super-focused bit?"

"No, the other part."

"Oh, that. I think I better hold off—dangle it out there as an incentive to get you out of the house. I'll tell you when I see you face-to-face."

"Okay. I'm leaving—" The sound of a door closing echoed through the house and wiped the grin off my face.

$\mathcal{I}$ COULD HEAR MOVEMENTS BELOW near the front door. I swallowed and carefully tiptoed to the doorway of the bedroom where I could see across the hall and down to the front door.

"Kate, what's happened?" Alex asked, his voice strained.

"They're back," I breathed.

Alex lowered his voice, but the intensity of his worry came through the quiet tones. "I told you to get out of there."

I whispered, "I would have had plenty of time to get out if you hadn't distracted me by proposing. I got caught up in the moment."

"Seems we're having our first fight as an engaged couple," Alex said.

"Wait a minute…they're talking."

I could hear Sylvester's voice clearly as it floated up the stairs. "I don't see what it matters if a plodding constable sees you mail something." Sylvester stood in the open front door, holding two suitcases.

Torrie was searching the overnight bag. "Because he was there yesterday. I don't like it. They're watching us. We'll mail every-thing else on the way. It will slow us down, but it will be safer."

I stepped back into the bedroom and pressed the phone close to my mouth. "They're leaving. Sylvester is about to carry out their suitcases. Where are you?"

"I'm on the high street now."

"Thank goodness. I'll wait until they leave, then meet you on the path that goes to the cottages."

"Got it. See you in a minute," Alex said, his voice businesslike and steady. "You better be there," he added.

"Wouldn't miss it for the world," I whispered. "There are things I can't wait to hear you say."

I think I heard him chuckle before I hung up.

I found Quimby's number in my call log and sent a text. *Torrie and Sylvester leaving Nether Woodsmoor now.* Then I eased back to the door, poised to head for the back staircase as soon as they left through the front door. I didn't move any farther. I didn't want a creaky floorboard to give me away.

"Where is it?" Torrie asked, her voice whipping up the stairway.

Sylvester, his hands weighted down with the suitcases, shrugged. "How should I know? You're the one who packed the bags."

"There were five mailing boxes when I packed. Now there are only four."

In the *luggage*—of course that was where the cash would be. I was an idiot. I'd been so focused on finding the trunk that I hadn't even thought to check the bags by the door.

The air crackled between them. I guess that was the trouble with teaming up with someone to betray a partner. You would have to wonder if the betrayal ended there, or if you were next on the list to be double-crossed.

Sylvester stepped up and put his face inches from hers. "Let's get this straight right now. I didn't take it. I'm not that sort. You better have a look upstairs."

She stared at him a moment. "Fine." She spun on her heel and headed for the stairs.

I hesitated for a second. If I went into the hall to go into one of the unoccupied bedrooms, they'd see me. I turned away from the door and darted into the bedroom's adjoining bath. I stepped behind the door and tried to calm my ragged breathing.

Except for the towels left on the floor, there was nothing in this room—surely she wouldn't come in here...? There was no shower curtain to hide behind and only a tiny round window. No way I could wiggle out of that—and this wasn't the ground floor, so I wasn't about to try that. A storage cabinet to one side of the sink had a large door. I might be able to fit in there. I closed one eye and looked through the sliver of space between the door and the frame.

Torrie stomped into the room, surveyed it with her hands on her hips for a second, then she marched over to the ironing board and checked the empty boxes, swiping them all to the floor when she saw they were empty. She checked under the wardrobe and the bed, then marched around the end of the bed, stepping on the pile of sheets and blankets on her way to the dresser on the other side of the room.

I caught my breath. Her footsteps had shifted the sheets slightly, revealing the corner of one of the slim boxes. I flinched each time Torrie yanked a drawer open then slammed it closed. Muttering under her breath, she dragged the trunk over a few feet, checked under it, then shoved it onto its side.

"Torrie, let's go," Sylvester bellowed. "It's just one blooming box. We have plenty."

"We can't leave it behind—then they'll know." Torrie moved

toward the bath, and I scurried for the cabinet. It was tiny—minuscule, in fact. How had I thought I might be able to get into it? Maybe if I'd been doing yoga for years and years, I could contort myself into that space, but I didn't have a chance right now. I grabbed a damp towel.

As soon as Torrie pushed the door open, I threw the towel over her head and shoved by her. I heard her tumble...into the bath, it sounded like, but I didn't look back. I sprinted across the room and snatched up the box from under the sheets. As soon as I picked it up, I knew it was what Torrie was looking for. It was sealed and had a weight to it that the empty envelopes didn't. Torrie sputtered behind me and yelled for Sylvester.

I burst into the hall, then paused. I couldn't go down the glass stairs with Sylvester at the front door. Chester had carried a gun. Sylvester might have one too. I didn't want to find out if he did, so I made for the door to the back stairs. My feet were loud on the bare wooden treads, and I pounded down as fast as I could. No use in trying to be stealthy.

Behind me, the door at the top of the stairs slammed against the wall with a resounding crack, and I heard Torrie shout, "Kitchen! She's going down that way."

I swung around the landing then flew down the last flight of stairs to the closed door. *Please don't be locked*, I prayed. The handle turned, and I shot into the dim kitchen at the same moment Sylvester came through the hallway from the sitting room. I scuttled around the island to the door to the garden.

"Stop right there," he commanded. The light glowing from the island illuminated a gun he had pulled from a holster under his shoulder. He leveled the barrel at me.

Reflexively, I put my hands up as Torrie thundered down the steps. I still had the envelope gripped in my left hand, and as soon as Torrie came into the kitchen, her eyes widened. "You? The police still didn't take you in? Good grief. We couldn't give them any more evidence."

"You mean Gil." I was breathing hard from my sprint down the stairs, not to mention the fear and adrenaline pumping through me. "He wasn't dead. He's in the hospital, but expected to recover," I said, hoping it was true.

Torrie said, "You're lying."

"No. He was stunned and unconscious, but not dead."

She looked at Sylvester. "What are you waiting for? Shoot her. We can't have *another* witness."

Sylvester looked uncomfortable. "Not a good idea," he said. I felt as if a band around my chest had loosened a bit even though his extended arms didn't waver. "We can tie her up and leave her here. We'll be out of the country before anyone finds her."

I didn't love that plan, but I liked it better than Torrie's idea.

She advanced on him. "Are you crazy? She *knows*. She's obviously figured out what we did—"

"What you did," Sylvester said quickly. "I didn't kill anyone. You heard what she said. The photographer guy isn't dead. That means you're the only murderer here. I just helped you move the money."

"Oh, you have standards now?"

"One dead body is enough. Like you said, Arabella was never going to split it with us."

Torrie nodded. "Never—grasping, greedy thing that she was. If the public knew what she was really like then she never would have been so popular," Torrie said, clearly expounding on one of her favorite topics. "In fact, Arabella would think the whole thing was incredibly clever in a way. She'll be more famous now than ever—and she'll always be young and beautiful and tragic in everyone's mind. It's what she wanted, eternally youthful."

Part of me marveled at the coldness in her tone when she talked about Arabella and the underlying sense of triumph in her manner. Torrie had truly hated Arabella. The whole crying jag after her death was a performance—but Torrie had been an actress, too. A very good one. The other part of me that wasn't busy being appalled was alternating between being terrified and trying to work out if I could make a dash for the door. Would I be able to get outside before Sylvester shot at me? Why did it have to be such a spacious kitchen? And why was there nothing handy on the counter? No pots or pans or knives or even a cutting board. Only the gas cooktop with stovetop grates...they were cast iron, weren't they? Could I pick one of the grates up and fling it at Sylvester...?

Both Torrie and Sylvester were on the other side of the island from me. *Lunge forward and grab the grate, throw it, and run.* It might work.

"...messy to leave her alive," Torrie said. I'd missed some of what they were saying, but I heard those words loud and clear. "She's seen us. She knows about the money and about Gil. It's really the only thing we can do."

The money, I thought. Of course! I did have a bargaining chip. I lunged forward, but I didn't grab the stovetop grate. I twisted a knob to the IGNITE position. A couple of loud clicks sounded then the gas flame whooshed to life.

Sylvester said, "Hey," and moved a step closer, but by then I'd cranked the knob to high. The flame flared blue in the dim kitchen. I tossed the envelope on the burner and bolted for the door in a crouching run. Torrie made a strangled sound and cut in front of Sylvester as she dove for the stovetop.

I came out the back door, pelted across the terrace, and down the steps to the garden, slowing only enough to make sure I didn't lose my footing on the steps. I plunged into the deep shade of the garden. My heart stopped for a moment as a figure separated from the shadows around a clump of trees, but then I saw it was Alex, and I ran to him.

"I thought I better meet you here," he said against my hair.

I heard sounds of running footsteps on the terrace and tensed. A door was shoved back against a wall with a clatter, and then I heard diminishing shouts of, "Police. Hands in the air," from inside Tate House. "On the floor...both of you," the shouts continued, and I relaxed back into Alex's arms. "Much better idea, to meet here."

CHAPTER 32

"SO YOU GOT BOTH TORRIE and Sylvester?" I asked Quimby, who was seated at my kitchen table. He had been asking Alex and me questions for nearly an hour, and it looked as if he was wrapping up. I figured I'd better ask my question while I could.

Alex was beside me and had a firm grip on my hand. After the chaos died down at Tate House and Alex and I had permission from the police to wait for Quimby at my cottage, we'd returned there, and I'd brewed a strong pot of coffee. We were now on our second pot.

Alex and I had been a little too absorbed in each other to take in much of what had happened with Torrie and Sylvester. Now that Alex and I were sorted—I felt a little giddy, and it wasn't just from the adrenaline high that came from running for my life—I wanted to hear what had happened with Torrie and Sylvester.

Quimby nodded as he rubbed his deeply shadowed eyes. He'd been up all night. His suit was rumpled, and he had a layer of stubble on his face. He had gratefully accepted the large cup of coffee I offered him. "After I heard what Gil Brayden had to say and I got your text, I went directly there."

Quimby had told us that Gil had come around in the hospital and when he found Quimby at his bedside, he'd repeated everything he told me in Alex's cottage. Quimby continued, "I'd called and asked the local officers to meet me there. We had the situation under control within a few minutes. We apprehended Sylvester Hibbert first. Once he saw the other officers, he dropped to his knees. Torrie Mayes went back through the house and grabbed a large bag, which hampered her progress. She didn't make it off the grounds of Tate House. Both of them are in custody."

I said, "Even with millions waiting for her in Jersey, she still wanted more. And she thought Arabella was greedy."

"Well, the bag was full of five hundred euro notes." Quimby removed a large plastic bag and set it on the table. "I thought you might want to see this."

It contained the charred remains of the box. It was a considerably smaller package than it had been. Below the curled and blackened edge of the box sat two fat stacks of pink notes with seared edges. Quimby tapped the plastic. "This denomination, the five hundred euro note, will be a thing of the past soon. They are being phased out—for good reason."

"Smuggling?" asked Alex, reaching down to pet Slink, who was curled at his feet.

"Yes. Law-abiding citizens don't have much need for them. It's the criminals who want them. Makes it easier to move cash. They take the pounds they get here from drug sales and convert them into euros through shady money exchanges then iron the bills as flat as they can get them. Five or six million euros only weighs about ten or twelve kilograms, an easy fit for a suitcase."

"So that's why they had the ironing board set up at Tate House," I said. "I should have known something was up when I saw it in Arabella's room. She certainly wasn't the sort to do her own ironing. But they were mailing most of the money, right, in boxes like this, not putting it in suitcases?"

Quimby said, "Correct. It's quite a good way to move the money, actually. The flat boxes could be mailed at a postbox. Nice and anonymous. Since they broke it up into tiny shipments, they could get the money out of the country without worrying about taking a suitcase through customs at an airport. Different regulations regarding the post make monitoring it more difficult, not to mention the sheer volume of material that's processed. The mail is one of the easiest ways to smuggle currency, a fact that I'm sure Arabella picked up from Lund."

"They must have had several boxes packed and ready to go because I saw a stack of them on the kitchen table the day I saw Gil in the garden, and Torrie was still dropping them in the mail after Arabella died. I saw her mail a package before they got the crowbar."

Quimby nodded. "That's what Sylvester Hibbert tells us. He began talking right away. He's quite anxious to cooperate. He said Arabella had several boxes lined up and ready to go when she died. They continued mailing them to the address in Jersey, intending to go there and pick them up. They only got the trunk open yesterday. They searched for the key, but when they couldn't find it, they pried it open. Mr. Brayden's attempt to 'sell' the key to them came a little too late. By then he was a liability, which they tried to take care of."

Alex took a sip of his coffee and said, "I get that Arabella stole the money from Stevie and that Gil Brayden saw an opportunity. He snatched the bracelet with the key, hoping he would get his money. What I don't understand is why Torrie worked out an elaborate plan with the wires in the garden, but didn't have a better plan for the trunk. Why would she wait until the last minute to move it out of Arabella's room?"

I glanced toward Quimby, but he waved his hand and settled

back in his chair, obviously glad to have a few minutes to enjoy more coffee before he had to leave. I turned to Alex. "Because she couldn't move it until Arabella was dead, and Arabella wasn't going to do yoga outside until the weather was nice. Those days of rain and drizzle probably extended Arabella's life by a few days. Torrie told me she didn't know Arabella was going to workout in the garden that day. And she didn't know about Arabella's meeting with Gil, either. When Torrie came back and found out Arabella was dead, she was as surprised as we were. She worked herself into a frenzy to buy some time away from me to get upstairs and move the trunk. Everything was moving faster than she'd expected. She must have thought she'd have time to replace the wires with her sections of pre-cut wires, which would make the lighting look completely normal and the death would be written off as a tragic accident."

"She knew how to do that, rewire the lights?"

I lifted a shoulder. "The information is online for anyone to find." I glanced out of the corner of my eye at Quimby. After he'd had a few swallows of the coffee and settled at the table, I'd told him about the note and the computer searches. He frowned at me now, but didn't rehash the warnings he had given me earlier about withholding evidence and obstructing an investigation. He'd had quite a bit to say on both subjects, but instead of arresting me, he'd dispatched someone to collect the laptop from Alex's cottage and alerted his office to watch for the envelope I'd sent him.

He put his cup down as he said, "When you found Arabella's body, you threw everything off. Torrie planned to be the one to 'discover' her body, but only after the wiring had been put back in place."

"So she did go into the garden and the shed. Is she really allergic?" I asked.

"Sylvester Hibbert says she is, but that she took antihistamines to keep her allergies down and then risked going into the garden to set up the wires. She wore long sleeves and pants to protect from stings."

"She thought about so many things," I said, "but there were so many she couldn't control, like you showing up too early. She lost it for a second when she found out a DCI was already at Tate House," I said, "but she recovered as best she could. More coffee?" I asked, mostly as a distraction, so that Quimby wouldn't backtrack to my subterfuge with the note. He waved me off, so I said quickly, "What will happen to Stevie Lund? He really wasn't trying to kill Arabella."

"That's probably the one and only time he's not guilty of something he's accused of. Don't worry. By tonight, Stevie Lund will be living a very different life than he is now. No sports cars or designer suits." I raised my eyebrows, and Quimby continued, "After I interviewed Gil Brayden, I sent word to the drug task force about the woman who lived near Lund's flat, but they didn't need her information. They arrested Lund this morning, caught him attempting to transport a suitcase full of cash to one of his mules."

"All those suitcases of cash," I murmured.

"I'll never look at luggage the same way again," Alex said.

Quimby smiled briefly. "Quite."

"What about Arabella's sister, Violet?" I asked.

"What about her?" Quimby asked.

"Did she know about the money? I saw her this morning, leaving Tate House before I went in. She'd said she was leaving Nether Woodsmoor so I was surprised to see her."

Quimby frowned as he tapped a note into his phone. "That is interesting," he said and had me describe the encounter in detail.

His phone rang, and he answered then sat up straight. "Gone? How?" He listened a moment, barked some orders about getting officers to the train station, then ended the call. He pushed back his chair. "Brayden left the hospital sometime in the early morning hours. Just walked out." Quimby left so quickly that Slink barely had time to rise and trot after him to the door.

I settled back into place beside Alex. "I'm not at all surprised that Gil slipped away without them knowing. He's probably halfway to London by now. I wonder where he'll go? He did say he wanted to go somewhere warm when he said he wouldn't talk to the police."

"Probably somewhere far away from this mess—South America maybe. I have no doubt that he'll land on his feet."

"Yes, I suppose that's true. He does know how to take care of himself."

"Gil Brayden is the last thing I want to talk about," Alex said.

I settled into the curve of his arm. "I couldn't agree more."

"IT'S SO OFTEN about money, isn't it?" Beatrice said as we walked down the steps to the gravel drive in front of Parkview. The interview in the Tapestry Gallery had gone off without a hitch earlier today, and I had just finished the final inspection, making sure we left the room exactly as we found it, when Beatrice arrived and asked if I could spare her a moment.

You don't turn Lady Stone down, so I'd given the drapes a final tug then walked with her through the elegant rooms to the front of the house and down the wide steps to the drive.

At the base of the steps, she turned and looked up at the mellow golden stone. Her gaze ran across the banks of windows and up to the stone pediment with its figures carved in relief. "Marriages made, land bought and sold, dowries settled. So many decisions made—good and bad—for money."

She was not generally a philosophical person, but I had been thinking the same thing over the last few days as the tangle around Arabella's death had been sorted out. "Arabella was certainly all about the money."

Beatrice sniffed. "Quite the ruthless person, too. Now that other young man, the photographer, what happened to him?"

"Still no word. I doubt he'll be found," I said, picturing Gil on a beach somewhere.

"And the other security guard, was he involved?" Beatrice asked.

"Chester Hibbert? No, he's much more of a by-the-rules kind of person. Quimby told me that Arabella, Torrie, and Sylvester kept the theft and transfer of the money from him. Apparently, once Sylvester worked out what they were doing, he wanted in, but insisted they keep it from Chester because he might turn them in."

"I see. Well," Beatrice said, "I'm glad that's sorted. Quite disturbing to have something like that going on here in Nether Woodsmoor."

I agreed, understanding why she was asking the questions. She wanted to make sure all was well and back to normal in her little village.

"Oh, that reminds me, we have an inquiry about a possible event, Painting at Parkview. I believe the organizer, Violet Emsley, was part of the recent incident at Tate House. Do you know anything about her?"

"Arabella was her sister," I said. "But Violet wasn't really involved with the mess at Tate House." Quimby had called me with a few follow-up questions for his reports. While I had him on the phone, I'd asked him about Violet. "Quimby told me that they investigated her. Violet didn't know about the money and wasn't involved in the plan to murder Arabella. She only came to Nether Woodsmoor to see her sister."

And to attempt to get some funding for an art school, I added mentally but didn't mention that to Beatrice. Instead, I said, "Violet told Quimby that she'd decided Tate House would be an ideal location for an art retreat and that was why she stuck around. She made several attempts to get inside and see the grounds and the house."

I wasn't sure I believed that last bit, about Tate House being a good location for an art retreat. But maybe it was the truth, if Violet was actually planning an art event in the area.

"Odd that she'd want to use Tate House after what happened there," Beatrice said.

"Yes, I thought so too, but she said she thought it could be a memorial." Cynically, I wondered if Violet had wanted to grab onto some of the publicity surrounding Arabella's death to get the word out about her art school, which was in the works, according to Quimby. I shifted my gaze from Parkview to the gardens. "But I think Parkview is a much better location for an art retreat. The gardens alone would keep an artist busy for years."

We both turned at the sound of a car coming up the drive. It was Alex at the wheel of the MG, which had survived running off the road without a scratch—well, without a new scratch. Because of its age, it already had some signs of wear and tear. The day was pleasant, and he had the top down. The wrap party for the final episode had already kicked off, and he was here to give me a lift to the party. We planned to announce our engagement there, and I felt a flutter of nerves, but they were good nerves—excitement and happiness, not worry or strain.

Beatrice turned to me and said in a brisk voice, "Now, I want you to know that there is an opening on the calendar, the third Saturday of September. Parkview would be a lovely location for your wedding. Sir Harold and I would enjoy it greatly if you'd have it here. We'd waive the normal fee, of course, as part of our wedding gift."

"Ah—I—um." Stunned, I swallowed and tried to put together a coherent sentence. "But it's not—um..."

"Official?" Beatrice said. "Yes, I know. But it's obvious," she said as Alex braked at our side.

"Hello, Beatrice," he called. To me, he said, "All finished in the Tapestry Gallery?" I nodded, still processing what Beatrice had said. Did everyone already know about Alex and me? We'd wanted to keep our news to ourselves until the end of filming. I hadn't told anyone, not even Melissa or Louise.

I slid into the passenger seat, and Beatrice closed the door. "Discuss it with Alex and let me know. We're so happy for you." She patted the door once then climbed the steps back to Parkview.

Alex shifted into first, and we motored along the drive under the arching branches of the oak trees. "What was that about?"

"Ah—Beatrice says she and Sir Harold would love for us to be married at Parkview on the third Saturday of September."

Alex burst out laughing. "Figured it out did she?" We came out from the shade of the drive to the road. Alex shifted up through the gears, and the wind flicked my hair around my face. We came to a rise that gave us a view of Parkview looking elegantly formal, its honey-colored stone glowing against the undulating green countryside. Alex let the car roll to a stop on the edge of the road. "What do you think?" Alex asked looking at the view. "Should we get married there?"

We hadn't talked about the ceremony, and Alex was a very low-key person. "It depends. What sort of wedding do you want?" I asked.

"I want you there and my family and friends—that's all that matters to me. What do you want?"

"Same thing—mostly," I said, thinking of the havoc my mother could cause. "You haven't met my mother yet."

"She'll want to be there, of course."

"Without a doubt. Getting me married off has been her one unchanging goal and desire in life. Since that will be happening, maybe that will, um, take the edge off." I hoped that would be true, but I felt a wiggle of doubt about the statement. "If we are married at Parkview, we could use the photos on our website to show the versatility of the location."

"That's my girl. Always thinking about business."

"Not all the time," I said, and we exchanged a smile before I looked back at the view. "I think it would be lovely."

Alex nodded. "Then let's do it."

THE END

Stay up to date with with Sara. Sign up for her updates and get exclusive content and giveaways.

Want more Nether Woodsmoor and Parkview Hall? Don't miss Kate and Alex in Death at an English Wedding, which is available in ebook, audio, and print.

WEDDING BELLS ARE RINGING in the English village of Nether Woodsmoor for location scouts Kate and Alex. They are tying the knot at one of England's most elegant stately homes, but when a wedding guest is murdered and suspicion falls on those closest to Kate, she and Alex must put their plans for happily ever after on hold. If they can't figure out who sabotaged their big day, their honeymoon may be over before it begins.

Death at an English Wedding is the seventh installment in the popular Murder on Location series from USA Today bestselling author Sara Rosett, which features an English village, quirky characters, along with dashes of humor and romance.

THE STORY BEHIND THE STORY

THE TITLE CAME FIRST WITH this book. I loved the idea of writing a story around an English garden. Originally, I'd intended it to be a cottage garden like the one in front of Kate's house, but as the story developed, I realized Arabella Emsley would require a grand garden. I used the Wollerton Old Hall Garden as inspiration, particularly the Yew Walk along with some gorgeous images on Pinterest. (You can check out the images and inspiration on the *Death in an English Garden* Pinterest page.)

I also found the research into currency smuggling fascinating. Like Alex, I'll never look at suitcases the same way! And it was fun to use an iron and an ironing board as a clue. Chatsworth House in Derbyshire is the inspiration for my Parkview Hall, and part of it was swathed in scaffolding and white drape when I visited it on a research trip.

For an in-depth analysis of money in Jane Austen's time, check out the illuminating book *What Matters in Jane Austen? Twenty Crucial Puzzles Solved* by John Mullan. Thanks to Celina Grace for recommending it to me and for helping me sort out the mail details.

visiting Nether Woodsmoor and plan to return ne more book. We have to get Alex and Kate ff, but I'm sure there will be some mayhem ve to keep you updated on new releases. To be r reveals, get exclusive excerpts of upcoming books as well as find out what new mystery authors I've discovered lately, sign up for my occasional newsletter at SaraRosett. com/signup/2 I'd love to keep in touch.

OTHER BOOKS BY SARA ROSETT

This is Sara Rosett's complete library at the time of publication, but Sara has new books coming out all the time. Sign up for her newsletter to stay up to date on new releases.

Murder on Location — English village cozy mysteries

Death in the English Countryside

Death in an English Cottage

Death in a Stately Home

Death in an Elegant City

Menace at the Christmas Market (novella)

Death in an English Garden

Death at an English Wedding

High Society Lady Detective — 1920s country house mysteries

Murder at Archly Manor

Murder at Blackburn Hall

The Egyptian Antiquities Murder

Murder in Black Tie

An Old Money Murder in Mayfair

Murder on a Midnight Clear

Murder at the Mansions

On the Run — Travel, intrigue, and a dash of romance

Elusive

Secretive

Deceptive

Suspicious

Devious

Treacherous

Duplicity

Ellie Avery — Mom-lit cozy mysteries

Moving is Murder

Staying Home is a Killer

Getting Away is Deadly

Magnolias, Moonlight, and Murder

Mint Juleps, Mayhem, and Murder

Mimosas, Mischief, and Murder

Mistletoe, Merriment and Murder

Milkshakes, Mermaids, and Murder

Marriage, Monsters-in-law, and Murder

Mother's Day, Muffins, and Murder